DARK PARADISE

A Ryan Weller Thriller

EVAN GRAVER

CHAPTER ONE

Naomi lay staring at the ceiling of the V-berth cabin. Her breathing had slowed, and the residual effects of the adrenaline had left her drained, her veins and muscles shriveled in the aftermath. She'd suffered through the sweaty groping and humping of her body by a man she'd come to hate. There were no more tears, only prayers for the end of this captivity and torture.

Her captor had introduced himself as "Captain Billy" to Naomi and her husband, Matt Shaffer, a week earlier. She'd since learned his full name was Billy Ron Sorenson, a former businessman from North Carolina. Naomi and Matt had hired Captain Billy to take them from Spanish Town on Virgin Gorda to Guadeloupe. Billy had seemed a happy-go-lucky man, who'd picnicked with them on white sand beaches, shown them the splendor of the coral reefs under the crystal-clear sea, and strangled her husband to death.

Two days ago, they'd found Billy rifling through their possessions. Matt had confronted him, and the men's angry shouts had turned to punches exchanged in the tight confines of the sailboat's cabin. Then Billy had overpowered Matt and taken him to the deck, choking him with one hand and grabbing a long filet knife off the galley counter with the other.

Naomi remembered her piercing shriek as she charged in to protect her husband. Their honeymoon, which they'd elected to extend indefinitely, had become a nightmare. Captain Billy held out the knife, stopping her short with its wicked point. The long, thin blade glinted in the cabin's weak battery-powered lights. He held her at bay while he strangled Matt, leaning his whole body on Matt's neck as the smaller man flailed beneath him. She watched the life seep from her husband's body.

In desperation, she snatched the kettle from the swinging trivet and slammed it into Billy's hand. He dropped the knife and jumped at her. She smacked him repeatedly with the solid steel kettle, but the crazed man kept coming. He tackled her and, in the fall, she hit her head and blacked out.

When Naomi had come to, she was naked and bound to the V-berth bed by a short length of dock line. She screamed and jerked on the rope, and the skin on her wrists had torn, blood trickling down her arms. Then the cabin door had slammed open and Billy stood in the frame. He'd looked wild with his blond hair spilling over his shoulders. His sweat and the low light accentuated his well-defined abdominal muscles; his mouth twisted up in a lustful sneer. He hadn't tied her legs, and she'd fought with him, getting in several good kicks to his chin and chest, but he'd kept coming and overpowered her. Her mind had shut out the events of the next days.

She was weak from hunger and ravenous with thirst. In desperation, she'd twisted her sweaty body to allow her access to the rope tied between her wrists and the wooden rail above the mattress. One by one, her fingernails had broken off while trying to untie the knot, so like a rat, she gnawed at the ropes. Slowly, the strands frayed.

Naomi rolled onto her side, seasick in the rolling waves of

the storm that had overtaken them last night. It hadn't stopped Captain Billy from using her body. She'd lain so he couldn't see the frayed rope and hadn't fought him. Now, the heavy swells and lashing rain covered the sounds of her movements. The longing to be free and to quench her thirst with gulps of cool water overtook everything else. Desire swelled in her belly, filled her chest, and threatened to explode out of her. It was an all-consuming, tingling sensation that rushed through her tired limbs, making her work with haste. As she chewed, she jerked at the ropes, trying to break them. Gnaw. Jerk. Gnaw. Jerk. Gnaw. Jerk.

"Come on," she pleaded in a low whisper. She'd been begging the universe to help her since she'd awoken in this tiny, floating prison. *Why, God, did you create someone so evil?*

Suddenly, the rope broke, and the momentum of the jerk and the snapping of the rope threw her back on the bed. She lay there for several seconds, stunned that she was free, then rolled off the bed and stood on shaky legs. Her fingers probed the door's lock until she slid it open, but the door only moved a fraction of an inch. She pressed her eye to the slit and peered through it. A shotgun lay nestled in the cushions of the settee, and a boat hook had been wedged between the door and the table.

Sitting on the floor, Naomi pushed her dark hair off her forehead and braced her back against the bed. She put her feet on the door and pushed with all her might, watching splinters form in jagged lines across the wood around the boat hook's handle before they popped through the lacquered finish.

The door broke open, and a cool rush of air blew over her. She shivered as she climbed to her feet, not knowing if it was from the wind wicking away the sweat from her naked body or fear of the monster lurking in the cockpit. Quickly, she sliced off her bonds with a kitchen knife.

Naomi jerked when the salon door slid open accompanied by a blast of wind and water. She shrank into a corner. Her hands searched for the shotgun, fingers closing around the metal barrel.

Captain Billy Ron Sorenson swung through the companionway door, not bothering with the steps. He landed on his feet and spun to dig something from a cabinet. Naomi swung the shotgun.

The wooden butt smashed into the captain's head and he fell forward to his knees. Blood coursed from a scalp wound, turning his neck red. Instead of knocking the man out, however, the blow seemed to incense him. As he touched the back of his head, he bellowed in anger and pain.

Why had she done that? She should have just shot him. Naomi twisted the gun, sliding the butt up under her right arm. Her finger found the trigger, and her thumb skated across a raised, ribbed piece of metal where the buttstock met the receiver. She glanced down and saw it was the safety. Her thumb pressed the slide forward, and a red circle appeared. The gun was ready to fire.

Squatting by the cockpit stairs, Billy Ron glared up at Naomi. Anger darkened his scowl, the muscles along his rugged jaw making his stubble twitch. Fire roared in his eyes. Then, as he stood, he smiled. Naomi remembered that smile from the first day they'd met. It had endeared him to her, made her believe he was capable and confident. Now, she saw it for what it really was: the face of a madman.

Billy Ron held out his hands. "Now look, honey, I know you think you want to kill me, but if you fire that gun in here, you're gonna sink my boat."

The smoothness of his voice now grated on her nerves. She aimed the barrel at his chest.

Killing someone was wrong. It was a sin. A commandment, *thou shall not murder*. But this wasn't murder; this was self-defense. What he'd done to Matt was murder. The man before her was a murderer. She thought of Captain Billy pressing his hand into Matt's neck, the shade of blue Matt's cheeks had turned as he struggled to breathe. She thought of the way he'd come at her the first time in the V-berth and the brutal way he'd assaulted her. Naomi's finger curled around the trigger.

The big gun boomed. Fire spit from the barrel, and the sound wave reverberated inside the fiberglass hull.

At the last instant, Billy Ron leaped sideways. Naomi worked the slide, praying there were more shells in the magazine.

Billy Ron scrambled to his feet.

Before she could fire again, the boat lurched. She lost her footing and grabbed the table for support. While she was distracted, he jumped on her, punching her in the stomach and trying to wrench away the shotgun. He pushed her to the cabin sole.

Naomi's hands clutched the gun in desperation. It had turned sideways, wedged between their bodies. His hot, wet flesh pressed against hers, and she bucked and fought like a wildcat. She got a hand free and tried to press her thumb into his eye. With a roar, he punched her in the jaw.

The blow made her jerk back, smacking her head against the deck. Blackness swirled her vision. His hands clamped around her neck, and Naomi felt him spreading her legs with his. Her throat worked to draw in air, lungs fluttering like butterfly wings. He stared at her with those piercing blue eyes.

Naomi let go, too tired to fight anymore. She was ready to find Matt.

CHAPTER TWO

Mango Hulsey locked his dinghy to a battered concrete post with a length of chain running through the dinghy's gas tank, around the motor, and through the stainless-steel stern eyes. As his father had always told him, a lock keeps an honest man honest. The thieves on Martinique were notorious. Even the kids playing along the waterfront had a mischievous streak and liked to "borrow" dinghies to use as dive platforms or cut the mooring rope and watch the inflatable boats drift away on wind and tide.

He straightened and stared across the water at their sailboat, a steel-hulled Amazon 44 named *Alamo*. Mango took his backpack from his wife, Jennifer. He tossed it over one shoulder, and she looped her arm through his.

He was five-ten and broad in the shoulders, although the last year of living aboard the sailboat, he'd lost some of his muscle mass. He couldn't hit the gym regularly, but he used elastic resistance bands and swam countless laps around the boat at anchor. Jennifer had the slim physique of a runner and could still sprint a five-minute mile. She loved the long-distance runs and had competed in several marathons.

Mango's blond hair ruffled in the Les Trois-Îlets anchorage's constant wind. It seemed no matter where they went in Fort-de-France Bay, the wind found them. It tugged at Jennifer's shoulder-length, dirty blonde hair as Mango opened the rental car's passenger door for her. She slid in, seeming thankful to be out of the wind. They'd chosen to anchor here because it was more central than the larger marina in Le Marin at the southern tip of the island. Plus, this anchorage was quieter, more secluded. They'd come to treasure these little coves since they'd set out to sail around the world a year ago—except they hadn't made it out of the Caribbean.

He and Jennifer had purchased *Alamo* in New Orleans after their first boat had been stolen by Mexican pirates. Mango had teamed up with Ryan Weller and gone in search of the pirates. They'd found that Aztlán cartel kingpin, Arturo Guerrero, was using the stolen sailboats to smuggle guns into the United States. Ryan and Mango had gone into Tampico, Mexico, looking for a way into Guerrero's compound, but Guerrero's *sicarios* had quickly apprehended them. After meeting with Guerrero, they'd escaped, and Ryan had killed Guerrero before he could board a helicopter and flee. The new cartel leader had placed a two-million-dollar bounty on them.

After that, Mango had accompanied Ryan during his investigation of the arms dealer supplying Guerrero. When they'd almost died escaping a sinking cargo vessel, Jennifer had put her foot down and demanded he sail off into the sunset with her. They'd island hopped south, slowly making their way toward Panama. Neither of them was in a hurry. They enjoyed taking their time, investigating the islands. If they liked what they saw, they dropped anchor and stayed for a few days, or a few weeks. If they didn't like the island, they sailed away. Mango considered it a perk of having a floating home.

He drove with his left foot, keeping his right leg tucked back against the seat. Even though he had a state-of-the-art prosthetic leg with tiny servo motors and computer-controlled robotics, he still didn't have the nerve endings that would allow him to feel the pedals.

He'd been a member of the Coast Guard's elite Maritime Security Response Team, doing ship boarding exercises in the Persian Gulf. He'd mistimed the jump from their boat to the ladder of a freighter, and his leg had dropped between the two, breaking the bones beyond repair. He'd adapted to the artificial limb, but he still battled depression from the loss of it, and at being mustered out of the service. The depression had almost ended his marriage. When it threatened to overtake him, he thought of those who had it worse than him—like his friend, Greg Olsen, who used a wheelchair after shrapnel from an IED had severed his spinal cord, or the quadriplegics he'd known during his stint in rehab. Those were the true heroes, and it had taken him a long time to see his good fortune.

The road wound around the bay, through the historic district of Fort-de-France and into the mountains. Jennifer wanted to look at the three thousand varieties of tropical flowers growing in the Balata Gardens. Mango was going for the swinging catwalk built through the tree canopy. When they tired of looking at flowers, they planned to tour Habitation Clément, birthplace of rhum agricole, and sample the wares.

Life was good aboard their sailboat. As long as the boat remained afloat, there were no problems. While Jennifer often worried about the local thieves on the islands they visited, Mango never gave it much thought past ensuring their valuables were tucked away in the hidden compartments and that he'd locked the cabin door. Material possessions could be replaced. He never envisioned having his philosophy tested, but he soon would.

CHAPTER THREE

Billy Ron Sorenson watched as an ancient black man tread through the shallow water along the thick mangroves of Fort-de-France Bay. He carried a seine net and cast it to capture the small bait fish swarming along the nutrient-rich plant roots, then emptied the net into a bucket tied to his waist. When he had a full bucket, he carried it to a small canoe and emptied it into half of an old plastic barrel.

Billy Ron wiped his mouth with the back of his hand, the long blade of a carving knife he gripped gleaming in the sunlight. He didn't want to kill the old man, but he needed the canoe. They were far enough back in the swamps that it would take the old man a long time to raise an alarm, and by then, Billy Ron planned to be long gone.

Fortune had smiled on him, as she always had. A passing trawler had plucked Billy Ron from the water and saved his life. The fishermen had given him hot tea and warm blankets and dropped him in Les Trois-Îlets. He'd grabbed the waterproof pouch he kept his passport and cash in before abandoning ship, but it wasn't much, and the fishermen had felt sorry for him and given him a few dollars. He'd used them to buy himself one decent meal. Billy Ron found it hard to think with an empty belly, and his was growling again. It was time to find another boat and restart his business.

Before the bitch had shot a hole in his boat and sent it to Davy Jones's Locker, he'd operated a small charter service, ferrying his clients between the islands. Sometimes it was just from one island to another, sometimes it was a run from Trinidad to the Dominican Republic. He'd taken advantage of a few women like Naomi. She'd been his favorite, even though she'd gotten loose and tried to kill him. Well, she was dead now, and he was here.

Why she hadn't shot him in the back, he could only guess, but it didn't matter. Naomi's first shot had damaged the electrical system and kicked off the Hydrovane self-steering, then the storm waves had pushed the bow around and the flooding water made the hull sluggish. The old boat had lurched, and Billy Ron had attacked. As he strangled her, he'd had his way with her until her eyes grew dull and her chest quit rising and falling. It was more exhilarating than any other woman he'd killed.

The old black fisherman shuffled through the shallow water, dragging his canoe. As he approached, he saw Billy Ron crouched among the mangrove roots in ankle-deep water. Billy Ron's face, hands, and arms were a mass of mosquito bites and mud he'd smeared on himself to keep the mad, little blood suckers away.

The old man spoke to him in the lilting accent of the islands—the slow drawl that let you know there was never any hurry—but he spoke French. While Billy Ron couldn't understand the words, he could hear the inflection and the tone. The old man was scolding him for hiding.

Billy Ron felt a hunger deep in his soul. It wasn't the same as with a woman; they stirred his sex drive. Men were just targets of opportunity, and lately, the bloodlust had been singing in his ears.

Across the bay, the ferry steamed through the sun-dappled waters of Fort-de-France Bay toward Les Trois-Îlets. He had to get on with this. He needed to get to the sailboat at anchor in the bay. He'd watched the couple, he assumed owned the boat, leave earlier and didn't know how soon they would return, but he wanted as much of a head start as possible.

He gestured to the canoe in a way that said, *let me have it*.

Worry creased the old man's face, either from the lack of understanding or the way Billy Ron brandished the knife. Billy Ron gave him a wry smile and gestured again, but the man just shook his head.

"Give it to me, old man."

Again, the fisherman shook his head, then backed away.

Billy Ron felt the dark fury rise inside of him. He lunged. The knife caught the man in the chest, the point striking bone and sliding off, driving deep inside his fragile chest cavity. Billy pressed the man under the water and held him there until he stopped struggling, blood swirling around his hands and arms in the gin clear water. He jerked the knife from the fisherman's chest and wiped it on the old man's clothes.

Billy Ron closed his eyes and let the energy from the kill wash over him. It felt so good.

The canoe sliced easily through smooth water, and Billy Ron was aboard the sailboat in a matter of minutes. He tied off the canoe and used the big carving knife to jimmy the cabin door lock. As he staggered to the refrigerator, he glanced around the well-appointed cabin and smiled at his choice of boats. This one would do nicely, and it had a steel hull. No one would be shooting this one out from under him.

He grabbed the first water bottle he saw and drained it in long gulps, letting the cool water flow over his chin and trickle down his sweaty chest. Then, he tossed the bottle into the sink and smiled as he reached for a beer. He rolled the bottle across his forehead before chugging it. The next one went down just as fast. The third he sipped while he rummaged through the chart table and the cabin's drawers. His smile grew broader when he found a pair of engine keys. He savored the fourth beer as he fired up the Yanmar diesel and hoisted the anchor.

Moments later, he was motoring out of Fort-de-France Bay, making for the open seas.

CHAPTER FOUR

It was well past sunset when Mango and Jennifer returned to the small parking lot where they and other boaters parked their cars overnight. They walked to their dinghy carrying two bags, one with groceries and the other full of rhum bottles. Mango set the bags in the boat and slung off his backpack. Jennifer held a small flashlight to help him see as he unlocked the chain and pulled it from around the post.

"The mast light isn't on," Jennifer said.

Mango straightened and gazed toward where their sailboat was anchored. Or, at least, where their sailboat had been anchored.

He leaped into the dinghy and started the motor with two yanks of the cord. Jennifer jumped aboard and they roared away. Mango disregarded the normal etiquette of idling through the anchorage so as not to disturb the other boats, instead slaloming through at high speed, racing toward the spot *Alamo* had rode on anchor for the last week.

"What the hell, bro!" he exclaimed. Their boat was nowhere to be seen. He chopped the throttle, and the dinghy drifted over their previous anchorage.

Mango gripped the engine tiller and tamped down the anger threatening to explode from him. He had to keep it together for Jennifer, but inside, he was seething. This was the second sailboat he'd lost.

He blinked his eyes hard, trying to make the Amazon 44 sailboat reappear.

Jennifer spun on the front seat to face her husband, tears glistening on her cheeks. "What are we going to do?"

Mango gritted his teeth, the anger still a white-hot fire in his belly. He turned to look at the other boats in the vicinity. Several were brightly lit, and people had come out to see why he'd disturbed their peace. He pushed the motor hard to starboard, cracked the throttle, and the little boat headed to port.

They came alongside a double-ended sailboat, and Mango rapped on the hull. An older man with neatly combed white hair wearing a pink polo shirt and pleated khaki shorts appeared in the cabin hatch, holding a miniature schnauzer.

"Hey, Gene," Mango said.

"Ah, Mango, I thought you left. Where's your boat?"

"Someone stole it," Jennifer blurted.

"What?" Gene stepped into the cockpit to look past them at the empty bay.

"Did you see anything?" Mango asked.

"As a matter of fact, I saw your boat heading out. I thought you had left without saying goodbye." He paused in thought, then mused, "I did find it strange that there was a canoe tied to the stern."

"Did you see who was on it?" Jennifer demanded.

"A man," Gene replied. "I assumed you were at the helm, Mango. I can't see so well without my glasses. I'm terribly nearsighted."

"Can I use your radio?" Mango asked. "I'd like to put an alert out to the cruiser network."

"Certainly. Come aboard." Gene gestured for him to do so.

Mango sighed in relief. "Thanks, bro."

Jennifer tied the dinghy's bow line to one of the sailboat's midships cleats, and the couple scrambled aboard the double-ender. In the salon, Gene's wife, Mary, gave Jennifer a hug and poured her a glass of wine while Mango put an alert out on the cruiser network using Gene's VHF radio.

After Mango rehung the mic in its holder, he accepted a beer from Gene. He took a drink and rested his head on his hand. "I'm not sure what else to do."

Gene picked up the dog and stroked her head. "When we were in the Bahamas, something similar happened. The man who'd lost his boat put pictures on Facebook and posted rewards on many of the cruising forums. Someone spotted his boat in the Florida Keys and the police arrested the thief. I presume you could do something like that as well."

Mango retrieved his phone from his backpack and scrolled through the pictures, looking for a profile shot of *Alamo*.

"If you'd like, you can use my computer," Gene offered.

Mango gratefully accepted Gene's offer and posted pictures of *Alamo* on several social media pages and forums, offering a reward of five thousand dollars for information leading to the return of the boat.

When Jennifer had finished her second glass of wine, Mango helped her into the dinghy and headed for the dock, where he refastened the chain, wrapping it around the post he'd removed it from an hour earlier. He drove them to the Hotel Bakoua. The couple had eaten dinner in the hotel's restaurant several nights ago, and the valet recognized Mango when he stepped from the car.

"*Bonsoir, monsieur.*" The valet switched to English. "Welcome back."

"Thanks, Pierre," Mango said, reading the kid's name tag.

"Are you eating dinner? Le Chateaubriand is just about to close."

"We'd like to get a room."

"Excellent, *monsieur*. I will get your bags." Pierre stepped around to the trunk.

"We don't have any," Jennifer said, her voice trembling.

Pierre cocked his head, then grinned. "Ah, *une aventure d'un soir*." He translated when Mango and Jennifer looked puzzled. "An adventure of the night. You say ... ah, a one-night stand?"

Mango laughed and put his arm around his wife's shoulders. "Exactly, Pierre."

The young valet grinned and got into the driver's seat. Mango and Jennifer stepped into the hotel and paid for the only room they had available, a seaside luxury suite. Mango filled out the guest information using their false names, Steven and Jillian Smith, a concession to the Aztlán Cartel's bounty.

"Welcome," the concierge said with a smile. She handed over the keys, and the couple headed across the hotel grounds toward their room.

"We need clothes for tomorrow," Jennifer said, looping her arm through her husband's.

"We can get what we need from a shop in town." He bumped her with his hip. "You can buy a new bikini."

"Is sex all you think about?" she chided with a smile.

"Every thirty seconds, according to the scientists."

"You're incorrigible."

"Don't you know it—and enjoy it."

"I do," she conceded, "but I'm worried about our boat."

"Me, too, babe." Mango patted her hand and held up the bag containing the rhum. "Let's get to the room and have a drink."

He needed one to steady his nerves. Mango was trying to hold it together for Jennifer, but inside he was wracked with guilt and anger. As he poured their drinks, he silently vowed to find the son of a bitch who had stolen their boat and hang him from the yard arm.

CHAPTER FIVE

The water churned with sediment, and each step Ryan Weller took stirred it even more. He tugged at the umbilical of air hoses and safety lines connecting his Kirby Morgan hard hat diving helmet to the compressor on the barge one hundred and twenty feet above him. He glanced at his dive computer. He'd been working almost an hour, breathing twenty-nine percent nitrox. The extra eight percent of oxygen helped limit the nitrogen collecting in his tissues, but he still needed to do several hours in the decompression chamber. He hated riding the iron coffin. The best part about it was climbing out.

"You have ten more minutes, Ryan," Stacey Wisnewski said over the communications line. The fiber optics made her sound like she was in the helmet with him.

"Roger that," Ryan replied. "I can send up one more container."

A massive cargo container ship had lost its steering during a storm on its way to St. Croix, and the ship had rolled hard to port, spilling containers into the open ocean. Fortunately, they weren't deep, and the insurance company was paying

Dark Water Research to raise them from the seabed. So far, he, Travis Wisnewski, and the team's new diver and engineer, Mike Cochran, had raised a hundred. They had seventy to go, according to the ship's manifest and insurance documents. Most were in a jumbled pile, with others scattered along the drifting route of the ship. They'd used GPS to pinpoint the containers' locations, so all the tug had to do was push the barge over the coordinates and hover in place while the divers attached the lift sling and the crane operator hoisted the containers aboard.

Ryan concentrated on latching the crane cable to the cargo box's lift points, then scrambled out of the way and told Stacey to lift the container. He stood in the muck, watching the forty-foot-long steel box ride out of the gloom toward the brilliant Caribbean sunshine.

"Ready to come up?" Stacey asked.

"Yes, I'm clear."

The slack went out of Ryan's umbilical, and he too rose from the depths. As he did, light filtered through the water. There was no need for the helmet-mounted lights he used at night, and he'd forgotten he'd turned them on this morning when his dive had started at six o'clock.

He reached up to flip them off and caught movement out of the corner of his face plate, which blocked most of his peripheral vision. What looked like a long, gray torpedo scooted along the edge of the gloom. Ryan's eyes focused on the eight feet of natural predator. The blue shark turned, and Ryan saw the large pectoral fin, looking like a surfboard sticking out of the its side. It always made him do a double take. It seemed like the big pelagic creature was simply curious though, and Ryan didn't think it would harm him.

He vented his helmet, blasting a burst of bubbles into the water, and the shark retreated into the haze. It was uncommon to see a blue so close to shore. They preferred to cruise the depths. Old blue must have heard the noise or smelled something coming from one of the containers and come up the underwater walls to investigate the containers.

Minutes later, Ryan was standing on the deck of the barge *Miss Carolina*. He stripped to his underwear and hopped into the recompression chamber. Stacey blew him down to fifty feet, where he'd spend the next two hours. The barge had a larger chamber than the single person tube on their salvage vessel, *Peggy Lynn*. He dried off and lay back on the bunk. Time to catch some z's.

The changing air pressure woke Ryan. He peered at the clock hanging outside the chamber window. He'd done his time, and they were bringing him up.

"Rise and shine, Diver," Stacey said through the crackling speaker. She had taken to calling them all *diver* when they were underwater or in the chamber.

She cracked the door open, and fresh air rushed in. Even though the chamber was air-conditioned and shaded, it still got hot inside from the sweltering tropical sun. Ryan slid outside and stood, swaying in the heat. There was no breeze on the dead-still water. In the distance, the green rise of St. Croix's hills shimmered. He ran a hand through his brown hair. It needed a trim, but here on the open ocean, he didn't worry so much about it. He bent and touched his fingertips to his toes, feeling every muscle in his six-foot frame stretch across his bones.

He glanced at Stacey, who had gone to the far side of the barge to the tender station. Her bright purple hair was fading, and the roots were showing brown where her hair had grown longer. She turned and gestured for him to hurry. He grinned. They'd once flirted shamelessly with each other when they'd worked together in Key Largo at a dive shop, but now, she all but ignored him. She only had eyes for her husband, Travis.

Ryan pulled on the pair of shorts waiting for him on the

deck beside the chamber and slid into a pair of boat shoes to protect his feet from the barge's steel decking and grating. He flipped a DWR T-shirt over his shoulder and strolled toward where his home between jobs, a Lafitte 44 sailboat named *Windseeker*, lay alongside the barge. Normally, he'd leave her in port and live on their salvage vessel, *Peggy Lynn*, but the weather had been perfect, so he'd brought his boat. It was nice to have a solitary retreat.

Windseeker rubbed her fenders against giant tractor tires mounted on the side of the barge. He cast a critical glance over the gleaming teak he'd hand-rubbed with oil to look like varnish—a testament to the boredom he felt between salvage jobs. The sailboat looked good, and he took pride in her being shipshape. He slipped off the barge and dropped the three feet to *Windseeker*'s deck. As he made his way to the cockpit, he eyed the lines, guides, stays, and ropes for wear. Whoever Joulie Lafitte had gotten to work on the boat had done an exceptional job.

His good mood dampened as he thought about the beautiful woman he'd left in Haiti. She'd broken up with him and told him not to come back. With the current unrest in her country, he was glad he wasn't there, but he still missed her.

After staying out of relationships for the ten years he was a Navy explosive ordnance disposal tech, he'd fallen into two: one with an insurance investigator, and the second with a Haitian warlord. Both had ended with him being kicked to the curb. Maybe it was a sign. Or maybe they weren't the right ones.

He glanced at his watch and flipped on the single-sideband radio. Not only could he listen to reports on the weather in the Caribbean, he could hear the latest cruiser safety and security news. It was entertainment on those long, lonely days on the open ocean and for a sailor, knowing the weather was crucial in making judgments about when to sail, what direction the winds were from, and if there were storms brewing. The same applied to divers. Working underwater in inclement weather was just as hazardous as sailing through it.

While he listened to the weather, he brewed a pot of coffee, put some bread in the toaster, and scrambled two eggs. The weather looked excellent for the next few days until a low pressure moved in from the south, bringing rain and wind. They'd have the containers loaded on the barge and be relaxing on the beach in St. Croix by the time it showed up.

He ate with efficiency, finishing the meal quickly before wiping the dishes clean. Both were habits deeply ingrained from years of living on a boat and his stint in the Navy. Finished with his chores, Ryan crossed over to *Peggy Lynn*. He found Captain Dennis Law and Mike Cochran on the bridge. Cochran worked for DWR and was on loan until Ryan found his own diver and engineer to join his private crew of salvors.

"How's she doing?" Ryan asked, leaning over Cochran's shoulder. Cochran had the flat-screen monitors tuned to the camera on Stacey's dive helmet.

"She's a first-rate diver. With her working, we should get most of 'em bastards up today."

"Good." Ryan glanced at the dive schedule. Travis was in the chamber, Stacey in the water. When she came up, she'd go straight to the chamber, and Cochran would dive at noon.

"Damn big blue shark down there," Cochran said.

"It was."

Ryan refilled his coffee mug. Beside the twelve-cup brewer sat a half-empty bottle of Jim Beam, Captain Law's choice for doctoring his coffee. Since Ryan had hired the old captain to raise gold bars from a sunken freighter off the coast of Haiti, his drinking had slowed, but he still enjoyed the taste of whiskey in his coffee. Ryan thought maybe it was to cover the horrible taste of the overly strong brew. Even Ryan needed a little sugar to smooth the taste, and he normally liked his coffee black, like his soul.

"I'm going over to check on Anthony," Ryan said. They'd hired a young kid from a local commercial dive shop to act as tender.

"He's doing an excellent job." Cochran rose from his seat at the computer monitors. "I'll go with ya."

The two men stepped over to the barge and walked across the deck to the tender station. Emery Ducane, the man everyone called Grandpa, leaned against the bottle rack containing their breathing gas supply. The octogenarian's wild, white hair stuck out from under his black watch cap. His equally white beard had a tobacco stain trailing from the right corner of his mouth. He eyeballed the two men, both fifty years his junior, and spit over the railing.

Ryan glanced over the gauges on the blending station to check the gas mixture and pressures. Everything looked copacetic. Anthony stood by the edge of the barge, holding the thick umbilical that trailed over the side, and disappeared into the water.

"How's she doing?" Ryan shouted over the loud rattle of the compressor.

"She good," the young islander replied. The youth had stripped to his shorts, black skin glistening with sweat, his thin arms and legs corded with muscle.

Ryan said, "Keep a close eye on her. This is one of her first commercial jobs."

Anthony made an OK sign with his fingers. As divers, they had converted from giving the thumbs-up, which meant "go up" in diver sign language.

Cochran motioned Ryan away from the loud compressor. Once the sound was less overwhelming, he said, "We should send Anthony down. We could use another diver to speed up the job."

Ryan nodded. "Who will be the tender?"

"You or Travis."

"What about you?"

Cochran shrugged and gazed across the horizon at St. Croix. Ryan concluded the man wanted to be on the beach, not diving.

"Okay," Ryan agreed. "We'll put him in."

Ryan walked to the dive station, and Cochran meandered back to *Peggy Lynn*. If Anthony was any good at computers and repairing gear, he'd trade the kid for Cochran. Cochran had been Greg Olsen's choice of replacement and seemed more interested in staring at the monitor than doing any actual work. He took his turn in the water and worked hard while under, but he was lazy when he could get away with it. Ryan didn't want that attitude infecting his crew.

"Anthony," Ryan hollered.

The kid turned.

"You want to dive?"

Anthony nodded enthusiastically. He'd brought his helmet and gear when he'd come to the barge.

"You're up when Stacey gets out of the water."

He tucked the umbilical into the crook of his arm and held up double OK signs beside his wide grin.

Ryan slapped him on the back then sipped his coffee. The crane had lifted four cargo containers since she'd gone into the water. He pressed the squawk box button. "How are you doing down there?"

"I'd be better if that damned shark would leave me alone."

Ryan glanced at the clock. "You've got fifteen minutes left."

"Any way we can cut that short? I think I peed myself when the shark rubbed against my back."

"All right. Are you hooked onto a container?"

"Yes. He's been circling this one like crazy."

"It must have some meat in it. Finish getting it hooked and we'll pull you up."

"It's ready now. Get me the hell out of here."

"Copy that, stand by to come up."

Ryan stepped over to Anthony and shouted for him to bring Stacey to the surface. He glanced at the clock. Ryan put his straight hand against his forehead to indicate shark. Anthony nodded and began taking in Stacey's slack.

Ryan went to the barge's dive locker to check the gear then went back to *Windseeker*. With the job came paperwork, and he was tired of shuffling it. He'd just sat down at the navigation desk when the handheld VHF radio squawked.

Jerry, the crane operator, asked, "Hey, Ryan, can you come to the barge?"

With a groan, he rose and made his way across to the rigger's station, where Jerry and two crewmen stood staring into an open container.

"What's up?" he asked.

"Think we found what your shark was interested in," Jerry said.

Ryan peered into the container. He closed his eyes and breathed through his mouth to avoid inhaling the stench of bloated bodies and decaying flesh. His stomach lurched.

"What should we do?" Jerry asked.

Ryan turned his back on the ten dead bodies. "I'll call the U.S.V.I. police and have them come out. Close that up and set it to the side." *What a horrible way to die*, he thought.

Jerry nodded, and the two crewmen closed the container.

Ryan went back to his boat. The stench of death lingered in his nostrils as he sat at the chart table and woke up his laptop to find the number to the St. Croix police department. The big blue must have had the same smell in its nostrils and Ryan wondered why more sharks hadn't been prowling around. He used his sat phone to call the police and asked them to send an investigator.

He shuddered at the thought of the panic and fear the people must have felt when the container rolled off the ship and filled with water. Ryan swore and got up from the navigation table. He couldn't concentrate on the paperwork. He poured a shot of tequila, slugged it down, and went topside to the cockpit. The breezeless ocean air, mingling with diesel smoke from the crane and compressor, was laden with humidity. The relentless sun beat hard on every surface, baking them to oven temperatures.

Human traffickers used cargo containers to smuggle people. To pay off the high price the traffickers demanded, the people trapped in the container were often forced into a form of slavery for the rest of their lives. At least their deaths had set them free. He stripped off his shirt and let the sun burn him as he made his way across the barge to the crane operator.

As he approached, Jerry gave him the puzzled look. He responded by holding two fingers to his lips. With a smile, Jerry dug out a pack of Marlboro Reds. Ryan lit the cowboy killer and took a deep drag. It was good to be alive on an ever-turning earth.

He finished the cigarette while leaning on a railing, staring into the silty water and watching Stacey come up the ladder. Anthony pulled her helmet off and helped her strip out of her wetsuit. She wore a bright purple bikini.

Grandpa stood by the recompression chamber, opening the hatch so Travis could come out. He pecked his wife on the lips as she passed and entered the chamber. A minute later, Stacey was being blown back to their working pressure.

Travis pulled on shorts and walked over to Ryan. "What's the deal with that container?"

"It's got dead bodies in it."

"Really?"

"Yeah," Ryan said. "I called the police. They're sending someone out."

Travis nodded.

Ryan straightened. "I need to get more paperwork done. Anthony is going in next."

"Anthony?"

"Cochran suggested it," Ryan said. "I think he's avoiding his turn."

Travis frowned. "He'll need to dive after Anthony so we can get the rest of the boxes up."

"I think we need to send him back to DWR."

Travis nodded in agreement.

Ryan walked to *Windseeker* and settled into his work. Being the boss sometimes sucked.

At noon, he stood and switched on the SSB again, changing the frequency to the safety and security briefing. He rinsed his coffee cup and refilled it before doctoring it with rum. He had his own vices and demons.

The speaker crackled, and a voice he hadn't heard in six months came through loud and clear. He spun to stare at the radio.

"This is Steve Smith. Yesterday, someone stole our sailboat *Alamo* from Fort-de-France Bay in Martinique. She's a steel hull Amazon 44. You'll recognize her by the distinct pilot house, dark blue hull, and white topside. She'll have a similar colored jib."

Ryan stood in disbelief with his mouth open. The airwaves sang with people asking questions about the theft. He took a slug of coffee, burned his lip, and then grabbed his sat phone. He dialed Mango Hulsey's number, but he didn't answer, so Ryan jumped on the SSB.

When Mango came on, Ryan said, "Where are you now?"

"At a hotel on Martinique," Mango replied.

"Call me. You got the number?"

"Yes," Mango said.

A minute later, the phone rang.

"Tell me what happened," Ryan said without preamble.

Mango reported what he knew and told Ryan where they were staying. While he listened, Ryan spread a chart of the Caribbean on the table and used a ruler to determine the distance between his position and Martinique. After a few calculations, Ryan said, "It will take me a couple days to get there and then we'll find your boat."

"All right, bro," Mango said eagerly.

"See you in a few days." Ryan ended the call, scrambled up on the barge, and jogged across to *Peggy Lynn*.

When Ryan entered the bridge, Dennis said, "We heard."

Ryan glanced between Travis, Dennis, and Cochran. "I'm taking off for Martinique."

"What about the police and the dead people in the container?" Travis asked.

"You guys can handle that, and we only have a few more days on this job. Use Anthony and get it done. Hire someone off the beach if you have to."

Captain Dennis nodded. "Go help Mango and Jennifer."

While Ryan trotted back to his boat, he made plans in his head. He dropped into the cockpit and started the engine. When he started forward to get the bow line, Travis untied it and tossed it to him.

"I'd love to come with you," Travis said.

"I know, but I need you to stay here and get this job done. I'll talk to Greg about Cochran."

Travis gave him an OK sign.

Ryan engaged the prop drive, and the big sailboat eased away from the barge. He tapped the fuel gauge. The wind needed to pick up. He didn't have enough fuel to motor to Martinique. Stepping to the chart plotter, he put in Les Trois-

Îlets. The distance calculations propagated on the screen. At six knots, it would take fifty-five hours to travel the three hundred and thirty-one miles to the French island.

Ryan ran the motor at half throttle. The cruise would take longer, but he needed to conserve fuel. He wished he had Greg's big Hatteras GT63, *Dark Water*, to make the marathon run in less than a day.

With nothing to do but wait while the autopilot steered *Windseeker* on a southeastern route, Ryan ran calculations for the Amazon's travel radius. He looked up the specs of Mango's sailboat, trying to determine how far away the thief would be now if the thief had left yesterday and sailed around the clock—assuming he hadn't ditched the boat or sunk it. When he finished, Ryan had six expanding circles drawn on a chart around Martinique. Three were red, showing motoring distance for the last three days; the other circles were blue, showing the sailing distance.

Ryan went back outside and scanned the horizon. A massive crude tanker steamed off his starboard bow. He felt antsy. This cruise was taking too long, and the thief was still out there.

He reached over and shoved the throttle forward. To hell with the fuel.

CHAPTER SIX

The fuel gave out before he reached Martinique. For six long hours, the boat sat motionless in the sun, while Ryan prayed for the wind to fill his sails.

Finally, a ghost of a breeze flapped the limp jib and main. Ryan urged the wind to rise. He had places to be and stuck in the doldrums was not one. Once the wind filled the sails, there wasn't any stopping him.

He put on as much canvas as he could and raced toward Martinique. The nap during the doldrums had done him wonders, and he sailed into Fort-de-France Bay twenty hours later. Without an engine, he'd have to drop anchor while under sail. He sailed directly at Les Trois-Îlets—though, while he could speak some French, he could never get the pronunciation right, and it always sounded more like "Les Toilets." It was just as easy to say, "The Three Islands."

When he decided on his anchorage, he spun the boat to tack upwind. He'd laid out the scope of his anchor rode along the deck, having previously checked the charts for water depth. He ran forward, ready for the sail to luff. As soon as the wind came out of the canvas and the boat stopped making way, he tossed the anchor overboard.

When the wind started to push the boat backward, he dropped the mainsail. The wind caught the jib and pushed him back even quicker. Ryan jerked the line connected to the jib's roller furler and the jib rolled smoothly onto the forestay while the anchor rode slid off the boat's deck. He felt the anchor bite into the sand, and the boat stopped with a jerk that nearly knocked him off his feet.

Over the sound of the wind, he heard another sound. Ryan turned to see an older man standing in the cockpit of a double-ender, watching him and clapping. A small dog barked.

Ryan bowed then began securing the sails. He straightened the main between the lazy jacks before putting a cover on it. For the long ocean passage, he'd put his dinghy on the bow. He unstrapped it and slid it over the rail, then mounted the Honda ten horsepower outboard. After locking his cabin, he motored across to the double-ender.

The man who had clapped was still in the cockpit when Ryan came alongside, and the miniature schnauzer was standing on the gunwale, yapping.

"Fine piece of seamanship you displayed over there," the man said, rising from his seat.

"Thanks." Ryan grinned, proud of his skills. "My name's Ryan. I'm looking for a couple of friends of mine, Steve and Jillian Smith."

"Name's Gene." He scooped up the dog, and it stopped barking. "I saw them yesterday. They came by and used my radio to listen for reports of their stolen boat over the safety and security net."

Ryan nodded. "That's why I'm here. Did you see who stole *Alamo*?"

"I told the Smiths that I saw a man in the cockpit, and he was towing a canoe."

"Nothing else?" Ryan asked.

"No," the elderly boat owner replied.

"Where's the Hotel Bakoua from here?"

"Around the point." Gene pointed to the north. "You'll see the boats moored outside the hotel's breakwater. You'll need to clear customs at the ferry terminal across the bay."

"Thanks, Gene," Ryan said and glanced at the sun. "Suppose they're still open?"

"They won't be by the time you get there."

"Okay, I'll see you later."

He motored away, opening the throttle to the stop, the seafloor zipping by under crystal-clear water. Rather than round the Pointe du Bout peninsula to beach at the hotel, he slipped into the marina nestled in the peninsula's fork. He filled the two diesel cans he'd brought with him and asked if he could leave his dinghy while he walked to the Bakoua. The marina staff showed him where to dock his boat, then gave him directions to the hotel. Ryan walked along the narrow streets most famous as the birthplace of Josephine, wife of Napoleon Bonaparte.

When he found the hotel, he asked the clerk to call the Smiths' room, remembering at the last second that they were traveling under assumed names. Ryan had his own fake passport but chose not to use it. Someday, the bad guys would catch up to him, and he'd have to deal with it; until then, he wasn't hiding. He'd done that for six months, and even then, the cartel had found him in Key Largo.

The clerk replaced the phone receiver in the cradle. "There is no answer in their room, *monsieur*."

Ryan nodded and asked for directions to the restaurant. He could wander the grounds and look for his former DWR partner-in-crime without being questioned by the staff.

Before he reached the restaurant, he spotted Mango hunched at a bar, the gleaming metal of his artificial leg a dead giveaway.

"I'll have what he's having," Ryan said to the bartender and sat on a stool beside his friend.

Mango slapped Ryan on the back. "You made it, bro."

"Are you drunk?"

Mango grinned. "Not yet, but I'm working on it."

"Where's Jennifer?"

"She's pissed at me and went for a walk."

"What did you do now?" Ryan asked.

Mango held up his shot glass and stared at Ryan through the liquid inside it.

The bartender set a shot in front of Ryan. Her name tag said Aimee, and she had dark skin and long braids holding the black hair back from her oval face. Her white shirt and blue shorts did little to hide her figure.

He picked up the shot glass. "What's this?"

"Tequila," Aimee said.

He downed it without salt or lime, then tapped the bar for another.

"Whoa, now she's gonna be pissed at you, too, bro," Mango said, slurring his words.

"We got work to do, Mango."

He sighed. "Yeah, we do."

"Any leads yet?" Ryan asked.

Mango shook his head. "Nope. We put posts on every social media site available, from Facebook to FarmersOnly."

Ryan laughed. "What about the cruiser net?"

"Nothin'."

"I made some calculations on the way here," Ryan said. "I figured out speed and distance and have a general radius the guy could have traveled."

"Yeah, me too." Mango downed the shot and waved at the bartender.

Aimee glanced at Ryan when she set his shot down, and he made a tiny hand gesture to tell her not to serve Mango anymore liquor. She gave him a wink and walked away.

"Hey!" Mango called after her.

Ryan cut him off. "We've got too much work to do for you to be sitting here feeling sorry for yourself."

Mango crinkled his eyebrow, lip curling disdainfully. "Shot blocker," he muttered. Then he grabbed Ryan's shot and downed it.

"Get this joker some coffee and a glass of water," Ryan told Aimee. He gave her a wink and laid a fifty euro note on the bar. He kept an assortment of currencies on his boat for the different islands.

Aimee replied with a wink of her own.

"Any idea where the blonde went that was with him?" Ryan asked.

"She's at the pool."

"Thanks." Ryan stood. To Mango he said, "Don't wander off."

Mango gave a sloppy salute. "Roger that, good buddy."

Ryan walked through the hotel grounds to the infinity pool where Jennifer was lying on a chaise lounge. He stretched out on a chair beside her and placed his hands behind his head. The pool looked as if it extended right into the placid blue waters of the tiny cove. Beyond the protective seawall, several sailboats rode at anchor.

"Wherever there's trouble in paradise, the great Ryan Weller rides to the rescue," Jennifer said mirthlessly.

"Do you want me to leave?"

"No." She gave a heavy sigh. "I'd like people to stop stealing my boat."

"I'm here to help. If you don't want me to, I'll go away." He swung his legs off the chaise and rose.

Jennifer grasped his hand to stop him from leaving. "I'm sorry I'm cross. It just seems like every time you show up, my husband's life becomes forfeit, but please stay and help us get our boat back."

"Okay." Ryan sat, but she didn't let go of his hand. "Let's get your husband sobered up and start this project."

"Have you seen him yet?" she asked.

"I talked to him at the bar and got the bartender to swap out the tequila for coffee and water."

They found Mango where Ryan had left him, his head in his hands and elbows on the bar. Aimee was refilling a water glass, and she smiled at Ryan.

Ryan smiled back. "Let me have one of those and something for the lady."

"I'll have the same," Jennifer said.

Aimee moved to fill the order.

"So," Ryan said, sitting between the husband and wife, "what do we know?"

"Nothing—we know nothing," Mango said.

"Come on, dude. Don't quit on me. We suspect a lone male stole your boat. If he sailed around the clock, he could be three hundred and forty miles from here."

"Not if he was towing a canoe," Jennifer added.

Aimee came back and set the water glasses on the bar. "I heard about the sailboat theft. You said he was towing a canoe?"

"That's what our eyewitness said," Ryan said.

The young woman looked concerned. "There was an old man murdered out in the mangroves. The police say he was casting for bait and his canoe was missing."

"Do you know who I can talk to about it?" Ryan asked her.

"My brother is an inspector," she said.

"Can you introduce me?"

She grew suspicious, backing away from the counter and casting a wary eye on him. "Why are you asking?"

"If the canoe is missing from the murder site and our boat thief had a canoe tied to the stern of the sailboat when he left the harbor, the murderer might have stolen their boat."

"Oh, sweet Mother Mary," Jennifer whispered.

Aimee nodded and walked to the end of the bar. She picked up the phone and made a quick call. When she returned to where Mango, Jennifer, and Ryan were sitting, she said, "My brother, Mathieu, will speak to you. He wants me to bring you to the station when I am done with my shift."

"When is that?" Mango asked.

"In an hour, *monsieur*, but you will not be going. I won't take a drunk to meet my brother."

"Take him to the room, Jennifer. I'll go with Aimee to see the inspector."

Jennifer helped Mango stand, and he leaned on her as they wobbled to their room.

As they left, the front desk clerk appeared, standing a respectful five feet away and eyeing Ryan. "Excuse me, *monsieur*."

"What do you want, Jacques?" Aimee asked, her voice a scathing rebuke.

"This man is not registered at the hotel. I saw him wandering the grounds and talking with the guests. I am asking him to leave before I call security."

Aimee snorted, her face twisting into a frown. "This man is my guest."

Jacques sneered at her, turned his nose up, and stormed away.

Aimee flipped her braids over her shoulder. "He is a petty little man."

"Maybe I should get a room," Ryan said.

She grinned mischievously. "Maybe you should."

"I'm staying on my sailboat."

Her grin remained. "I like boats."

They chatted until her shift was over then walked to the parking lot.

"How will you get to the police station?" Aimee asked.

In Haitian Creole, Ryan told her he would ride in her car. He'd been listening to the natives and found their Creole to be similar to the Haitian he'd picked up during his stay in Cap-Haïtien.

Aimee's mouth hung open for a moment as she stopped at a scooter and picked up a helmet from the seat. She recovered with a smile and replied in Martinican Creole.

Ryan only understood half of what she said. In English, he replied, "I'll just ride on your scooter."

She threw back her head and laughed, then yammered at him in French.

Ryan held up his hands. "I don't speak French, either."

"Good, it will keep you on your toes." She threw a leg over her scooter and started it. "Are you getting on?"

Ryan slipped on behind her, feeling like a monkey on a football with how big he was compared to the diminutive machine. Aimee took them through the narrow, twisting streets, weaving around cars and potholes. Eventually, she stopped in front of a bright yellow house surrounded by lush flowers.

"Wait here. I want to change clothes."

Ryan stood on the sidewalk and admired the hard work the homeowner had done to manicure the gardens and shape the draping vines to the stone retaining walls and trellises. Steps led from the rear of the house, up the retaining wall to the next street.

Aimee came out wearing a blue sundress. She mounted

the scooter again, and Ryan climbed behind her. Again, she negotiated the streets, this time to the police station.

The two-story building, with its faded yellow clapboard siding and porch and balcony running the length of the front, looked more at home in a Spaghetti Western. The white bars covering the doors and window matched the balcony railing. Ryan expected Doc Holliday to step off the porch and say, "I'm your huckleberry."

Aimee parked and shut off the scooter. Ryan slid off, thankful to be on solid ground, and followed her into the building. She and the desk sergeant chatted in French before he called over his shoulder for Mathieu, all the while smiling dopily at the inspector's pretty sister.

Inspector Mathieu Courbon was tall and lean. He wore his hair close-cropped, and his uniform had crisp, military creases in it.

"Sista, is this the man?"

Aimee nodded.

"It is good to meet you, *monsieur*." Mathieu extended his hand.

Ryan shook it and introduced himself. "I'm helping the Smiths find their stolen sailboat. An eyewitness saw the boat towing a canoe as it was leaving the harbor. I think your murderer and my thief are the same man."

"I heard about da Smiths' boat. Ah did not know there was an eyewitness."

"I believe the thief has left the island," Ryan said.

Mathieu nodded. "I believe that as well. Why are you interested in this case?"

"The Smiths are my friends, and I want to help them."

The inspector nodded again. "This be a dangerous man."

"Do you have any leads?" Ryan pressed.

"No, we don't."

"Where was the man killed?"

"Back in de mangroves. I get you a map, but the water washes away all de evidence."

Ryan shrugged. "You never know."

"This I do know. I investigated da scene."

"I'll take a look, anyway."

Inspector Mathieu brought out a map and spread it on the counter. He pointed at the spot and gave Ryan the GPS coordinates. "If ya find anything, you let me know?"

"I will."

"Good. What else can I do for you, Mr. Weller?" Mathieu said.

Ryan asked, "Do you know where I can rent a plane?"

"Are you a pilot?"

"No. I want to search for the sailboat from the air."

"How do you know where to look?" Mathieu asked, resting his forearms on the counter.

"I don't, but I can make an educated guess based on times and distances."

Mathieu nodded. "I know a man." He gave Ryan the information, then excused himself to return to his office.

Ryan and Aimee walked outside and climbed back on the scooter.

"Where to now, Yankee?" she asked, grinning over her shoulder.

"Marina Pointe du Bout," Ryan said as he wrapped his arms around her slim waist.

It took ten minutes for them to reach the marina. Aimee followed him to the dinghy and climbed in.

He turned toward her; brow furrowed. "Where are you going?"

"I'm coming with you. My father was a fisherman, as was his father."

"I have the GPS coordinates," Ryan said. "I'll be okay."

"I grew up in the mangroves. You will need a guide."

Not wanting to waste time arguing, he moved to untie the painter and they climbed aboard. They stopped at *Windseeker*, where he emptied the ten gallons of diesel into the tank. Now he could move her to marina, top off her tanks, and have dockside power for air conditioning. First, he wanted to see where the old fisherman had met his demise.

As they raced across the bay, Ryan couldn't stop yawning. The long sail had worn him out and he needed sleep. Aimee diverted his attention by pulling her sundress over her head, revealing a matching blue bikini. Suddenly alert, he wished this was more of a pleasure cruise.

Ryan glanced at his handheld GPS, keeping the boat on the line leading to their destination. Ten minutes of high-speed driving brought them to the mangrove shallows where the old man's body had been discovered. Ryan wasn't optimistic they'd find anything, and after a half hour of searching among the shifting sands and mangrove knees and roots, they called it quits and motored back across the bay. The rush of wind caused by the speeding boat blew away the cloud of mosquitos that had descended on them in the mangroves.

He came abreast of *Windseeker* and tied off the painter. Aimee looked at him quizzically.

"I'm about to fall asleep," he told her. "I've been awake for almost twenty-four hours and need to crash. You can take the dinghy back to the harbor, and I'll bring the sailboat in tomorrow."

Aimee smiled coquettishly. "You can drive me there in the morning."

CHAPTER SEVEN

Each day they didn't find *Alamo* was another day she could be farther away. They knew time was of the essence, but questions nagged at Ryan's thoughts. What if the thief had sunk the boat, or ran it aground in some forgotten mangrove swamp? He could be days away from Martinique or right around the corner. No one on the cruiser's net had seen *Alamo*, either. If the man had changed her name or altered her shape, they might never find her.

When Ryan and Aimee walked into the dining room of the Hotel Bakoua the next morning, Mango and Jennifer were already sitting at a table, looking glum. Jennifer glanced between the newcomers after they were seated. A sly smile crept across her face. Ryan gave her a *don't go there* glare, and she laughed.

"What's the plan?" Mango asked.

"A pilot will meet us at the airport," Ryan said. "We'll take a tour of the island and see if the boat is here, then we'll pick a direction and work our way out."

"What we need," Mango said, "is satellite coverage."

"I'm not sure we can get satellite coverage for a stolen boat," Ryan said.

"You could talk to your friend," Mango said.

"Let's see what we come up with in next couple of days," Ryan said. "I owe *our* friend too many favors already."

"And you know he'll collect at some point," Mango said.

"That's why I'm worried." Ryan knew Floyd Landis, his old DHS handler from when he'd worked for Dark Water Research, would eventually collect on the many favors he'd already done. Ryan wanted to avoid adding to the mounting list of goodwill he owed Landis.

The waiter arrived with menus, and Ryan and Aimee ordered. When they finished their meal, Aimee said she needed to get ready for her shift at the bar, but that she'd be glad to help search for the Smiths' boat when she was off work.

Mango drove Jennifer and Ryan to the Martinique Aimé Césaire International Airport. They bypassed the main terminal, stopped at the small fixed base operator's building, and trooped to the front desk, where Ryan asked for Leon De Ridder. The receptionist directed them to Hangar Twelve.

Approaching the hangar, they saw a twin-engine Piper Aztec equipped with floats that would allow it to land in the water. A stocky white man with dark hair stood on a ladder beside the port engine. He had the cowling up and was wiping the oil dipstick on a rag.

He turned as the three stopped at the entrance to the hangar. "*Oui?*"

"We're looking for Leon De Ridder."

A smile lifted the man's cheeks. "I am he. Come. Come." He motioned for them to enter the hangar.

Ryan glanced around the space. The plane sat on a pristine floor of polished concrete. Under the plane's port wing were long black-and-chrome toolboxes. One drawer was open, and Ryan could see foam padding inside, with cutouts for each tool. To the right of the plane, a sofa and chairs formed a lounge area. They faced what Ryan guessed was a seventy-five-inch flat-screen television, playing a soccer match. On the right side of the TV was a bookcase laden with technical manuals, books on flight, vinyl records, and two models of the Piper. Mounted on a wall to the TV's left were several plaques and certificates. The first was from a flight school in France, the second a discharge certificate from the French Foreign Legion. That made Ryan's eyebrows rise.

"What can I do for you?" Leon asked in a heavy French accent.

Mango stepped over to the shorter man and said, "My wife and I had our sailboat stolen. We want to hire you so we can look for it."

Leon nodded and closed the engine cowling. "How long ago did they steal your boat?"

"It's been four days," Mango said. "We have a chart with sailing and motoring distances on it."

"Let's have it." Leon motioned to a workbench.

"You were in the Legion?" Ryan asked as Mango spread out their chart.

Leon glanced at the discharge certificate. "Suppose you can read, then."

"I was Navy EOD. Mango was Coast Guard."

The pilot looked unimpressed. He leaned over the chart and studied it while wiping his hands. "It's too much ground to cover. You'll never find it."

"We have to try," Jennifer pleaded. "It's our home." Her eyes dropped to the floor, then in a less adamant voice, she added by way of explanation, "We're cruisers."

Leon shrugged. "It's your money. I get paid by the hour and you pay for the fuel."

"Cash or charge?" Ryan asked.

Leon grinned. "As you Americans like to say, cash is king."

Ryan reached into his backpack and pulled out a banded stack of bills. He tossed it to Leon. "That should buy us a few days."

Leon fanned through the stack of hundred-dollar bills, noting the ten-thousand-dollar band. He walked over to a wall safe, opened it, and put the money inside. After he'd closed the safe and spun the dial, he turned and grinned at his new employers. "Have you any pictures of the boat?"

Mango produced one and handed it to Leon, who carried it over to the plane. He climbed into the cockpit and clipped the picture to the dashboard between the two sets of instruments, then stepped back out of the plane.

"If you want to travel around the island, I suggest you speak to my friend Angelo. He runs a helicopter tour service. I'll take you and you." Leon pointed at Mango and Jennifer. "We'll check the ocean and farthest points. EOD will check around the island."

"Sounds like a good plan," Ryan said.

Jennifer and Mango agreed, and fifteen minutes later, the Piper Aztec lifted into the sky.

Ryan went in search of Leon's friend Angelo. He found the Martinican prepping a Eurocopter AS-350B in another hangar. He was a big man, beefy in the chest and arms. While Ryan was muscular from years of working out and the rigorous training he'd done in EOD, he felt dwarfed beside Angelo. When the larger man greeted him, Ryan explained his mission.

"Do you have a picture?" Angelo asked.

He produced a photo.

Angelo studied it carefully before handing it back. "What we need to do is take overhead photographs of the marinas and anchorages. Then we feed the pictures into a computer program that will search for the same characteristics and shape as your boat."

"Do you have a program like that?" Ryan asked.

Angelo shrugged. "No."

"I know someone who can make one for me. I need a camera. Do you have one?"

"I know where you can buy one," the big man said.

"Point me in the right direction."

Angelo pointed across the runway at the airport terminal. "There's a camera shop in there."

"Fuel the bird, and I'll be back in a few minutes."

"You're paying the fuel bill, Yank."

Ryan sighed and pulled out his credit card. This endeavor was becoming costly. He swiped the card through the reader and paid four hundred and twenty dollars for sixty gallons of aviation fuel before using Mango's car to drive to the main terminal where he purchased a Cannon digital camera with a telephoto lens. When he was back in the car, he called Ashlee Calvo's extension at Dark Water Research in Texas City, Texas.

Ashlee had helped Ryan on his last two jobs. She'd located the wreck of the *Santo Domingo* after two hurricanes had moved the freighter over a mile on the seabed. More recently, she had helped him bust a cargo container theft ring in Puerto Rico. If anyone could build him the software he needed, it was her.

When she answered the phone and heard Ryan, her voice filled with excitement. "Hey, Ryan. When are you coming back? Don and I are getting married next May. Don wants you to be a groomsman."

Ryan sighed, not wanting to watch other people get married when his relationships seemed to crumble from the beginning. Still, he told her he would be there which allowed him to change the subject and explain why he had called.

"Email me the photo of Mango's boat, and I'll get started on an algorithm," Ashlee said.

"I'll send it to you now, then email the photos when we get back from the flight."

"Have fun," she said.

Ryan caught her before she could hang up. "Hey, Ashlee."

"What?"

"Can we keep this between us? I know Greg is busy with other stuff."

"I sure will," she replied and hung up.

Ryan called Mango. "Hey, do you have a camera with you?"

"No, why?"

Ryan explained the plan to photograph the boats from the air.

"I'll bring one tomorrow, but I'm pretty sure I'll recognize my own boat."

Ryan drove around to Angelo's hangar. The pilot spooled up the helicopter as Ryan climbed into the copilot seat. They needed to find this boat soon, or it might disappear forever, and this whole exercise would be a waste of time and money. While Ryan hated admitting defeat, he knew Mango and Jennifer had enough money to buy another boat and continue with their voyage.

By the time they landed four hours later, Ryan felt like he'd spent more time staring at the tiny camera screen than looking out the helicopter's window. His bottom hurt from shifting in the uncomfortable seat. As the rotors wound down to a stop, he climbed from the cockpit and walked toward the hangar. The muscles in his cramped legs protested. After a dozen yards, he stopped to stretch. Getting old sucked.

Angelo joined him on the walk to the office. "Will we go out again tomorrow?"

"Yeah," Ryan said. "We'll go south."

"Why?"

"The winds are from the east, and it'll be easier to tack downwind than beat up island."

Angelo nodded. "Then I will see you in the morning."

Ryan took a taxi to the marina, leaving the car for Mango and Jennifer. He went straight to his boat and downloaded the pictures from the camera to his computer, then emailed them to Ashlee. He searched through the photos, trying to make a visual match, but saw nothing close. If he were the thief, he'd have sailed north and then turned east, letting the following wind drive him to Panama.

A knock startled him from his visual search. Aimee's lilting voice came through the open cabin door. "Permission to come aboard, Captain?"

"Permission granted." He chuckled as he turned back to the computer. He heard her soft footsteps come down the ladder and track across the cabin sole. She was barefoot, wearing her work uniform. In her left hand, she carried a bright-colored tote bag. She slipped an arm around his shoulder and kissed his cheek.

He closed his eyes, savoring the warmth of her body pressing against his. Why had he fallen into this trap again? They'd only just met. He steeled his heart and blackened his soul to keep her from burrowing inside, but he knew he'd always carry a piece of her with him.

"How was work?" he asked to break the silence.

"Good." She kissed his neck. "Can I take a shower?"

"Yeah." He gestured toward the forward head.

Her fingers trailed across his shoulders. "Are you busy?"

"Yeah ... sorry. Go ahead without me."

"Too bad." She left him with another kiss on the cheek.

Ryan rubbed his eyes. His distrustful mind wondered how many men she had been with, and if she had tried to seduce each one into giving her a different life or taking her away from Martinique. What was her game? Did she want to help find Mango's boat, was she looking for a weekend romance, or was he just being cynical?

He stared at the computer. When he heard the water running, he stood and walked to the head's door. Gingerly, he tested the latch. She had locked it.

He returned to the desk and tried to focus on the pictures.

An incoming email notification window appeared in the lower right of his computer screen. He clicked on it when he saw it was from Ashlee. She hadn't found a matching boat, and Don had said hello.

Then, his sat phone rang. Greg Olsen's number appeared on the tiny screen.

"What the hell is going on in Martinique?" Greg asked.

Ryan explained the search for the Hulsey's stolen sailboat.

"Why didn't you call me?"

"Because we have it handled," Ryan said.

"Do you know how I found Mango and Jennifer when we needed backup to take down Jim Kilroy?"

"No."

He could hear a smirk in Greg's voice. "I have a tracker on their boat."

"Really?" Ryan asked. "Do you have a tracker on mine, too?"

"Yes."

"Big brother *is* watching."

Greg laughed. "I wouldn't be doing my job if I didn't know where my people are."

"How about you start doing your job and tell me where *Alamo* is?" Ryan snapped.

"I would, but the transmitter isn't responding."

"Great," Ryan muttered.

"I like the direction you're going with the photos," Greg

said. "Keep sending them to Ashlee, and she'll run them through the program."

Ryan heard the door to the head open, and he glanced down the short passageway. Aimee wore a towel and held her tote. She paraded past him to the rear berthing, letting the towel drop as she came abreast of him.

He rose to follow. "I'll talk to you later, Greg."

CHAPTER EIGHT

If there was heaven on earth, Billy Ron Sorenson had found it in the tiny cove of Petit Tabac in the St. Vincent and Grenadines Tobago Cays Marine Park. He lay in a hammock suspended from *Paradise Gone*'s cockpit sun dodger, a beer in one hand and a cigar in the other.

He'd gotten rid of the name *Alamo* by spending a few hours rubbing off the transom letters and painting on new black ones in sweeping cursive. The letters tapered from a large P and meandered up and down the transom like a drunk had painted it—though, to be fair, he had been. He brought the beer to his lips. A lot of men had died at the Alamo. This wasn't his last stand.

After leaving Fort-de-France Bay, he'd headed southeast, following the wind and searching for a secluded spot in which to hole up. Those were tough to find in the Caribbean, but with the end of cruising season approaching, the anchorages were clearing out. July meant hurricane season, and the eastern winds would push him to Panama, where he could hide in the San Blas Islands. His plan was to restart his charter business and maybe find another girl. He grinned.

Definitely find another girl. A sweet, shapely one like Naomi had been.

Many of his problems had solved themselves when he'd stolen this boat. During his high-speed run from Martinique, he'd investigated the cabin, finding several hiding spots the owners had built into the cabinets and woodwork. In one, he'd found a Glock 19 pistol; in another, he'd found a combination of U.S. dollars and euros totaling fifty thousand dollars. Now, he was styling and profiling. He let out a Ric Flair *woo*!

All he had to do was get to Panama without getting caught by some do-gooder trying to collect a fee for reporting him to the owners. He'd come into port at Union Island to get diesel and restock the fridge and pantry. Flush with his newfound cash, he'd splurged on food, but mostly beer and rum.

Billy Ron alternated between puffing the cigar and sipping his beer. He'd been here several times, bringing charter clients to the tiny island made famous in the movie *Pirates of the Caribbean: The Curse of the Black Pearl*. The ship's crew mutinies against Captain Jack Sparrow and maroon Sparrow and Elizabeth Swann on the tiny spit of sand and trees. They discover a rum cache left by smugglers and get roaring drunk before passing out. When Sparrow comes to, Elizabeth has set the rum ablaze to attract help.

Billy Ron's guests liked to find the tree from the movie and mimic Sparrow's exaggerated paces, looking for the underground hiding spot of the rumrunners. Idiots. Of course, there was no hidden cache of rum, but he always gave them plenty of rum—or rum punch for the ladies—and let them explore and take pictures. Sometimes if there were kids on the charter, he'd put on an eyepatch, wave an old cutlass, and roll his r's like a proper pirate.

Those days were behind him now. He'd have to find new

haunts and attractions. Maybe he could ferry backpackers from Columbia to Panama, around the Darien Gap.

The sound of an outboard interrupted his thoughts. He swung his feet from the hammock and stood to see which direction the boat was heading. A small inflatable was coming straight for him, carrying two people. As the boat approached, he could make out a man and a woman in their early twenties. *Probably trust fund babies*, Billy Ron thought.

When the boat came alongside *Paradise Gone*, Billy Ron looked down into the face of a sweet angel with a halo of windblown blonde hair. He licked his lips. Blood surged in his groin and adrenaline sang in his ears. She was a tasty treat in shorts and a bikini top revealing an ample amount of cleavage. She gazed at him with bright green eyes, her lips thin and her nose pert, reminding him of Jennifer Aniston. *Damn*!

His gaze flicked to the male. He was skinny, with the thin ropiness of youth. He wore shorts, but no shirt, allowing Billy Ron a view of the boy's concave belly and bony rib cage.

What the hell is this chick doing with him? Gotta be the money.

"I'm Pammie, and that's my brother, Mike," the girl said.

That explains it, Billy Ron thought as he leered at her.

She said, "We're on *Barefoot* over there."

He turned and looked across the water in the direction she was pointing. He knew the boat was an Island Packet 495. He'd checked it out on the way into town, along with the other boats in the anchorage. He liked this Amazon, but his last boat had been an Island Packet, and he loved their dependability and solid feel in the water. The Amazon felt heavy in comparison.

"Nice boat." Billy Ron spotted a cooler in the dinghy. "Having a picnic?"

"There aren't many people in the anchorage, and we thought we'd invite you," Pammie said. "We're going to the beach."

"Mighty nice of you," Billy Ron said. "I'm Steve Smith."

"You by yourself?" Mike asked.

"Yeah, me and the missus had a falling out. She went back to North Carolina. I changed the name on the stern. Ain't no paradise no more."

"Sorry to hear that," Pammie said. "Hop in and we'll take you to the beach. We have plenty of food." She patted the cooler between her and Mike.

Billy Ron shrugged. "You need any beer or rum?"

"Bring a six-pack," Mike said.

"And bring those abs of yours," Pammie added with a grin. "They're hot."

Billy Ron grinned back and squeezed his muscles, making his abdominals ripple. Pammie giggled, Mike frowned.

Billy Ron grinned wider. *This could be fun*.

He grabbed a six-pack of beer and climbed into the dinghy. Mike gunned the engine, and they raced across the short stretch of water to the beach. They braced themselves as he ran the dinghy onto the sand.

Billy Ron piled out with his beer in one hand and the dinghy painter in the other. He marched up the sand and tied the painter to a tree. Stuffing five beers under his arm, he opened one and took a long swig while he watched Pammie bend and stretch to spread out a blanket and arrange the food.

They had a bottle of chilled wine—*pretentious snots*—and a bottle of rum. *Much better*.

Mike removed the cork and poured a dark red liquid into plastic wine glasses. He passed one to Billy Ron, who declined. Reds always gave him a headache, and most of them were too dry for his taste. He'd choked them down to satisfy clients, but he always knew he'd need a Tylenol after. He watched Pammie lean forward, glimpsing a wonderful view down her bikini top. Maybe he could cure his headache in other ways.

She glanced up at him and caught him staring, but he grinned. That grin disarmed even the most cynical of foes. Pammie beamed and sat up, brushing her hands on her shorts. She fiddled with a diamond stud belly button ring.

Oh, yeah, she was flirting with him. He would have fun with this one.

Another cruiser joined them; some guy named Archie. He was tall and lean with a powerful bearing. Billy Ron had seen guys like him before; former military who were always vigilant. He'd have to watch his back now. The two kids were easy prey, but this asshole intruding on his party wouldn't go down without a fight.

They rapidly finished the food and drink. Billy Ron told them he had plenty more on *Paradise Gone* and had to tell the newcomer about how his wife had left him. His tale brought a look of pity and heartache to Pammie's face. He created little details to make the story more realistic, like how they'd fought about going home and how she'd given up on their dreams. When he wanted to stay, she had called him a fool and hopped the next flight back to the States.

They fell for it hook, line, and sinker, and followed him back to the boat. Lounging in the salon, Billy Ron and his friends drank rum and beer. They toasted to their adventures and to new love. Pammie kissed him hard on the mouth.

Mike remained passive, but Billy Ron saw the apprehension in the boy's eyes.

He put his arm around Pammie's shoulders and winked at her brother. The man blushed and glanced away. *He's queer as a three-dollar bill*, Billy Ron thought. *Ain't no room for no queers on my boat*. He kissed Pammie again and watched Mike's face turn red. *Was it shame or envy?*

Archie didn't seem to notice anything but the way Billy

Ron held Pammie. The man's mood had turned somber as he drank. He hadn't partaken the way the others had, and that bothered Billy Ron. Archie was too watchful.

The rum was just about gone, and the sun had set a long time ago. Billy Ron's hormones were raging. This little woman had spun him up. He wanted her brother to watch as he took his sister. It was the bloodlust singing in his soul. The drink brought on the blackness. He had to get rid of Archie.

As if on que, Archie stood. "We should go. It's been a long day."

"Don't bother yourself with these kids, Arch," Billy Ron said. "They're capable of taking care of themselves."

Archie looked hard at Pammie, but she turned away, burying her face in Billy Ron's neck and giggling. She pulled back. "Make him go away, Mike."

Mike stood; his thin frame as skinny as the mast running down through the cabin. "She wants you to go."

Archie glanced at each of them. "We've all had too much to drink. Let's go sleep it off."

Pammie snuggled up to Billy Ron, wrapping both arms around his left arm and nestling her head on his shoulder. He liked the sensation of her flesh pressing into him. "I'm going to sleep it off right here."

"You heard the lady," Billy Ron said, his voice low and menacing as he stared Archie in the eyes.

Archie held up his hands in surrender. "Talk some sense into your sister, Mike."

Mike said, "She wants to stay here. I'm staying with her."

"I don't think it's a good idea," Archie said, lowering his hands. He looked at Billy Ron. "You know they're drunk kids. Let 'em go."

"They're old enough to choose," Billy Ron said. He liked the idea of Mike staying close and protecting his sister. The combination of booze and his body's chemicals were making him light-headed. The world swirled before him in a haze. He let the booze slide over his brain and fog out the contempt Archie had shown him.

Archie reached across the table and grabbed Pammie's arm.

"What are you doing?" she demanded.

"You're not staying with this asshole," Archie replied, trying to pull her free.

The comfortable buzz took a back seat to the adrenaline hammering Billy Ron's veins. He came to his feet fast. "The lady says she's staying, and you need to leave my boat. Ain't no one done nothing wrong yet, but you keep pushing her and I'm gonna step in."

Mike stepped between the table and Archie. "Leave it be, Archie."

The kid has guts, Billy Ron thought.

Disgust filled Archie's voice. "Are you going to let him do whatever he wants to your sister?"

"It's not your business, mister."

"The hell it's not," Archie stiffened. "I won't let you rape a drunk woman."

Billy Ron's eyes flicked to the filet knife on the counter. He also had a folding tactical knife in his pocket he'd found while rummaging through the V-berth's hanging closet.

"She's given her consent by telling you to beat it," Billy Ron said, bringing himself nose to nose with Archie.

"Please, don't fight," Pammie squealed.

"Ain't nobody fightin', honey," Billy Ron said. "Old Archie was just leaving. Ain't that right, Arch?"

"Not without these kids."

"Then you ain't leaving."

Billy Ron's hand lashed out for the filet knife, fast as a snake, and sliced it across Archie's belly. The man clutched his stomach, blood flowing through his interlaced fingers.

Pammie screamed and started to rise. Billy Ron spun and backhanded her across her cheek, knocking her to the settee.

Mike backpedaled, holding his hands up to protect himself. The knife flashed in and out of the boy's frail chest. Then, Billy Ron stabbed him again, burying the blade to the hilt until the point of the eight-inch blade poked through the man's back. Mike toppled backward.

Billy Ron clutched him with his hand, laying him gently on the cabin floor. "I'm sorry, Mike," he whispered. "I wanted you to watch."

Mike's eyes fluttered, the light fading as comprehension dawned on his face.

Billy Ron smiled. "That's right, boy, I wanted you to watch me with your sister. She's one fine piece of ass. I'm going to take my sweet time with her."

Mike struggled to say something. His words came out as gasps of air, crimson blood bubbling from his mouth. Then his body went limp.

Billy Ron let the boy's head drop to the deck. He rose, turning to face the injured Archie.

"You wanted to be the big man." Billy Ron pointed the bloody knife at Archie, who was struggling toward the cockpit steps on his knees. "You made me do this, Archie. You and your big mouth."

Archie sagged against the steps, turning to look at Billy Ron and the gore that dripped from the man's hand. The knife gleamed in the overhead lights. The cabin smelled of copper and excrement.

Through labored breaths, Archie said, "You won't get away with this."

Billy Ron snickered. "You know how many women I've killed?"

Archie shook his head.

Billy Ron laughed, deep and hearty. "A bunch." He shook

the knife at Archie while he scolded, "If you'd just gone home like a good little boy, you'd be alive tomorrow."

"I couldn't let you ..." Archie shuddered.

"And I'm still gonna. I just got the added fun of killing you."

Archie turned away, burying his face in the crook of his arm. He let out a sob and slid to the floor.

Billy Ron smiled and stepped forward, raising the knife. "Let me help you."

Pammie moaned as Billy Ron wiped Archie's blood from the knife. He took two quick steps to her, picking up a towel from where it hung on the stove door handle. With practiced ease, he tied it around her head in a makeshift blindfold.

The girl reached for the towel, but Billy Ron pushed her hands back.

"What's going on?" she asked, her voice small and hollow.

"Your brother and Archie got into a fight, honey. I don't want you to see what's happened. Please," he implored, "don't take off the blindfold."

"Is Mike okay?"

"No. Archie had a knife and—"

"But you had the knife. I saw you cut Archie."

"You don't remember so good, Pammie," Billy Ron told her. He kept his voice low and soothing. He needed her to stay calm. If he could maintain control of the situation, he could get her off the boat and away from this crime scene. Archie had been right about one thing; he wouldn't get away with this. He'd never left any of his victims where they could be found.

"I saw ..." Pammie put her hands over her eyes.

"You hush now, girl," Billy Ron scolded. "Come on."

He pulled her to her feet and guided her to the ladder. He was thankful for the dark night and the lack of fellow cruisers. Billy Ron set Pammie in the cockpit, then went back into the cabin. He stuffed the money and pistol into a backpack along with a few supplies. Before he closed the cabin door, he shut off the lights.

He helped Pammie into the dinghy. She sobbed quietly beneath the towel. When Billy Ron had them underway, she pulled off the blindfold and stared at *Paradise Gone* as it receded into the night.

It didn't take long for them to reach *Barefoot*. Billy Ron tied off the dinghy and helped Pammie aboard. She went to the rear stateroom. When he brought her a glass of water, he found her curled up in a ball, sobbing. He handed her a white pill which he told her was Tylenol but was actually the date rape drug Rohypnol. She took the pill without question. Soon she was sound asleep. Billy Ron gazed at her limp form, feeling a deep desire to force himself upon her, but he turned away. He had to stay focused, but to satisfy his craving, he pushed up her bikini top and cupped her breasts.

Outside, he climbed into the dinghy again and putted to Archie's boat, a forty-two-foot Bluewater Coastal Cruiser. The man must have had plenty of money to motor all the way from Florida. Billy Ron climbed onto the narrow swim platform and forced the lock on the sliding door. He spent the next hour tearing the boat apart, searching for money and valuables. In a cache below the water pumps, he found five hundred bucks. In a second cache, behind the false front of a kitchen cabinet, he retrieved another grand. He also took Archie's passport and driver's license. In the right get-up, Billy Ron fancied he could pass for the man and use his two credit cards.

The sun was just lightening the eastern sky when he checked on Pammie. She was still sound asleep. His need for her was a physical ache.

"No," he told himself firmly. There would be plenty of time for that later. When he could take his time and enjoy it.

Back in the cockpit, he started the engine and weighed anchor. He wanted to be gone before someone found those bodies. He steered toward the channel leading out of the marine park.

He had a new woman and a new boat. Life was looking good.

CHAPTER NINE

Angelo had the Eurocopter gleaming in the morning sun. He stood on a ladder, polishing the windshield as Ryan and Aimee approached. She had the day off work and wanted to fly in the helicopter. Ryan had warned her it would be a long and boring day, but he'd given in to her pleadings.

Ryan turned at the sound of a plane, spotting the Piper Aztec speeding down the runway and waved as it lifted into the sky.

"Was that Mango?" Aimee asked.

"Yes." Ryan turned back to Angelo.

The big man was off the ladder. "Where do we fly today?"

"St. Vincent," Ryan said, sliding his backpack off and dropping it into the copilot's footwell.

He turned back to see Aimee gazing up at the pilot. They were chatting quietly. Angelo had a goofy grin on his face. Ryan had seen that look before. He remembered times when he'd had a similar smile.

"Hey, Angelo, let's go."

Angelo glanced up and grinned. "Yes, boss." He climbed into the pilot seat after helping Aimee into the back. The three of them settled headsets over their ears and adjusted the boom mics before Angelo started the helicopter and took off, flying toward St. Vincent.

The island was one hundred and sixty kilometers from the airport on Martinique, making it around one hundred miles. Angelo had explained his helicopter's capabilities in metric, and Ryan had to do the calculations on his own, although the more time he spent away from the U.S., the more familiar he was becoming with the metric system. The Eurocopter had a max range of four hundred miles, and it could cruise at one hundred and twenty-two knots, or one hundred and forty miles per hour. The knot thing he'd figured out shortly after joining the Navy, although he still needed a calculator to give him an exact number.

Ryan photographed the boats along St. Vincent's eastern shore, where the six main anchorages were, after circling the island. Then they flew to Barbados before returning to Martinique.

By the time they landed, he was ready to give up the search for the boat. He doubted Mango had found her either. Ryan emailed the photographs to Ashlee before the helicopter settled onto the hangar ramp. He zipped up the camera and laptop into his backpack and exited the bird with a moan. It felt good to stretch after the long hours of sitting still. Ryan's leg ached where he'd been shot during a firefight in Afghanistan. The scar tissue bothered him more as he aged.

Angelo came around the bird's nose and stopped Ryan. "Are you and Aimee dating?"

Before Ryan could answer, Aime said, "We're just friends."

With benefits, Ryan thought, but he kept his mouth shut. He could see the pilot was smitten with the bartender. And just like that, Ryan was single again. It wasn't the first time he'd introduced a quasi-girlfriend to another man and lost out. He'd done the same for Stacey and Travis. He shrugged and left Aimee to get a ride home with the pilot.

He didn't want to go to the Hotel Bakoua and listen to Mango and Jennifer's negative reports, so he went to his boat. He stopped at the marina restaurant and ordered a margarita to go with his steak and fries. After eating, he sat in his boat's cockpit and called Travis to see how the cargo container recovery had gone. Travis reported they were done and enjoying a few days on the beach before heading to Puerto Rico for another job.

"Did you see the news in Haiti?" Travis asked.

"No, I've been busy," Ryan said. "Why?"

"They caught several American ex-special operations guys and a former DHS agent running around with a car full of automatic weapons." Travis sounded almost suspicious when he added, "You're not in Haiti, are you?"

"Nah, man, I'm in Martinique with Mango."

"Well, be safe wherever you are."

Ryan said his goodbyes, hung up the phone, and scrolled through his contacts to the screen showing Joulie Lafitte. He stared at her face, running his thumb across the screen toward the *call* button. He tossed the phone onto the bench opposite him and went below, returning a minute later with two bottles of Bière Lorraine Ambrée and a pack of cigarettes. Sitting, he lit a smoke and cracked open a beer.

He didn't want to admit this to anyone, especially himself, but he was lonely. He had thought by now he would be married and maybe have a kid or two. Here he was in his mid-thirties, living on a sailboat in paradise with no one to share it with.

The two beers went down smooth and fast. Ryan picked up the phone and called his mom.

CHAPTER TEN

Ryan met Mango and Jennifer at the hotel restaurant for breakfast. There was no better way to start the day than by sitting at an open-air table and staring out at the beautiful ocean. They were tired of searching, and no one was eager to go out. Mango said his eyes ached from the glaring sun reflecting off the vast stretches of the open, empty Caribbean Sea. The plane had burned through Ryan's initial investment. The helicopter had sucked down even more.

After the waitress served the sailboat hunters their food, Mango lamented, "The man could be practically to Panama by now."

Ryan nodded, trying to stay positive. No one wanted to give up, but the odds of them finding *Alamo* decreased exponentially every day. No word had come through the cruisers' network and none of their social media posts had yielded results.

Jennifer sighed. "We might as well look for a new boat. Do you suppose the insurance company will cover a second stolen boat?" It was a question they'd speculated on endlessly.

Neither Jennifer nor Mango had the courage to make the phone call. They didn't want to hear more bad news.

"I suppose I need to call our agent," Mango said, glumly staring into the cup of fresh coffee the waitress had just poured.

"What kind of boat are you looking for?" Ryan asked before sipping from his own steaming cup.

"We've been looking at those big catamarans," Mango said. "They don't heel as much, and they have lots of room."

"You can each take a side," Ryan joked. The boat's cabins were built in the catamaran's hulls, and depending on the layout, there could be two large staterooms in each.

"We talked about doing a charter business in the South Pacific," Mango said. "We can live on one side and rent out the other."

They ate in silence. Ryan glanced over at Jennifer, who was scrolling through boat listings on her phone. He felt encouraged that they were ready to move on from *Alamo*, but it was still a heart-breaking loss. He'd been through the same thing when he'd lost his Sabre to Mexican pirates.

Jennifer squealed with delight. "You have to see this boat. It has a freaking bathtub, Steve Smith. A freaking bathtub!" She held out the phone for Mango to see.

Mango took the phone and scrolled through the pictures.

"What is it?" Ryan asked.

"It's a five-year-old Lagoon Fifty-Two." Before he passed the phone to Ryan, he said, "It's at the marina in Le Marin."

"Let's go look at it," Jennifer said, jumping up from her chair. "I don't care if we find *Alamo*; you're buying me a boat with a bathtub."

"Calm down, honey."

Jennifer turned, cocked her hips, and placed her fists on them. "Let's go, Steven."

"Yes, ma'am." Mango laughed, then looked at Ryan. "Are you coming?"

"Might as well. We could use the day off. I'll call our pilots and let them know."

"Great. Let's go," Jennifer said, already heading for the car.

"Looks like you're buying a new boat," Ryan said. "Is she always like that when she wants something?"

"When we first met, I didn't ask her out right away, and she hounded me for two weeks until I did. So, yes, when she wants something, she goes right after it."

"You poor bastard." Ryan swallowed the last of his coffee.

With a big, dopey grin on his face, Mango said, "You have no idea how blessed I am, bro."

Mango drove them to Le Marin to meet with the yacht broker. The office was a tiny one-room affair in a neat little clapboard cottage beside the marina. Hanging on the outside wall beside the door were pictures of boats for sale. Ryan glanced over the listings before following his friends inside.

They sat in plastic chairs, sweltering in the stuffy office save for when the oscillating fan swung around to blow warm air across their hot bodies. A sign on the desk said in French and English that the broker would return in fifteen minutes.

Ryan didn't need to be in the office. He stepped outside and walked along the marina's fence. He stared at the forest of sailboat masts, wondering where *Alamo* had gone and if they'd ever see her again. Mango and Jennifer had their whole lives stowed on the boat, not to mention the money and guns stashed throughout the various hidden holds. The thief had already killed to steal a boat, and if a man would stoop that low just to commit an act of thievery, then there was no telling what else he would do. Ryan wanted a chance to find out. He wanted to get his hands around the man's neck and let him see how it felt to have the life seep from his body.

Ryan tried to clear out his thoughts. When had he become so jaded that he could take a life with ease, or even contemplate the murder of another man? Yes, he'd killed men in battle while serving in the Navy, and had taken lives since, but they had been for self-preservation. He didn't think he'd killed anyone in cold blood or could. He also didn't underestimate the darkness that lurked in his soul. Ryan had stared into the darkness and he didn't think it would be hard to slip over the edge.

"You coming?" Mango shouted.

Ryan turned to see Jennifer and Mango standing beside the marina entrance gate. They were with a bald black man wearing blue slacks, a white dress shirt, and boat shoes. Ryan guessed he was in his mid-fifties. Mango introduced him as Lionel, and as they walked through the gate, Lionel gave them the boat's history and explained why she was for sale. The original owners had purchased the vessel intending to start a charter service. They had ordered the boat new and outfitted her to their specifications, including the jacuzzi tub. After two seasons of sailing *Margarita*, the couple had tried their hand at charters, but had moved back to England when they had trouble making ends meet.

Ryan's first impression was of a sleek, space-age yacht with the fit and furnishings of the million-dollar boat she was. He couldn't imagine walking away from a boat of this caliber. Her hull was a polished white with a large '52' on each sponson. The boxy salon extended above the deck, with tinted windows wrapping around the front and sides. Her cushions were a beautiful, vibrant blue. A large fiberglass sunshade covered the rear deck, and a soft Bimini shaded the flybridge. Raymarine electronics studded the nav station, which also provided a sweeping view of the twin foredecks and the trampoline—the netting strung between the two hulls at the bow.

They entered the salon through sliding glass doors. The

wrap-around counter and kitchen were bigger than the salon on Ryan's *Windseeker*. To the left of an interior navigation station, a flat screen television would rise from the console at the touch of a button.

On the starboard side, the master suite took up the whole hull with a large bedroom, walk-in shower, and hanging closet. In the port hull were two cabins with private heads and a dive locker. Jennifer laid in the tub and stretched out. With a smile, she said, "I don't have to see any more."

Despite Jennifer's declaration, Mango and Ryan opened every hatch, cabinet, drawer, and bilge cover. They looked at the marine survey the owners had authorized before flying to England and made notes of the things the boat needed.

When they'd finished their inspection and had gathered in the salon, Ryan said with a bit of envy, "This is an amazing boat."

"Can we take her out?" Mango asked Lionel.

The broker agreed, and the motley crew fired up the twin seventy-five horsepower Yanmar diesels and headed for open water. They spent the afternoon putting the boat through her paces and hoisting every sail onboard. The rigging differed slightly from their V-bottom boats, but they agreed the ship handled wonderfully, making eight to ten knots in the heavy breeze.

After returning the boat to her slip, they walked to Lionel's office, where Mango made an offer.

Instead of writing the offer price on the paperwork, Lionel leaned back in his chair. "Might I suggest a lower price. The sellers are desperate, and the poor boat has been here for a long time. I know this is undercutting my commission, but let's ask them to take off one hundred thousand."

Mango nodded. *Margarita* had a price tag north of a million dollars and if he could get it cheaper, all the better. "I like your thinking, Lionel. Let's offer eight hundred thousand and see if they negotiate."

"Very good, sir." Lionel filled out the paperwork and Mango signed his name.

"I'll email them right away. It's quite late in England and I doubt we'll hear from them until tomorrow. I'll call you when I do."

On the way back to Les Trois-Îlets, Mango's sat phone rang.

"Can you answer that?" Mango asked Ryan.

Ryan said, "Hello."

"Hey, is this Steve Smith?" the caller asked.

"Steve's driving; I'm Ryan. Is there something I can help you with?"

"I think I found his boat," the caller said.

"Hold on." Ryan pushed a button. "I put you on speaker. Start from the beginning."

"My name's Jim. I think I found your sailboat."

"Awesome. Where?" Mango asked.

Jennifer leaned forward between the seats to hear better.

"There's a boat in the cove at Petit Tabac," Jim said. "She looks like the one you're describing, but she has the name *Paradise Gone*."

"Have you called the police?" Mango asked.

"No, I called you so you can look at her and decide if she's yours."

"Thanks," Mango said.

"If she's yours, you can stop by my boat in the Tobago Cays and pay the reward. I'm on *Mistress of the Sea*. I can see your boat from mine."

"Thanks, Jim," Mango said. "We'll be right there."

Ryan hung up and called Leon De Ridder. The pilot answered on the third ring.

"Hey, Leon, this is Ryan Weller. Can you fly us to Petit Tabac tonight?"

"Shouldn't be a problem."

"We'll be there in twenty minutes."

"I'll be ready when you arrive."

Fifteen minutes later, they pulled into the FBO parking lot, scrambled out of the car, and raced to the hangar. They helped Leon push the plane onto the apron. After closing the hangar doors, all four crowded into the Piper Aztec and took off.

The hot June sun was still well above the horizon when Leon called the Union Island Airport for clearance to land near Petit Tabac. Though they had once been privately owned, the government had purchased the tiny islands between St. Vincent and Grenada to develop the Tobago Cays Marine Park into a tourist attraction. As they coasted in for a landing, Ryan saw a small boat racing toward them.

"Is that going to be a problem?" he asked Leon.

"Nah, just the park rangers coming to collect their fee."

"There she is," Jennifer said. Mango leaned forward to look through her window. A sailboat matching theirs lay at anchor, casting a shadow on the rocks and coral beneath her. In the clear water, *Alamo*—or *Paradise Gone*, now—seemed to hover in the air. She rode easily in the horseshoe bay, surrounded by blinding white sands and lush green palms.

Leon landed the Aztec on the smooth water and coasted them to a stop with the noses of the pontoons buried in the sand. He shut off the engines, jumped out of the cockpit, and tied the anchor rope to the port pontoon leg before carrying the anchor up the beach and dropping it in the sand.

The rangers beached the red-and-white patrol boat and hopped out as Ryan, Mango, and Jennifer eased from the plane. Ryan expected the rangers to pull their guns, so he kept his hands well away from his body until he saw the rangers didn't have weapons.

The ranger who stepped out of the boat said, "We're here to collect your entrance fee. It's thirty dollars for the plane and ten dollars a person. How long do you plan to stay?"

Mango approached the rangers' boat and handed over seventy East Caribbean dollars. "Just long enough to see if that sailboat is mine. She was stolen from Martinique. We've been looking all over for her."

The man handed Mango a sheet of paper with a list of park regulations on it. "I haven't seen anyone aboard in several days."

"Can you take me and my friend over to her?" Mango asked.

The ranger glanced back at his partner, who remained at the stern helm station.

"For ten dollars," the driver said. Both he and his partner wore light gray polo shirts, khaki shorts, and inflatable life vests.

Mango forked over the money, and he and Ryan helped push the boat off the beach before climbing aboard.

Ryan clamored to the stern and sat beside the driver. "I'm Ryan." He extended his hand.

"Tillman Lewis."

"You said the guy hasn't been around in a few days?"

"It's not unusual for a cruiser to leave their boat at anchor and fly home."

The rising tide had swung the stern of the Amazon toward the island, and they could clearly see the outline of the word *Alamo* under the drunken scrawl of *Paradise Gone*. Mango cupped his hands into a megaphone and shouted to Jennifer, "It's her."

She threw her hands up in triumph.

When they were alongside, they caught a whiff of something rotten.

Ryan cursed. He knew that smell. Not long ago, he'd opened a cargo container and inhaled the perfume of dead and decaying bodies, now he smelled it once again. He turned to Tillman. "You better come aboard."

They tied off the rangers' boat to *Alamo*'s rear starboard cleat. Ryan, Mango, and Tillman climbed into the sailboat's cockpit.

Mango pointed to the cabin door. "The lock's busted."

Tillman pulled the door open, and the full odor of ripe dead bodies hit them. Tillman vomited over the side of the sailboat, and Mango joined him, adding an acrid smell to the already pungent bouquet of aromas.

Ryan covered his nose and went down into the cabin. When he glanced at the two bodies sprawled across the cabin's floor, he felt the bile rise in his throat. He choked back the burning acid and climbed out of the cabin. Once upwind, he took deep breaths of cleansing air. From here, he could see Jennifer still standing near the plane, shading her face with her arms.

She cupped her hands to her mouth and shouted, "Is everything okay?"

Ryan formed his own hand megaphone and yelled, "No!"

CHAPTER ELEVEN

Tillman and Mango each went into the cabin to gaze at the morbid scene. When they'd had their fill, all three men huddled on the foredeck with the cabin door closed. Even then, they could smell the decay. Flies buzzed around their heads and mosquitos dive bombed them in the warm evening air.

"I must call the police on Union Island," Tillman said.

"You're not going to investigate?" Ryan asked.

The park ranger shook his head. "No. We collect fees for the park, not investigate crimes."

"How soon will the police arrive?" Mango asked.

The ranger glanced at the setting sun and shrugged. "They have a boat, but never any fuel, and it's getting dark." He shrugged again. "Who can say?"

"All right. Can you take us back to the plane?" Ryan said.

During the gentle ride to the beach, Tillman called the police and reported the grisly double murder. They would send an investigator.

"Have you had any reports of abandoned or missing

boats?" Ryan asked when Tillman had replaced his radio mic on the dash.

"No," Tillman said. "Like I said, cruisers often leave their boats in the anchorage for long periods of time."

"I'd think they'd want to move them with hurricane season coming," Mango said.

"Yes, they will," Tillman said.

The rangers dropped Ryan and Mango on the beach with Leon and Jennifer. As they pulled away, Mango gave Jennifer a sanitized version of what they'd found.

Jennifer held the back of her hand over her mouth and her eyes glistened with tears. "I'll never go in there again."

"What now?" Leon asked.

"Let me make a call," Ryan said. He stepped away from the group and dialed Floyd Landis.

Landis answered by saying "Let me guess, you need another favor?"

"This is more a heads-up, than a favor. Mango's boat was stolen, and we just found it in Tobago Cay Marine Park with two dead bodies onboard."

Landis was silent for a long moment, and Ryan could hear the man clicking the ball point of his government-issued pen in and out.

"You boys are always getting into trouble," Landis growled. "What do you expect me to do about it?"

"There's two dead men in Mango's boat. Maybe they were after the bounty, maybe not. Either way, you should care about the safety and well-being of a man who served under your command."

"The loyalty speech from Ryan Weller. This is rich."

"I'm asking you for help. The local police seem to have their hands full. At least run the prints and help me figure out who these guys are. If the guy who stole Mango's boat killed those two, then that makes three in the last week."

With a sigh of resignation, Landis said, "Get me the prints and I'll see what I can do."

Ryan waved away a cloud of mosquitos converging on him now that it was dark, and the wind had died. His companions had retreated into the airplane. "Thanks, Landis. I don't care what they say, you're a good guy."

"Flattery will get you nowhere. Someday, I'll collect on these favors."

"I'm counting on it," Ryan said and ended the call. He should have taken the fingerprints when they were on the boat with Tillman, but he hadn't wanted to disturb the scene or show he was anything more than a boat bum helping his friends.

He climbed onto the pontoon. "I need to go back to the boat."

"You'll have to swim," Leon said.

"You don't have a life raft?" Ryan asked.

Leon pointed to the rear of the plane. "Just my emergency one, and you're not taking that."

Ryan asked, "Any chance you could motor us out there so I can jump off the wing onto the boat?"

The pilot reached down to start the engines.

Ryan crouched on the starboard wing behind the open door, allowing it to block the wind and water whipped up by the propeller. The landing lights cast brilliant cones of light in the darkness. He gripped the anchor line, which he'd retied to the starboard float leg and run over the wing. As Leon brought the wing within two feet of the sailboat, he shut off the starboard engine. Ryan waited as the plane drifted. Leon goosed the port motor and fought the controls to keep the plane in a straight line until the wing tip came alongside *Alamo*'s cockpit.

With long strides, Ryan sprinted across the wing and leaped the gap onto the boat. He landed hard, driving his sternum into the cockpit bench. Despite the seat padding, the impact knocked the wind from his lungs. He heaved and gasped until the air came back in, then the pain from the fall radiated through his body. Ignoring it as best he could, he stood and gathered in the rope. Leon shut off the port engine, and the plane drifted forward while Ryan secured the line to a cleat.

He wished he didn't need to breathe when he caught a whiff of the dead bodies. Making his way forward, he clicked on a flashlight and swung open the broken cabin door. Breathing through his teeth, he went to the engine room and drained diesel fuel onto a rag from the fuel filter. He held the rag under his nose to block the stench.

He heard a thump in the cockpit and swung around to see Mango coming down the steps.

"Hold the flashlight," Ryan said, handing it to him.

Mango took the flashlight and the rag, holding the latter under his nose. Ryan squatted beside the first body—a young man so skinny he could count the ribs in his bony chest. A while back, Landis had mailed him a smartphone loaded with Homeland Security applications. He used an app on the phone to take the boy's fingerprints, then moved to the other man.

"Take this." Mango handed the flashlight back. He stepped to the chart table and opened the lid to retrieve his own flashlight before moving forward to the V-berth. While Mango did whatever he was doing, Ryan searched the cabin, letting his flashlight beam cut through the darkness and illuminate one tiny section of the interior at a time.

Under the table, he spotted a woman's clutch.

"Hey, Mango, you got a pair of gloves around here?"

"In the chart table."

Ryan pulled on the gloves. They were leather and made for handling lines, not evidence, but he'd make do. He fished out the clutch and dumped its contents on the table. A tube of lipstick, a handful of euros and U.S. dollars, a California driver's license, a pack of cigarettes, and a lighter spilled out. The lipstick tried to escape off the table when the boat rolled gently. Ryan caught it and stuffed it into the bag along with everything but the driver's license. He thought about having a cigarette.

He photographed the driver's license, which read, 'Pamela Rachel Walcott.' Mango came out of the aft stateroom carrying a black duffle bag. He stepped over the dried puddles of blood to stand beside Ryan.

"You know this girl?" Ryan asked.

Mango shook his head. "I've never seen her before."

Ryan stuffed the license into the clutch and tossed the bag back under the table. "You ready to get out of here?"

"Just need a few more minutes, bro. I've got some shit I don't want the cops to find when they tear apart my boat."

"Did the thief take anything?" Ryan asked.

"About fifty K in cash and a handgun," Mango said. "But that's what I wanted him to find."

Ryan nodded while Mango ducked into the aft stateroom. He had similar hiding places on his boat, too. Once the thief found the first spot, they generally quit looking.

He took a whiff of the diesel rag and bent to pat the boy's pockets. Neither he nor the other man had identification on them. Ryan snapped photos of their faces, then went up to the cockpit, where he sent the fingerprints and the pictures of the license and faces to Landis.

Mango emerged from below, shouldered his duffle, and after Ryan stuffed his phone into the bag, stepped across to the plane. Ryan remained on the sailboat, untied the plane's anchor line, and pushed against the wing. The two floating objects swung away from each other, the boat pivoting on its anchor chain.

When the wing tip cleared the sailboat, Ryan scrambled out onto the slick metal surface and flopped onto his belly. He felt his body sliding along the wing's slick incline.

The port engine started, sending a vibration through the plane's skeleton. Ryan's fingertips scrabbled over the smooth surface, searching for purchase, finding nothing but the smooth rivet heads.

He slid off the wing, sinking deep into the warm water, watching the shimmer of the plane's landing lights. The buzz of the propeller was loud in his ears as he kicked for the surface. This was going to be a wet ride home.

CHAPTER TWELVE

Ryan was up before the sun and ran a long route along the shorefront of Les Trois-Îlets. He hadn't had a good run in a long time. Running squares around a barge deck littered with hoses, tools, and chains had its hazards, but he did it to keep in shape. When he returned to the dock, the sun was peeking over the horizon, and Jennifer sat in *Windseeker*'s cockpit with two large bags.

"You okay?" Ryan asked, stepping into the cockpit and unlocking the cabin door.

"I'm fine," she said.

Unconvinced, he asked, "You sure?"

She nodded. "I'll be all right. We found our lost boat and ..."

"Everything is going to be okay," Ryan tried to reassure her. "The bad guy is long gone. He's not hanging around after what he did."

"I know. It's ... I feel horrible just thinking about it."

"It's not your fault," Ryan said. "We'll get the police to handle things, and then we'll get your boat back. Besides, you'll have a new home when you get the Lagoon. I'll stick around until we get everything transferred and cleaned up. You'll never have to go back inside *Alamo*."

"You promise?" she asked.

"Absolutely." He held out his arms to give her a hug.

Jennifer crinkled her nose and stepped out of reach. "You need to take a shower."

He laughed and ducked into the head. He showered, dressed in shorts, and stepped into the galley. Jennifer sat on the settee, sipping coffee. Ryan poured a cup. "Where's Mango?"

"He's returning the rental. I saw you running on the beach during my walk from the hotel."

"You should have joined me."

She shook her head. "The walk was enough."

He dug out a pan to fry eggs, cooked four, then toasted bread. They ate in silence, and when Ryan finished his second cup of coffee and rinsed their dishes, it was full daylight. He went to the marina office and paid for his stay. He'd previously filled *Windseeker*'s tanks with diesel and freshwater and had pumped out the black and gray water, so he was ready to leave. When he returned to the boat, Mango was standing in the cockpit, sipping a cup of coffee. Ryan started the engine, letting it idle while he pulled off the sail cover and stored it under a cockpit bench.

He had Jennifer go forward and undo the bow line while he handled the stern. She held them in place until he'd engaged the drive, then she hopped from the dock to the boat with practiced ease. Ryan envied his buddy. He had a wife who loved to sail, and he got to share life's special moments with her, like sunsets at sea, walks on deserted beaches, and scuba diving. She shared the trials, too. *Someday, I'll have that*, he thought. *Someday*.

They motored out of the marina and across the bay to the Fort-de-France Ferry Terminal. Ryan cleared his boat and himself through customs. Mango and Jennifer spent the next two hours showing the customs officials police reports and explaining the theft of their boat. When asked how they were leaving, Mango explained he was taking a plane to Union Island to speak with the police there while Jennifer went with Ryan on his boat.

Since their paperwork was in order, the official stamped their passports and registration and allowed them to exit the country. Jennifer and Mango spent a few moments alone before he took a taxi to the airport and she boarded Ryan's boat.

When they rounded the end of Martinique, Ryan set *Windseeker* on a broad reach to the southeast, taking them between Martinique and St. Lucia. He planned to stay on this course until they could tack about and run straight to Union Island, where they'd clear customs and pick up Mango.

The breeze was heavy, and they sailed into three-foot rollers. Ryan stood behind the wheel. He'd turned on the autopilot, but it kept kicking off. Ready to take over when it stopped working again, he rested his hands gently on the wheel.

Jennifer sat on the cockpit bench, providing hiking weight to the high side of the heeled over hull. She wore a green one-piece swimsuit with a transparent white diamond on the stomach and had her legs braced against the seat on the opposite side. Each wave jarred the little boat and shook their bodies.

She said something, but the wind masked her words.

"What?" He sat beside her to hear better, keeping one hand on the big stainless-steel wheel and bracing his feet like she was doing.

She pushed her hair from her face. "I said, 'Do you know what I miss?'"

"What do you miss?"

"I miss my family. I miss getting together with them on holidays and birthdays."

Ryan nodded. He'd been absent from a lot of family get-togethers.

Jennifer continued, "I have three sisters, two brothers, and twelve nieces and nephews. I miss them. I miss watching them grow up. Don't you miss your family?"

"Sure," he said. "I call my mom and dad, and talk to my brother and sister, but I don't know. I don't think I'm missing out."

"Doesn't it bother you that you're never in the same spot or you don't have a place to call home?"

"I have a home." He patted *Windseeker*'s hull.

"No, I mean, like, a wife and kids and stuff."

"Yeah." He shrugged. "I'd like to have someone to share paradise with. You and Mango are lucky to have each other."

"I just want to go home." She sighed. "I love sailing, but I want to see my family. As long as you and Mango have a bounty, I have to be Jillian Smith."

Something in her voice made Ryan glance from the sea to her face. She was wiping tears from her cheeks.

"I'm sorry," he said. "I had no idea things would work out like they have. I wanted to give Mango a job, and he was hell bent on going into Mexico with me. I tried to stop him. You know how stubborn he can be."

Jennifer crossed her arms and stared at the horizon.

Needing to fill the awkward silence, Ryan said, "I even threatened to steal his leg so he couldn't go with me."

"But you still let him go."

"He was helpful to have around. He saved my ass several times."

She turned her head and stared at Ryan. "You could return the favor and get this bounty lifted."

He looked away, unable to hold the fiery gaze she cast

upon him. "I've tried. Kilroy promised to remove the bounty when we delivered the weapons. Then, I figured if we faked our deaths by dying in a shipwreck, the cartel would forget about us, but they've never stopped looking."

Jennifer stood abruptly and made her way into the cabin. Ryan sipped his coffee and sat in the sunshine. This would be a long twenty-four hours if Jennifer didn't talk to him. He couldn't blame her. He missed his family as well, but he'd missed so much of their lives that he didn't know how he fit into them anymore. After leaving the Navy, it had been hard to reintegrate.

He'd worked for his dad at the family construction business in Wilmington, North Carolina, but when Greg Olsen had called him to be Dark Water Research's liaison with Homeland, he had jumped at the chance. He'd do it all over again to stop Arturo Guerrero from starting a war with the U.S. to reclaim the Desert Southwest, what had once been part of Mexico. He hadn't planned on a bounty or having to keep a constant vigil for those seeking to collect. His left wrist bore the scar from an assassin's garrote. He'd been able to jam his hand between the thin wire and his neck, saving his life. He still did physical therapy on it. Unconsciously, he rolled the wrist and flexed it to stretch the muscles.

He bumped the autopilot button, and when the electronics engaged, he let go of the wheel and opened the lazarette. He had a waterproof box stored there. It had shifted and was now just out of his reach.

As he wiggled his head and arm into the small hatch to grab the box, he saw a small piece of electronics epoxied to the boat's hull. If he hadn't stuck his head through the hatch, he'd have never seen the GPS transmitter. Two wires ran from the rectangular unit and disappeared through a hole in the lazarette's bottom. Ryan instinctively knew they connected the device to the electrical system.

He closed the lazarette, scanned the horizon, then climbed into the cabin.

"What are you doing?" Jennifer asked as Ryan removed panels from the deck and opened the engine access hatch.

"Trying to trace a wire."

"Is it part of the auto pilot?"

"No, something else I found. Can you hand me the flashlight from the drawer under the chart table?"

Jennifer brought it over and squatted beside him. He shined the light into the engine bay, guessing where the wire came through the fiberglass. After a few minutes of searching, he spotted it. One wire dropped behind the engine, and the installer had used a quick splice connector to join what Ryan assumed was the GPS's power wire to a wire with constant battery power. The other wire connected to a ground terminal.

He snapped off the light, replaced the deck hatches, then called Greg Olsen.

"What GPS transmitter did you put on my boat?"

"It's a Globalstar SmartOne C. The same as on Mango's boat. Why?"

"Where'd you have it installed?"

"In Puerto Rico," Greg said.

"No, moron," Ryan said. "Where'd you have it installed on the boat?"

"Oh, yeah, it's in the dash above the aft companionway door."

"Well, I've got another tracker onboard."

"Is Joulie following you?" Greg asked.

"I don't think so," Ryan said. "She knows all she has to do is call me."

"What make is it?"

"Hold on." Ryan led Jennifer up to the cockpit and

handed her the flashlight. "Can you read the manufacturer's name on the tracking unit?"

Jennifer burrowed into the lazarette and shouted, "It says Back2You."

Ryan repeated it to Greg.

"I'll check it out."

"Any numbers on the box?" Ryan asked Jennifer.

"No," she said, "just a bar code." After extracting herself from the hold, she adjusted the straps on her swimsuit.

"Send me a picture," Greg said.

"Okay. I'll hang up, have her take the picture, and then send it. Call me when you have something."

"Wait," Greg said. "Did you find Mango's boat?"

"Yeah, it's in Tobago Cay Marine Park. I'll tell you about it later."

"Roger that," Greg said, and Ryan ended the call.

Jennifer crawled back in the hole and took pictures of the three visible sides of the GPS tracker. Ryan replaced the lazarette cover, sat beside Jennifer on the cockpit bench, and sent the pictures. Then he remembered why he was digging in the lazarette in the first place and retrieved the waterproof box, taking out cigarettes and a lighter. He got one going, and Jennifer took one from the pack, too.

"When did you start smoking?" he asked.

She lit it and blew out a stream of smoke. "I haven't had one since college. I need something to soothe my nerves."

Ryan understood completely.

Jennifer said, "Don't tell Mango."

"Mum's the word, bro," Ryan said, mimicking her husband.

They smoked in silence. When they were done, Jennifer took their butts with her into the cabin.

Ryan climbed onto the cabin roof and stood by the mast, slowly turning to watch the horizon at all compass points.

Who was tracking him, and why? It could be Joulie, but she had sent him off with no hope of reuniting. The only other people interested in him wanted him dead. Why track him when they could just as easily put a bullet in his head or blow up his boat? How long had the tracker been there, and how complacent had he been to not notice it?

His curiosity got the better of him. Glancing through the forward companion hatch, he saw Jennifer at the settee. He dropped into the cockpit, slid the aft companion hatch closed so she couldn't overhear his phone call, and stood in the narrow space aft of it under the sun dodger shading the instrument panel bearing the compass, GPS, sonar, and radar screens.

Ryan dialed the stored number for Joulie and watched the radar sweep as the phone rang.

"I didn't expect to hear from you," Joulie said.

He'd missed her voice. "Did you put a tracker on my boat?"

"Why would I do that?"

He grinned as wicked thoughts popped into his head. "So, you can join me for a few days of rest and relaxation."

The Haitian warlord laughed. "You're the white devil. This is why I sent you away."

He tried to force away the disappointment. "That's a no on the tracker?"

Joulie said, "I did not put a tracker on your boat. What about your friend, Greg?"

"He said no."

"Then you have a mystery."

"Any chance you want to come to Martinique? I know a great little hotel where we could never leave the room."

"No, Ryan," Joulie said with an exasperated sigh. "We talked about this. I must go. Take care of yourself."

The phone call ended like a punch to his gut. He'd known

better. Angry with himself for expecting something other than a cold shoulder, he shoved the phone in his pocket, then cursed while punching the air.

The autopilot kicked off again, compounding his frustration.

"Sonofabitch!"

He leaped to the wheel and steadied the boat before the waves could turn her. Repeatedly punching the autopilot button did no good. He dropped on the bench and jammed his foot against the spoke, staring up at the telltales on the mainsail and the wind vane on the mast head.

His hands fumbled for the pack of cigarettes, and he lit one while leaning back against the hull. He wrapped one hand around the life rail stanchion for support, using his foot on the wheel to keep the telltales—short pieces of string—pointed straight aft, which meant the boat was sailing at optimal sped.

How long had the autopilot been acting up? He'd have to check the ship's log to be sure. Did it coincide with the placing of the GPS unit? He cocked his head as he thought. If the tracker operated like the ones that he was familiar with, it would send a signal every ten minutes. If the installer had spliced into the autopilot's wiring, then when the GPS sent its signal, it would draw juice away from the autopilot, causing it to kick out.

The easy solution to the problem was to rip out the transmitter, but he wanted to know who was watching his boat. If he turned off the GPS, he'd alert whoever was following him that he knew about the tracker. On the other hand, he liked the odds. He now knew someone had eyes on him, and he could watch for the watchers.

The autopilot finally turned on when he hit the button for the hundredth time, and he started a timer on the stopwatch mounted to the wheel pedestal. Four minutes later, the autopilot shut off and the bow drifted. Ryan kept pressing the reset button until the autopilot engaged light came on, then started the stopwatch again. After a quick glance around the horizon, he scrambled up on the cabin roof and dropped through the forward hatch.

He went straight to the chart desk and pulled out his log. Running his finger along each page as he scanned, he came to the first day he'd noticed the autopilot's problems. He glanced at the clock, trying to determine how long until the autopilot would kick off, then back at the log.

According to his notes, the problem had started in the Virgin Islands, before they'd begun the cargo container reclamation. Someone had known where he'd be and when. Did they have access to the DWR computers or someone who worked at the commercial dive and salvage firm? How had they figured out he was now on *Windseeker*?

Glancing at the clock, Ryan tucked the log away and went topside. He checked the radar screen, scanned the horizon, and took a leak off the stern. When he turned around, the autopilot had disengaged. The stopwatch read ten minutes, and as he reset the watch, he assumed the four-minute reading was because he had started the stopwatch in the middle of the cycle. He let the boat have her head, feeling the way the waves pushed against her and tugged at the hull. Above him, the mainsail slackened and cracked as it luffed in the wind.

Jennifer hurried topside. "What's going on?"

"Just seeing how she responds to a little weather."

The sail cracked again, and the boom bounced violently. Ryan turned *Windseeker* back on course, and the wind tightened the canvas.

He reset the autopilot and sat beside Jennifer. He lit a cigarette and offered one to her, which she accepted. They sat in silence, listening to the wind creak through the canvas and the lines. The bow plunged up and down, occasionally bursting through a wave and showering spray across the deck and the dodger.

Jennifer was the first to speak. "You know what else I miss, and I didn't realize it until I was down in your cramped little cabin?"

"What?" Ryan asked, somewhat offended by her description of the cabin, however true it was.

"A place to spread out. I like to sew and make crafts, and if I get my things out, I'd always have to put them away. When we were living in a house, I could lay out my fabrics and buttons and notions and have time to study them. I can't do that when we're underway."

"The Lagoon won't heel much, and you'll have more room than on *Alamo*."

"I miss little stuff, too, like seeing the same register girl at the supermarket. Oh!" She clapped excitedly. "I miss supermarkets and isles of food and shopping in the same place all the time."

"And a big fridge to store everything in," Ryan agreed.

"Exactly." She tossed her wind-tangled hair over her shoulder.

When they'd stubbed out their smokes, Ryan told her to watch the helm while he went below to rewire their GPS transmitter. He tossed the cigarette butts in a trash can, then pulled off the engine cover. He traced several wires but wasn't happy with the GPS robbing power from any of the other systems. The main fuse block had an extra slot, so he ran a wire between the block and where the GPS had been spliced into the autopilot. He fit a ring terminal to the wire, crimped it solidly, then screwed it to the fuse block. Next, he used another plastic splice connector and hooked the new power wire into the GPS, then cut the old wire just above where it ran into the splice for the autopilot. The GPS now had its own circuit.

He crawled into the aft bunk and listened to the gentle sounds of water whispering past the hull. He never slept on the bed during a passage, preferring to stretch out on the cockpit bench. The mattress was too comfortable for him to awaken from a two-hour nap to stand watch for another two hours. The two-on, two-off rotation worked well, but by the time he'd completed the passage, he was always worn out. Ryan was glad to have a companion on this voyage.

Despite knowing the topside was well-tended, his mind wouldn't shut off, mulling over the GPS transmitter, who had placed it, and why. He also wondered about Pamela Walcott and how they would find her before she became another victim of the Caribbean Killer, or should he be the Sailboat Slayer?

Jennifer woke him just past dark, and he made a pot of coffee before climbing into the cockpit with a thermos. She reported the autopilot had not kicked off since he'd rewired the GPS unit. Ryan poured coffee into a mug and settled in on the cockpit bench. He lit a cigarette, and Jennifer joined him, the burning cherries bright in the darkness.

When he'd been in the Navy, the ships had sailed in blackout conditions, and the crew was not allowed to smoke for fear of the enemy spotting their cherries. He'd heard different numbers for the distance a burning cigarette was visible, from five hundred yards to three miles. He pondered it now as they sailed in the darkness, the night, the water, the horizon all shades of black, distinguishable yet not.

A night sail always made him feel insignificant and philosophical. How could one not, he wondered, when the Milky Way stretched across the horizon, with stars looking so brilliant he felt he could reach out and touch them? Behind the boat would be a bloom of bioluminescence, the ocean's microscopic organisms giving off light as the sailboat passed by them. Jennifer had a point; there were things to miss about living on land, but there was no other place that made Ryan feel as alive as a night ocean passage, except maybe disarming a bomb in the pitch-black waters or in the middle of a firefight.

Jennifer said goodnight and went to the forward berth.

Ryan sat, staring at the stars and wishing he had someone to share his adventurous life. Someone he could make love to under the gorgeous moon. There was nowhere else in the world he'd rather live than right here on his tiny boat in a giant blue ocean.

CHAPTER THIRTEEN

They made Union Island the next morning. Ryan swung south to enter Clifton Harbor, keeping west of the Grand de Coi Reef, then aiming between the island and Newland's Reef to enter the small harbor. A boat boy met them at the entrance in a sleek, low wooden boat with a powerful outboard. The man driving the boat offered advice on where to moor. When Ryan refused a mooring ball, the man roared away, leaving *Windseeker* rocking in his wake.

Ryan followed the channel entrance and anchored in the lee of the patch reef. Another boat boy came by, and this time, Ryan locked his vessel before he and Jennifer climbed aboard for a ride to the ferry terminal where they cleared through customs.

Jennifer used Ryan's phone to call Mango. He was at the police station in Ashton. Ryan and Jennifer found a taxi to take them across the island. When they arrived, a uniformed officer led them to a small office. Mango sprung from his chair. While he hugged his wife, Ryan glanced around the room.

The name plate for the inspector sitting behind the desk read 'Ernest Browne.' He was a stout black man who wore the tan-and-blue uniform of the St. Vincent and Grenadines Royal Police Force. His shaved head gleamed, and the skin of his thick neck wrinkled and folded just above his clavicle. When he rose to shake hands, he spoke the Queen's English with his island accent. "Pleased to meet you."

The second man leaned against the wall in a pressed blue suit and dress shirt. He had a pair of aviator shades dangling from the jacket's breast pocket, and his wavy brown hair reminded Ryan of Sonny Crockett from *Miami Vice*. He stared right at Ryan, never looking at Jennifer. He casually pushed aside the hem of his jacket to reveal a badge clipped to his belt, and said, "Michael Harwood, FBI."

"FBI?" Ryan asked. "I thought Interpol would handle this."

Harwood crossed his arms, affecting a casual stance. "I know you were expecting Homeland, but this is my jurisdiction."

Ryan shrugged. "I don't care. We just need to catch this guy. Any word on who he is or who the two victims were?"

"Thanks to your prompt contamination of the crime scene, we found out the skinny kid was Michael Scott Walcott," Harwood said. "He's got a sister named Pamela. Their boat, *Barefoot*, is missing from their anchorage in Tobago Cay."

"What about the other guy?" Ryan asked.

"His name is Archie Darling," Harwood said. "His boat is still at the anchorage, but someone ransacked it. We suspect the thief was looking for money, or drugs, but we're not even sure if the killer was the one who tossed the boat. There are plenty of kids looking for an opportunity, know what I mean?"

"Do you have an ID on the killer?" Ryan asked.

"Not yet," Ernest replied. "Our major crimes unit came from Kingston and took fingerprints. Agent Harwood sent them to the FBI crime lab."

"What about looking for the Walcotts' boat?" Jennifer asked.

"We have our police force on full alert," Ernest said, "and we have alerted the neighboring districts to be on the lookout as well."

"I put an alert on the cruiser's network," Mango added.

Ryan glanced at him. "What about social media?"

Mango said, "I put pictures and information about the boat and Pamela on several sites. They've had lots of shares, but no information. I offered another reward."

"Did you pay the man for finding our boat?" Jennifer asked her husband.

"He was happy to take cash."

Ryan addressed both the inspector and the FBI agent. "Do you have any assets actively looking for the boat?"

"No," Michael said.

"So, we're back to doing aerial surveys again," Ryan said glumly.

Ernest eyed him. "This is a police matter now, Mr. Weller."

"Do you plan to do anything other than what you're already doing?" Ryan asked.

Ernest said, "No, we do not have the manpower or the budget to search for stolen sailboats."

"With all due respect, Inspector," Ryan said. "You're dealing with a double homicide, and we believe he killed a man in Martinique. We need to stop him before he kills again."

"What about the woman, Pamela?" Jennifer asked, wrapping her arms around herself. "She could be a hostage on her own boat. Who knows what that man is doing to her?"

"Three murders by the same man should constitute a freaking task force," Ryan argued.

Miami Vice held up one hand. "Slow down, there, cowboy. This isn't your deal anymore."

"Whose is it?" Ryan demanded. "Whose job is it to find a serial killer?"

"Not yours," Harwood snapped. "Now, go back to your vacation."

Ryan stepped close to the FBI agent, bringing them nose to nose. "Someone better tell me whose job it is, because there are two dead people on my friend's boat, and a serial killer sailing around with a kidnapped woman. You better figure it out damned fast."

Michael Harwood glared right back, fixing his brown eyes on Ryan's face. "Listen, Playboy, don't stick your nose where it doesn't belong."

Mango rose from the chair opposite the inspector's desk. "Let's get out of here."

Ernest cleared his throat and fidgeted with a pencil. "Please do not disturb your boat any more than you have."

Mango shoved through the inspector's door with Ryan and Jennifer on his heels. Outside the police station, Ryan donned his sunglasses and glanced around at the odd collection of police cars and motorcycles. "Miami Vice doesn't know who our killer is?" Ryan asked.

Mango sighed. "No, and I'm glad to be out of there. I have an air-tight alibi, but I felt like they were ready to lock me up."

"They don't sound very helpful," Jennifer added.

"I don't think they will be," Ryan said.

Jennifer glanced at the two men. "Now, what are we going to do?"

"I could use something to eat," Mango said.

"And I need a nap," Ryan added, stifling a yawn.

"What about that poor kidnapped woman?" Jennifer demanded. "Have you forgotten her already?"

"No," Ryan said. "We'll find her."

CHAPTER FOURTEEN

The pirogue carried four men. Through the binoculars, Billy Ron Sorenson could see two of them had rifles. Cursing, he threw down the binos, retrieved the Glock pistol he'd found on *Alamo*, and shoved it into the waistband of his boardshorts. Then, he checked his prisoner. She lay curled into a tight ball on the bed in the aft berth, bound with ropes at her wrists and ankles. This one was a fighter, more so than Naomi, but he'd broken her spirit with a good lashing. The monkey fist had left welts and bruises on her back. Hopefully, they wouldn't diminish her value with the buyers in Trinidad.

Last evening, he'd found a place to anchor and spent the night indulging his lustful desires with his unconscious victim. She'd awakened during his playtime and he'd had to subdue her again, which had made the sex even more pleasurable for him.

After he'd finished, he'd gone to the cockpit and drank rum and smoked cigars. It was wonderful to have a plaything again. But sometime during the night, he'd come to the realization that he needed to dispose of Pammie because the police would be looking for her and that meant they would be searching for him. While killing her would be the ultimate pleasure, he also needed more money to start his new charter business. That's when the idea of selling her had popped into his mind, and he knew from previous visits to Trinidad that the island was one of the epicenters of sex trafficking in the Caribbean. He'd take her there, sell her, and continue west to Panama.

That was his plan, anyway—now, he might have to fight off pirates. Back topside, he checked the progress of the pirogue. The big outboard shoved the little wooden boat easily through the waves, the bow skimming the low rollers, bouncing the passengers.

Billy Ron glanced up at the wind vane, then at the advancing pirates. Rapidly, he hauled the wheel over, and the sailboat swung onto a southeastern tack, heading for the Hibiscus oil platform poking over the horizon.

"I've got enough problems without these assholes," Billy Ron muttered as the trailing boat also changed direction.

The Island Packet wouldn't shatter any speed records, and with the low wind, they were barely making five knots. He started the Yanmar diesel. Now he had more maneuverability, and according to the GPS, he'd added another knot to his speed.

He glanced back at the pirogue. They'd closed the distance and were nearly alongside.

Billy Ron waited until the bow of the little boat had passed his stern. The first man had his hand out, reaching for the Island Packet's lifeline. He swung the sailboat hard to port directly in front of the pirogue and shoved the throttle against the stop. The big boat heeled over, and the pirogue's bow glanced off the sailboat's heavy fiberglass.

Billy Ron held up his middle finger and shouted, "Better luck next time, assholes!"

The pirate engineman had to chop the throttle to stabilize the boat, and the two gun-toting men dropped their weapons, desperately clinging to the gunwales as the little boat rocked and pitched.

The engineman quickly regained control of his boat, and Billy Ron saw the men retrieve their blacked out AKs with collapsible stocks. He pulled the Glock from his waistband as the smaller boat came alongside *Barefoot*. Leaning over the rail, he fired point blank into the face of the first pirate who was just reaching for the lifeline. The dead man toppled out of the pirogue, and the other pirate brought up his rifle to return fire while the engineman chopped the throttle again.

Billy Ron kept firing, striking the second man in the chest. The engineman threw the tiller over as soon as the pirogue's bow cleared *Barefoot*'s stern. Billy Ron fired at the pirates until the Glock's slide locked open. He dropped the empty magazine and slapped a new one into the handgrip. His thumb hit the slide release, and a fresh round entered the chamber.

"Come back here, you bastards!" Billy Ron shouted. "I've got more where that came from."

The pirates didn't return, and he dropped the sails and set a course to let the engine drive them toward the Dragon's Mouth, the northern approach to Trinidad. Billy Ron had seen the territorial limits drawn through the middle of the Mouth between Venezuela and Trinidad, and he knew better than to cross the line.

Several hours later, he motored through the strait between the island of Mona and Trinidad's Chaguaramas peninsula to reach the town of the same name, which stretched along the coast with several natural harbors separated by the massive Pointe Gourde peninsula. Over the years, the town had become a hurricane hole and was now home to several of the Caribbean's largest marinas. Billy Ron hoped to get lost in the nearly three thousand boats either visiting or calling Chaguaramas their home port. He steered for the north side of Pointe Gourde, toward the buildings sandwiched between the azure sea and the deep-green mountains.

After taking a mooring ball, Billy Ron combed his hair and dressed like the man in the passport he'd stolen off the boat in Martinique. He could barely button the flowery Hawaiian shirt he'd taken from Archie's boat, but Billy Ron made do and took the dinghy to shore, where he walked to the custom's building. He preferred not to go through the hassle of clearing himself into the country, but he also didn't want to deal with the police or other nosy yachties. He wanted to sell the girl and get the hell out of Dodge.

The customs process cost him two hours and almost four hundred American dollars. He was glad he had the cash he'd found on *Alamo* and on Archie's piece of shit, because he hadn't found any on *Barefoot*, even after interrogating Pammie. The kids had carried little cash, preferring to use their charge cards and let Daddy pay them off every month. What Billy Ron wouldn't give to have someone paying his bills. Maybe he wouldn't be in the predicament he was in right now.

Leaving the customs building, he walked along the waterfront, looking for a suitable bar. He needed something high class but with a touch of seedy underbelly. It didn't take long before he found what he was looking for at a place called The Peninsula Hotel.

Lush vegetation grew along the walkway leading to the bar, which sat near the center of the U-shaped building. From his stool, he had a view of the pool. He looked over a menu of services provided by the hotel, glad to see massages offered for reasonable prices.

The bartender brought Billy Ron a beer, and he pictured the woman tied up on *Barefoot*'s bunk. He rubbed his mouth with the back of his hand. Then he motioned for the bartender to come back.

The young black man picked up a glass as he approached.

Billy Ron lowered his voice and asked, "Do you get a happy ending with the massage?"

A smile crept across the bartender's face.

"How much?"

"Ya must ask at di spa, sir."

Billy Ron nodded. He sipped his beer, then leaned forward again. "Are they lookin' for help?"

The bartender looked startled. "Who?"

"The massage parlor," Billy Ron replied.

"Only di women work dere, sir."

"I'm not looking for work, moron, I have a girl who is."

"Oh." The bartender set down his glass and picked up another. He wiped the inside clean with a white cloth he'd kept slung over his shoulder. "Ya should speak to Junior Botus; he di owner."

Billy Ron nodded and ordered another beer. He nursed it for a while before ordering a third. When he walked out, he left a decent tip on the bar, certain that he'd recoup his investment when he sold the girl.

CHAPTER FIFTEEN

Chalk, as everyone called The Peninsula Hotel's bartender, watched the tall American walk away from the bar. He had a slight sway to his step, and his Hawaiian shirt fit too tight across his back and chest. Still, Chalk had liked the man—something about his eyes and the wide, conspiratorial smile, like the man had drawn him into his confidence and shared a secret.

But when he was out of sight, Chalk reached for the telephone. He pulled it out from under the bar and set it on the bar top before punching a number into the plastic keys and waited for Superintendent Winston Carlo to answer.

"Superintendent, dis be Chalk."

"Wuz de scene?" Winston asked.

"Der be a boy looking to sell a gyul to the massage parlor."

The two men continued to speak in the native Creole. Chalk relayed his conversation and how he'd steered the American toward Junior. Then he described his long, blond hair and tight shirt. Chalk added, "He a real bess ting, boy," meaning Billy Ron was an attractive man.

Winston said, "Have the massage parlor delay him. I'll be right there."

CHAPTER SIXTEEN

Billy Ron pushed through the door to the massage parlor, smiling as he inhaled burning incense and the smell of coconut. He'd had many massages in places just like this, some with happy endings but most with none. He approached the desk and asked to speak to Junior Botus.

"He'll be back in thirty minutes," the Asian receptionist replied.

Billy Ron nodded, eyeing her sleek black hair and the short-sleeved cheongsam dress.

"You want massage while you wait?" she prompted.

"Yeah." Billy Ron stretched. After the sail from Tobago Cays, he needed the relaxation.

The woman led him to a small room with a massage table. She instructed him to disrobe and pointed at the towel he should place over his buttocks after he'd lain on the table.

Disappointed she wouldn't be the one giving him a happy ending, Billy Ron took off his clothes and stretched out on the table. He put his face into the hole and stared at the floor. A minute later, he saw a pair of shoeless feet with bright red toenails and felt the hands of the masseuse on his back. He closed his eyes and relaxed with the pressure of her hands.

Billy Ron was unsure how long it was between the time he'd closed his eyes and the time the room door opened. The woman stopped running her hands along his spine, and he watched her shapely feet stop at the head of the table. A pair of black athletic shoes also appeared, and the woman scurried away.

Billy Ron lifted his head to see a middle-aged Indo-Trinidadian dressed in jeans and a soccer jersey. He had an oval face with close-cropped hair, dark eyes, and a pleasant smile. Billy Ron felt himself drawn in by the man's charisma.

"I'm Junior Botus," the newcomer said. "You have something to show me?"

Billy Ron sat up and swung his legs off the table, not bothering to cover himself with the towel. The Trinidadian kept his eyes on Billy Ron's face.

"Yeah," said the American, "I've got a girl for your stable."

"Where is she?"

"Close by," Billy Ron said. "Are you interested?"

"I am always interested in new girls."

"You'll like this one." Billy Ron stood and pulled on his shorts. He didn't bother to button the shirt before starting for the door.

Behind him, the shorter man said, "You dropped this."

Billy Ron spun. When he saw his bogus passport in the man's hand, he cocked his head. There was no way the passport could have fallen out of his pocket. Suddenly, he remembered the woman stepping out of the room for a few minutes. Had she rifled through his clothes and taken Archie Darling's documents? He took the passport and crammed it into the cargo pocket of his boardshorts.

Junior smiled at Billy Ron's expression and explained,

"When someone I don't know offers to sell me a gyul, I must make sure he is who he says he is."

Billy Ron smirked. "I got nothin' to hide, Junior."

The man laughed. "We go see your merchandise."

Billy Ron led the way out of the massage parlor and into a long corridor between two buildings. The high stone walls wore a tapestry of pink trumpet vines, the air rich with the scent of their blossoms, which Billy Ron thought looked more purple than pink. He kept glancing behind him to see if Junior was still on his heels. Every time, Junior gave him a reassuring smile. Then Billy Ron stopped dead in his tracks.

He was intimately familiar with the sickening sound of wood impacting flesh. Expecting to receive a similar blow, he spun into a crouch, scanning the alley. Junior lay crumpled in a heap, limbs askew. Above him stood a stout man with dreadlocks, gripping a baton in his right hand.

Their eyes met, and the man gave a gap-toothed grin. He collapsed the baton and jabbed it into the back pocket of his shorts. In a thick Jamaican accent, he said, "We need to go, mon. That mon be a cop."

"He said his name was Junior Botus."

"No, mon, that be Police Superintendent Winston Carlo. The bar mon call him."

"Shit," Billy Ron muttered.

"Let's go." The man led the way out of the alley to the street. They turned right and strolled away from the hotel.

"My name be Linford. I want to see your girl."

"How do I know I can trust you?"

"I'm no ragamuffin, mon. You be blessed up I found you when I did. I buy de girl from you."

"You got cash?" Billy Ron demanded.

"Soon come."

Billy Ron looked hard into the man's face. He knew the sex trade was a staple of Jamaica and Trinidad's underworlds, so it wasn't surprising to meet a guy like Linford here. This man had knocked out a cop, and if he was willing to do that to keep Billy Ron from being arrested for selling a woman, then he might as well trust the dude. Unless this was a set up and they'd arrest him when he produced Pammie.

Linford must have sensed his hesitation. He grinned and slapped on Billy Ron's back, before saying, "No worries, mon. Let's look at de girl."

"Yeah, mon," Billy Ron said, glancing at the other pedestrians. No one seemed to pay attention to them, but he cast a wary eye on passersby and glanced at the reflections in shop windows as they made their way to the waterfront.

They piled into the dinghy and rode to the sailboat. Billy Ron had draped a sheet over the transom to hide the name and hung clothes on the lifeline around the cockpit to make it look as if he'd done laundry. He needed to change the Island Packet's name and home port.

Once aboard, Linford followed him into the salon. Billy Ron moved the boat hook he'd jammed against the aft stateroom door and pulled it open. Pammie lay curled in a ball, hands and feet still bound. She whimpered into the gag duct taped across her mouth.

"Come on, girl, get over here," Billy Ron ordered.

When she didn't move, he crawled onto the bed and grabbed her by the hair. She let out a muffled scream as he dragged her off the bed. He forced her to stand, pulling her head back so Linford could get a good look at her face.

"She clean?" the Jamaican asked.

"As a whistle," Billy Ron replied. He had seen no evidence of STDs, and she hadn't told him she had one.

Linford took Pammie's chin in his hand and moved her head back and forth. Her wide, green eyes stared vacantly, and tears flowed down her cheeks.

"She's a little old."

"Hey, she'll make some sheik a nice fifth wife," Billy Ron retorted. He pulled her shirt up to show Linford her breasts. She stood meekly, letting the men ogle her.

Linford nodded. "You've been seasoning her."

"She won't be eyeballing nobody," Billy Ron said. He'd beaten Pammie several times to break her resistance and withheld food and water to ensure her compliance. There were other things he'd done, too. Things that made him smile but he wouldn't tell Linford about.

"I give you ten grand."

"Are you kidding? She's worth twenty-five."

"No, mon, I give you ten."

Billy Ron shook his head and frowned. He wanted more money for the exotic blonde. Maybe if Linford was the end user, the price would be higher, but the Jamaican was a middleman and he had to make money, too. Besides, he could live a long time on the money he'd found on *Alamo* plus the ten Linford would give him.

"I'll take it. Where's the money?"

"No worries. Soon come." Linford pulled Pammie's T-shirt down and made her sit on the bed. "When was the last time she had water?"

Billy Ron shrugged. "It's been a few hours."

Linford went to the fridge and brought back a bottle of water. He pulled off Pammie's gag and told her to drink. She drained the whole bottle in several long swallows.

Pammie looked up meekly at Linford. "Can I please go pee?"

He guided her to the head. After watching her use the toilet, he took her back to the bed and reapplied the gag. He motioned for Billy Ron to follow him topside.

In the cockpit, Billy Ron opened a beer and handed one to Linford.

"I call my people." Linford took out a cell phone, dialed a

number, and spoke in a patois Billy Ron couldn't understand. After ending the call, he instructed, "Start the engine. We motor to another location."

Billy Ron took in his laundry, started the engine, and used the winch to pull up the anchor. He hosed off the mud and sand that had accumulated on it as Linford steered them east, staying close to shore. Eventually, they rounded the bulging Pointe Gourde peninsula and entered a sheltered cove. Billy Ron could see the sunken hulls of several old boats pulled up into the mangroves.

Billy Ron dropped anchor and set out just enough scope to keep the boat from going aground or hitting one of the other wrecks. Then they opened fresh beers and settled in to wait for Linford's man.

CHAPTER SEVENTEEN

Pammie heard the familiar sound of the anchor chair running through the hawser and felt the boat snug to the rode. She knew she had to escape, but every time she'd tried anything resembling defiance, Billy Ron had raped, beaten, and starved her. The bottle of water the other man had given her had been her first drink in more than twenty-four hours.

She pushed her tongue through her lips and pressed it against the duct tape. Her saliva had loosened the binding. She rubbed her head against the comforter and gradually, the tape peeled back, and it fell away from her face. She took long, deep breaths through her mouth. As badly as she wanted to scream, she knew if she did, she'd receive more punishment. For now, she'd savor the small blessing of being free of the gag.

Afraid to move any more, she lay on the bunk with her eyes closed, sensing the shifting of the boat as the men walked about, listening to their steps on the fiberglass and wood. Their laughter and murmured words were too vague to make out.

This was a nightmare from which she desperately wanted to wake. How could Mike be dead? Did their father know Billy Ron had kidnapped her, and would he send someone to find her? She had her doubts. She'd made herself a royal pain in his ass for most of her life, cashed in her college fund, bought the sailboat, and coerced Mike into coming with her. This was all her fault.

Pammie buried her head in the comforter, wishing for someone to either rescue her or shoot her and put her out of her misery.

Night had fallen when she heard a vehicle approach. The motor shut off, and a moment later, she watched through the porthole as a light winked on and off several times. A signal? A feeling of dread pervaded her body, and her stomach knotted with a cramp so violent that it drew her legs to her chest. Bile rose in her throat, the acid stinging her mouth.

Billy Ron slammed open the cabin door. She remembered first seeing him, the ripple of his abs and the flowing hair. His good looks had belied the violence inside him. Pammie shuddered now as she saw the leer on his face. He jerked her off the bed, applied a new piece of tape across her mouth, and checked the bindings on her wrists and ankles.

Roughly, he half-pushed, half-carried her up the steps to the cockpit. The fresh breeze felt amazing after being cooped up in the stifling cabin, but after it wicked away her sweat, her skin turned clammy and cold. Billy Ron shoved her onto a cockpit bench and motioned for her to stay.

The darkness swallowed everything around them save for a bouncing flashlight on shore and the faint LED cockpit lights. The man who'd inspected her earlier climbed into *Barefoot*'s dinghy and motored toward the flashlight. They waited in silence until he'd returned.

Pammie was surprised to see a sturdy white woman climb over the rail. She had short brown hair and a tired face. Her expression said she, too, had been through something like what Pammie now endured, or more.

The woman sat across from Pammie, their knees touching. "My name is Gita."

Pammie guessed she was German from the name and accent.

"I'll be with you for this journey," Gita said. "Do you need anything right now?"

There were so many things she needed: to eat, to drink, to curl up in her father's lap and tell him she loved him and how sorry she was for being a little shit.

Pammie shook her head.

"Good. I'm going to untie your feet. Please don't do anything stupid. These men will hurt you badly."

Pammie nodded.

"Don't make eye contact with anyone. Keep your head down. Speak only when spoken to. Don't make trouble. Do these things and you will be all right, okay?"

She nodded again, keeping her eyes on the deck. Inside her head, she screamed, *None of this is all right*.

Gita cut Pammie's leg bonds and helped her to stand. She commanded, "Get in the dinghy."

Pammie stepped onto the bench, but stumbled, her balance affected by her bound hands. Billy Ron picked her up and set her in the dinghy. Her inspector sat in the stern, one hand on the outboard's tiller. He flashed her a gap-toothed grin, looking evil in the low light.

Billy Ron and Gita climbed into the dinghy, and they motored through the darkness to shore. Pammie remembered lots of trips to and from shore in the little dinghy, and how Mike had wired a switch under the motor to cut out the electronics to make it harder to steal. Her heart broke from her dead brother; she wanted to kick Billy Ron in the face for killing him. She knew there was nothing she could do. Maybe she could jump into the water and drown herself.

She decided it wasn't worth the punishment if they recaptured her. The stories she'd heard about women being gang-raped crowded into her mind. How many men were here? How long would the torture last if they disciplined her like that? She never wanted to know.

They ran the dinghy up on the sand. Pammie saw two dark figures behind the flashlight. Gita helped her rise from the boat seat and step onto shore. Her legs were weak, and she wobbled. One man stepped forward to grab her under the arm. He smelled of sweat and tobacco, and his hands were rough against her skin. They marched her to the open rear doors of the van sitting in the cone of light spilling from the flashlight. Gita forced her to sit on the bumper. With quick and expert care, she lashed Pammie's feet together before pushing her onto the hard, metal floor.

The door slammed shut, and once again, she was alone in the dark. Gita entered a side door, and the two men got into the front seats. She heard the engine start. *How will Daddy find me now?*

CHAPTER EIGHTEEN

Linford walked quiet as a ghost in the dark night. The knot in Billy Ron's stomach tightened. This was where it could all go wrong. They didn't have to give him a red cent. He expected Linford to pull a pistol from his pocket and pay him with lead.

The van started, and the headlights snapped on, illuminating the tiny beach and silhouetting Linford. If the mosquitos were bad before, their numbers tripled as they flocked to the light. Billy Ron swatted at a cloud that had permanently attached itself to his head since their arrival in the keyhole-shaped bay.

Linford reached behind his back.

Billy Ron held up his hands to plead his case. He wanted to live, not die by a bullet in the lonely mangroves. The irony of him leaving his victims in similar fashions was lost on him. He swallowed hard. "I don't want no trouble."

Linford held out an envelope. With a sigh of relief, Billy Ron took the packet and stuffed it in his pocket. The money would all be there, or it wouldn't be. Either way, he'd gotten paid.

"It's best you go now, mon," Linford said. "Leave de island and don't come back."

Billy Ron nodded.

Linford trotted to the van. The door slammed as he got in, and the van backed away. It turned and headed for the city.

Billy Ron stood in the darkness. The knot loosened, and his bowels shivered. He ran to the edge of the woods, dropped his shorts, and defecated.

It had been the same when he'd killed for the first time. Her name had been Diana, and he still remembered how his anger had given way to an exhilaration so mentally and physically intense that, no matter how many times he'd tried, he couldn't duplicate the feeling, except with Naomi. When he'd finally become aware of Diana's death, it had scared the shit out of him, literally. Facing his own potential demise had done the same.

He kicked his shorts off, ran into the water to clean his bottom, then rode to the sailboat in the dinghy. The darkness made it too difficult to motor the sailboat out of the harbor, so he found the insect repellent and applied a liberal dose to his naked body, trying desperately not to scratch the thousands of bites already dimpling his skin. He closed the boat up tight and pulled on pants and a long-sleeved fishing shirt, then dosed himself in spray again. Finally, he lay on the bunk with a bottle of rum.

Billy Ron spent the night tossing and turning. He might have dozed off; he wasn't sure. Even the half bottle of rum he'd consumed did little to assuage the heat and the itching. When the first rays of dawn brightened the harbor, he made coffee and tried not to scratch the bug bites. He sprayed the repellent over his body again and went topside with his coffee.

The mosquitos had disappeared with the morning sun and

a slight breeze. His belly growled. There was little food in the cabin. After studying the map, he decided he wasn't far from the Five Islands Yacht Club, and they had a restaurant.

He finished his coffee, peeled off two hundred-dollar bills from the stack Linford had given him, and shoved the rest into a hiding spot in the engine room. Then he hopped in the dinghy and roared out of the keyhole. In retrospect, he should have just sailed away.

CHAPTER NINETEEN

Superintendent Winston Carlo rubbed the knot on the side of his head as he leaned against the wall of The Peninsula Hotel, scanning the people walking along the street. The dotish bastard had caught him just above the right ear, and he'd gone down like a sack of potatoes. A hotel maid had found him sprawled on the cobblestone alley and called for help. The bartender and Winston's informant, Chalk, had revived him with a dash of cold water to the face.

After Winston had reported to his superiors, they'd sent him to the hospital for a night of observation and started a citywide crackdown on known or suspected sex slave rings in retaliation. They hadn't found Winston's attacker or the man who Winston had gone to meet, a man calling himself Archie Darling—though the real Archie Darling had recently been murdered. Interpol had emailed a document with the killer's real name after finding his prints on *Alamo*. Billy Ron Sorenson had left a trail of bodies through the Lesser Antilles, and the Trini police hoped he was still on the island.

Now, every officer was scouring the neighborhoods, the bars, and the flop houses. They walked the sidewalks and the back alleys searching for the suspected murderer. If Winston's supposition was correct, he had almost bought Pamela Walcott from the man. If he'd only known who he was dealing with, he would have taken backup. Winston's boss had told him to be thankful he wasn't the victim of the Sailboat Slasher, a name coined by a news reporter and perpetuated through social media.

Beyond the street, the wharves and docks bustled with ships coming and going. The bay had taken on a calm, oily look between the tree-studded hills. He fumbled out a bottle of pain killers and swallowed two. The pain throbbed in his head, and he breathed deeply to help ease it, bringing the scent of the flowers and cooking meat. Winston's stomach rumbled. Chalk always served a good lunch.

Before he could head for the bar in The Peninsula's courtyard, his radio chirped. Winston snatched if from his belt and adjusted the volume. The transmission came through crisp and clear.

"Possible sighting of the suspect at Five Islands Yacht Club. All officers in the area please respond."

Winston didn't bother to radio dispatch. He ran to his car. The yacht club was one and a half kilometers from his position.

When he reached the yacht club, he parked beside two police cars with a cluster of officers in dark blue trousers, gray shirts, and bulletproof vests beside them, their forage caps pulled low. Two carried shotguns.

Sergeant Cortez, a lanky rising star in the department, asked, "Superintendent, what do you want us to do?"

Winston waved his hand in a circle. "Surround the building." He assigned several men to guard the front and rear entrances.

Two more vehicles pulled into the parking lot. Officers in blue camouflage carrying H&K MP5 machine guns piled out.

Winston walked over to the special branch senior superintendent, a man with a creased brow and hard scowl, who Winston knew only by reputation.

"I don't want to spook him," Winston said. "Have your men spread out along the front and keep him contained. I'm going inside to see if we can lure him out."

Without waiting for a response, Winston went to the restaurant. There was no need to bother the tourists if their suspect was not among them. He pushed through the door and found a waitress. Holding up a photo of Billy Ron Sorenson the police department had received from Interpol, he asked, "Have you seen this man?"

"Yes, sir, he go to the outside bar." She pointed toward the waterfront.

"Where is Ramesh?"

"Come." She led Winston to an office door.

Ramesh rose from his desk, dwarfing Winston by nearly a foot and a hundred pounds of solid muscle. Winston had known Ramesh before he'd bought the marina, when he'd been a first mate aboard a variety of ships based in and around Trinidad. They'd met when Winston had worked a case involving the theft of goods from a wharf where Ramesh's ship had been docked. They'd become friends, and now Winston frequented the Five Islands's restaurant.

Ramesh grinned as he asked, "What brings de superintendent to see me?"

"We're looking for this man." Winston held up the photo. "He is in the bar."

"Aw shit!" Ramesh muttered in his deep voice, then, "Judith, make sure he still there."

The young waitress scurried away.

Ramesh said, "I like to get my licks on dat boy."

Judith returned several minutes later. "He is still eatin'. Damian say he ask about a gyul."

"Someone in particular?" Winston asked, wondering if the woman Billy Ron had asked about was Pammie, and if she had escaped.

Judith shook her head. "He wanted a ho."

Winston scratched his ear. Yesterday, the man had tried to sell him a woman; today, he was looking to buy sex with another. He held his radio up to his lips. "The suspect is eating at the waterfront bar. We're gonna lure him out. Be ready."

Ramesh picked up the receiver for an ancient rotary phone, spun the dial once and said, "Send me Bridgid," before hanging up. To Judith, he said, "Have Damian delay da bill."

Winston watched as the woman once again left the room. Ramesh was manipulating things better than Winston could himself. "You act like you've done this before."

Ramesh grinned. "Dat cockroach have no right in my fowl party."

Before Winston could remark about the chickens eating cockroaches, the office door opened. An Asian woman entered the room. In her four-inch heels, she stood eye to eye with Winston at five foot eight. Her lustrous black hair shone in the florescent light. Winston gulped, immediately feeling self-conscious. She was one of the most beautiful women he had ever seen. Her almond eyes sparkled with mischief, and her high cheeks carried just a trace of makeup.

"Bridgid, this be Superintendent Carlo. He's here to capture da Sailboat Slasher."

"For true. He here?" she asked.

"In the bar," Carlo said.

"He ask for a gyul. I want you to lure him out so Winston can arrest him."

"Yuh dotish awah?" *Are you stupid?* Bridgid asked.

Ramesh laughed. "It's okay, Pumkin. You just invite him to lime and bring him toward the office."

Winston added to the plan about what she was to do after inviting him to hang out. "When you get him out the bar of the restaurant, we will arrest him. Yesterday, he tried to sell a girl to me. We need to find her."

The fear in Bridgid's eyes shifted to resolution. "We go lime and you arrest him?"

"As soon as he's outside," Winston assured her.

The woman nodded.

"Go now." Ramesh shooed her out of the office with a gesture.

"Where you find her?" Winston asked.

"She too much for you, boy."

Winston smiled. "She too much for you." He brought his radio to his lips and said to his men, "Be on alert. Wait for my signal."

The two men walked out of the office, toward the bar built on the waterfront. Winston wanted to watch Bridgid in action, but he knew he had to stay out of sight. Billy Ron might recognize him and get spooked.

The bar was open on three sides, with a small food prep area and liquor storage forming the fourth side and blocking the view of the boatyard. There was the possibility that Billy Ron could escape on a boat. If Winston circled around the building and Bridgid led Billy Ron toward the office, he could scare him into the arms of the tactical officers guarding the parking lot. He explained this to Ramesh, who said he'd go to the bar to keep an eye on Bridgid.

Winston nodded to the officers he had posted by the rear entrance, explained the plan to them, and entered the prep area.

Through a window in a door to the bar, he could see Bridgid and Billy Ron. Bridgid smiled coquettishly and laughed as if all the man's jokes were funny. Then Billy Ron stood, and the two linked arms. Winston felt sick to his stomach. Ramesh would kill him if something happened to Bridgid.

As Billy Ron and Bridgid walked out of the bar, Winston hurried after them. He saw Ramesh give Bridgid a hand signal, turning her and her john toward the office. She leaned in and whispered something in Billy Ron's ear.

When they were halfway to the office, with Ramesh tagging along behind, Winston keyed his radio and said, "Now." Then he shouted, "Billy Ron Sorenson, you're under arrest!"

The killer spun, pulling Bridgid to him, causing her to stumble. One of her high heels snapped, and she let out a screech.

Before the police could converge on Billy Ron, Ramesh crossed the parking lot and seized Billy Ron by the wrist, the only part he could grab as Billy Ron pulled Bridgid back and forth in front of him as a shield.

Billy Ron let go of Bridgid, and she fell into the arms of Sergeant Cortez. Winston ran up behind Ramesh, but the big man had already smacked Billy Ron across the face several times.

The special branch officers approached with their guns shouldered and aimed at Ramesh and Billy Ron, who had fallen to his knees, a trickle of blood oozing down his chin.

"Let the boy go, Ramesh," Winston shouted.

Ramesh glanced around at the men aiming their weapons at him and released the serial killer. Billy Ron slumped to the ground. Ramesh turned to find Bridgid crying and clutching the sergeant. He gently pulled her from Cortez's arms while the cops forced Billy Ron onto his stomach and cuffed his wrists.

"Ah get my licks in," Ramesh said as he and Winston watched a crowd of armed men escort Billy Ron to a waiting police car.

CHAPTER TWENTY

Ryan Weller stared across the vista of undulating blue ocean, reflecting the sunlight into a blinding glare. To the right, the oil rigs hovered over the Hibiscus field. On their left, the green humps of Trinidad and Tobago's hills rose from the water. He held the Cannon digital camera steady in his lap, ready to bring it up and snap off pictures of sailing vessels. So far, he'd taken over a dozen photographs and knew that, as Lamar flew him around Tobago, he would have to take even more.

After taking a nap for most of yesterday afternoon, Ryan and Mango had found two new pilots to fly reconnaissance. When he, Mango, and Jennifer had gone to dinner, the news plastered pictures of *Alamo* and *Barefoot* across the television screen with shocking headlines about a Caribbean serial killer. Since no one knew the killer's name, they used a blank silhouette for his picture and called him the Sailboat Slasher.

While Archie Darling was reported to have taken up cruising after making a fortune shorting the stock market during its downturn in 2008, the media preferred to focus on the Walcott kids. They were the heirs to a Southern California real estate empire. Both their father and estranged mother had appeared before the cameras to beg for Pammie's release.

Landis had shed no new light on the situation, either, and suggested Ryan and the Hulseys cooperate with FBI Agent Michael Harwood, who was assisting Interpol and the St. Vincent and Grenadine police. Ryan had told Landis that Harwood needed all the help he could get, and that the agent worried more about covering his ass to avoid getting the agency in trouble with a rich donor than catching a serial killer.

Mango and Jennifer had spoken to the Interpol inspector while Ryan was napping. He had helped the St. Vincent's forensic unit run fingerprints.

Now, the hot airplane cabin and the steady drone of the propeller were lulling Ryan to sleep. His eyes drooped, his head tilting forward as his muscles relaxed. The camera clattered to the floor between his feet, startling Ryan and the pilot. He glanced around sheepishly and fished the camera out of the footwell.

"Boat up ahead," the pilot said.

Ryan raised his camera and sighted through the lens at a catamaran. "That's not it."

"You want to circle Tobago?"

"Let's look at the oil fields first." Ryan pointed at the skeletal platforms rising from the sea on their spindly legs.

Lamar slid the plane to starboard, made a long loop out over the Caribbean Sea, and came back from the west, angling toward Tobago. Ryan saw few boats on the glistening sea. He dug out a protein bar to feed his grumbling stomach and offered one to Lamar, who declined.

The pilot cleared them into Tobago airspace and circled the island counterclockwise to allow Ryan a view of the coast through his camera lens. Tobago had two major ports favored by cruisers, Scarborough and Charlottesville. There were several smaller coves for boats to anchor in, but they mostly stayed near the urban centers.

They'd just rounded the northeastern end of the island when Ryan's phone rang. He saw Landis's name on the caller ID and thumbed the *answer* button.

"Where are you?" Landis asked.

"Flying around Tobago. We're taking pictures of boats."

"Forget about it. Billy Ron Sorenson used Archie Darling's passport to enter Trinidad at Chaguaramas. The police just captured him."

Ryan breathed a sigh of relief. "Thank God. What about the girl?"

"No sign of her."

"Shit."

"I couldn't say it better myself. Submit an expense report, and I'll see if I can get you reimbursed for your flight time and fuel."

"Thanks, Landis," Ryan said. "Anything else you want us to do?"

"No. I heard about your boat's mystery tracker. Watch your six."

"Roger that." Ryan hung up, then said into the airplane's communication system, "Let's go home. They captured the killer."

Lamar smiled. "Roger that, boss." He tilted the plane toward the north.

Ryan called Mango to let him know they could stop looking and meet back at the airport.

"That's a relief, bro," Mango said. "The broker just called and said the owners accepted our offer for the Lagoon."

"That's awesome," Ryan said. "I'll see you soon."

The flight back to Grenada went smoothly, and they were on the ground thirty minutes later. Another thirty minutes and the trio of searchers had taken seats in the outside seating area of The Waterfront, a restaurant overlooking Clifton Harbor.

A waitress set steamed lobsters in front of Ryan and Mango and slid a salad under Jennifer's poised fork. She dug in before the men had unfolded their napkins.

"Are you happy they caught the killer?" Ryan asked her.

She held a hand up to cover her mouth, and around her partially chewed food said, "Yes."

"Me, too."

Mango said, "I'd have run for Panama or South America."

"Have you been thinking about killing your wife, kidnapping a woman, and sailing away?" Ryan asked.

Mango glanced at Jennifer, who had stopped eating to stare at him. "No. I'm just saying I'd have done something different."

The ringing of Ryan's phone interrupted them. He checked the caller ID. "What's up, Landis?"

"The Trini police got a confession out of Billy Ron. He said there was an argument on the sailboat, and he killed the two men. He sold Pammie to a Jamaican near Chaguaramas."

"That's not good," Ryan said.

"Just wanted you to know."

Ryan ended the call and set the phone on the table.

"I can't believe that prick sold her," Mango said, apparently having overheard the conversation.

"And dumb enough to stick around Trinidad afterward."

"The dude had fifty grand already—why'd he sell her?" Mango wondered.

Ryan shrugged. "This way he got something for her other than dumping her overboard. At least there's a chance they can find her."

"Sounds like a greedy bastard to me," Mango replied.

"I think the dude has a few more issues besides greed," Ryan said. "But greed always catches up with you."

"When will it get you, bro?"

Ryan glanced up from shoveling a forkful of steaming, buttery lobster into his mouth. "What are you talking about?"

"How many drug and arms dealers are you going to rip off before they come after you?"

Ryan shot back, "*We* only ripped off one drug dealer."

"Did you tell him about your new tracker?" Jennifer asked.

Mango looked between them; brow furrowed. "What new tracker?"

Jennifer smirked at Ryan, then said, "He found a GPS tracker on his boat and no one knows who put it there."

Ryan sat back and stared across the water. He took several breaths, keeping his face neutral. He wanted to blurt out that she'd smoked half his pack of cigarettes during the passage. Instead, he said, "That drug money is buying you a new boat."

Mango frowned, then nodded. "Yeah, it is."

Ryan went back to eating. The tracker had him worried enough. He didn't need to argue with his friends. After a few minutes, he asked, "When are you flying to Martinique?"

"In the morning," Mango replied.

"Then what?"

Mango shrugged. "We gotta come back here and get our kit off *Alamo*. I think I'll put her on the hard, get her fixed up, and sell her. Then we'll either find a honey hole for hurricane season or head for Central America."

"It would be better to take *Alamo* to Trinidad."

"You going to sail her down there?" Mango asked.

Ryan glanced at Jennifer. "I promised your wife I'd stick around and help you move gear so she wouldn't have to go back aboard *Alamo*."

"How thoughtful of you."

"I'll get the boat released while you guys are in Martinique and sail her to Trinidad."

Jennifer asked, "What about *Windseeker*?"

"I'll fly back and get her after we square everything away with *Alamo*. Besides, it would be a good place to leave *Seeker* when I go back to work."

Mango agreed and they ordered another round of beers.

Later that evening, the three of them rode with a boat boy out to *Windseeker*. Jennifer and Mango gathered their meager possessions before taking the boat back to shore. Ryan sat in the cockpit, watching them go.

Once again, he was alone.

He went down to the galley and dug out a bottle of rum. Back topside, he stretched out in his hammock and lit a cigarette. He gazed across the water at the lights of a bar. Music and laughter drifted to him on the humid breeze. After a hit from the bottle, he swung his feet off the hammock, stubbed out his cigarette, and climbed into his dinghy. Maybe going ashore would be the cure for his blues. Drinking with shapely, sunburned tourists was better than drinking alone.

CHAPTER TWENTY-ONE

Two Trinidad and Tobago police cars slid to a stop at the entrance to Piarco International Airport. The uniformed officers stepped from the first car, and Superintendent Winston Carlo climbed from the driver's seat of the second vehicle. He opened the rear door for Billy Ron Sorenson. Winston wore his usual jeans and soccer jersey with a concealed handgun on his hip. Billy Ron sported white prison-issued athletic shoes, baggy blue jeans, and a collared shirt. The outfit helped the prisoner blend with the crowd while the superintendent escorted him to Central Police Headquarters in Kingstown.

Caribbean Air had provided them with seats on a flight to St. Vincent and asked that the prisoner and the officers dress in plain clothes. The only concession to law enforcement were the handcuffs manacling the prisoner's wrists and Winston's concealed Beretta.

Winston doubted they would get any more stares if they were in uniform. The local and cable news channels had played Billy Ron's photo across their screens for the last twenty-four hours. It seemed everyone at the airport had seen the reports and now watched as the prisoner stepped from the car.

While it was a crime to sell another human being according to Trinidad and Tobago law, Billy Ron would stand trial for the murders of Archie Darling and Mike Walcott in St. Vincent before he did time for human trafficking. DNA evidence, fingerprints, and a confession would ensure he spent the rest of his life behind bars.

Billy Ron walked like a man headed for Carnival rather than the guillotine. His sentence in St. Vincent would be life in prison. Several years ago, they'd outlawed the death penalty, but Winston remembered when the St. Vincent government had hung three men in 1995. Grimly, he wished they still did, or that Billy Ron had committed the murders in Trinidad and Tobago waters, where they still had the death penalty.

The entry to the terminal was a round atrium with floor-to-ceiling windows and a glass roof flanked on the right and left by covered arrival and departure areas. The superintendent pushed the prisoner toward the terminal's automatic doors, and the two cops from the first car flanked them.

Billy Ron stumbled. When he came upright, he planted his foot and slammed his shoulder into the back of the police officer to his right.

The officer fell to the pavement. Billy Ron spun and sprinted toward the street.

Winston spun, drawing his pistol, and shouted, "Stop!"

He leveled the pistol on the back of the fleeing man, but there were pedestrians in the way. The other police officer brushed past him and ran after the fugitive. Winston sprinted after them.

Billy Ron angled toward a gray Nissan just pulling up to the no-parking sign behind the police cars.

The driver came to a stop and stepped out.

Winston yelled, "Get back in the car."

The driver looked up, puzzled.

"Stop!" Winston screamed again.

Billy Ron leaped into the Nissan's driver seat and threw the car into gear. He stomped on the gas pedal and shot away from the curb.

Winston came to a stop at the curb, bending to place his hands on his knees. He watched as the Nissan's owner sprinted after his stolen car in a vain attempt to stop it.

The police officer Billy Ron had knocked over came running up to the curb. He spoke breathlessly into his police radio, giving the getaway car's license plate number. In moments, Winston's cell phone rang. He knew who was calling without looking.

"Hello," Winston said, putting the phone to his ear.

"What happened?" Police Commissioner Walter Crick asked.

"Sir," Winston said, self-consciously straightening, "we were transporting the prisoner to Kingstown. He pushed over one of the sergeants assigned to escort him and jumped into a car."

"Find him, Winston. We do not need a murderer loose on our island."

"Yes, sir."

"I'm sending all available units to your location. Coordinate with the defense force. I want roadblocks and neighborhood sweeps."

Winston nodded. "We will get him. There's only two ways off this island."

CHAPTER TWENTY-TWO

There were actually three ways, but Billy Ron Sorenson wasn't going to swim. He couldn't fly an aircraft, and while boats were plentiful, he hoped *Barefoot* still rode her anchor in the keyhole. Everything he needed to escape was onboard, most importantly the money. He could steal any boat, but he wanted his money.

"Damn this right-hand drive car," he muttered. At least it was an automatic and he didn't have to negotiate shifting a manual transmission with his left hand and steer while handcuffed. Billy Ron gritted his teeth as he approached the roundabout leading out of the airport. If the curb hadn't directed him to the left, he would have naturally spun the wheel to the right and charged into oncoming traffic. He wove in and out of the cars, cutting a few off as he took the exit for Churchill-Roosevelt Highway.

He had to dump the car. The cops would have called in the license plate and were probably mobilizing roadblocks as he drove. Glancing in the mirror, he could just make out the lights of a cop car.

Billy Ron turned the car into a gas station and coasted to

a stop behind the building. He jumped out, moving awkwardly with his cuffed hands. He needed to get rid of the cuffs, too. A dumpster sat haphazardly against the block wall of the building. Beside it, a stack of tires held scum-covered water. He spotted a piece of electrical wire lying on top of the tires. The copper bent easily in his hands, and he worked the hooked end into the handcuff keyhole.

A moment later, he popped the left wrist free. The right took more time, but it yielded too, and he tossed the cuffs into the dumpster, making sure they disappeared under the bags of rotting garbage.

What the hell was he going to do now? Chaguaramas might as well be on the other side of the moon, but he had to go there just to find *Barefoot*. What if the cops had confiscated her? He put that thought out of his head. They were probably more concerned about finding the girl than the boat. They hadn't even asked him about it during his interrogation. Damn, what a pussy he'd been for confessing to killing Mike and Archie. His gut muscles still ached from the pounding the cops and that big bastard at the marina restaurant had given him.

The most direct route was an hour's drive on the CRH, if not more, and Billy Ron knew that in Trinidad, accidents happened frequently. Even if there was light traffic, he felt sure the police would have roadblocks or would at least be looking for him.

He needed to find a way across the island to his boat. If nothing else, he could walk, or maybe catch a Maxi Taxi, one of the brightly colored vans used for public transportation. He took one last look at the pile of rusted junk beside the dumpster and saw a long sliver of metal the length of his forearm. It had a point at one end and tapered gradually to where someone or something had twisted it off another piece of metal, leaving a jagged end. With a chunk of concrete, he pounded the jagged end flush, creating a makeshift knife. The points still dug into his palm when he wielded it, but at least he had a weapon, and he liked knives.

Billy Ron walked around the building and leaned against the corner, observing the cars coming and going from the gas pumps. A group of young men clustered at the far end. Beside them, several motor scooters rested on kickstands. A scooter would be perfect, especially if he could find a helmet, but he couldn't risk getting into a confrontation unless he had a real chance of winning. No, he'd have to wait for a more opportune time.

After several minutes of observing the parking lot, a cop car screamed to a halt beside the pumps, and an officer climbed out. Billy Ron backed away from the corner and ran to the rear of the building. He glanced around wildly. As soon as they searched the area, they'd find the stolen car.

He sprinted into the woods and kept running through the brush until he came to a street. He turned left and jogged to Factory Road. The cops were back to his left now, so he went right, staying along the high, block walls, all the while searching the driveways of the colorful houses for a vehicle he could steal.

When he came abreast of a small market, he slowed to catch his breath. The exterior wall around the door had been plastered with posters, advertising everything from beer to produce. A large chalkboard held the specials of the day. If he had any money, he'd grab a six-pack. He needed it. But what interested Billy Ron now was the bicycle sitting unattended by the steps.

Without hesitation, he grabbed the handlebars and ran. As he did, he stepped on the pedal, swung himself onto the seat, and sped away. The shiv he'd picked up at the gas station made bending his leg difficult, but he continued, not wanting to stop to adjust it. He made several turns to elude anyone who might have spotted him.

The pavement ended ten feet from the next road. He carried the bike through the grass, across a small ditch, and then remounted. He rode toward a massive housing complex with tan, green, and blue two- and four-story apartment complexes for as far as he could see. Even their roofs bore the colorful designs so prevalent in the Caribbean.

This road ended in a grove of trees as well, and he groaned. Dismounting the bike, he carried it into the trees and stopped at the bank of a river. Beyond it were open farm fields with dirt roads between them. Billy Ron waded through the calf-deep stream and up the gravel bank on the other side. He set the bike on the dirt and took off pedaling again. The shiv had slipped down his pants and now poked him in the calf with each circle of the pedals.

Screw it. He stopped again, reached into his pants, and removed the piece of metal before tossing it into the dirt.

Billy Ron worked his way east, finding himself also making his way north. He knew the CRH lay in that direction along with police barricades. He wanted to stay in the agriculture areas, thinking the police wouldn't search the fields unless someone reported a white man riding a bicycle. He wished he had a map so he could come up with an escape route to Chaguaramas and the sailboat.

As the road rounded a bend, he headed east again. Being a creature of habit, he followed the main routes. He also thought the smaller two-track dirt roads would dead-end, and he preferred to not have to double back. But he was getting sick of this bicycling shit and ready to find a faster means of transportation—and, man, was he thirsty. His shoes, one size too big, were wet and water squished from his socks each time he pressed the pedal. This sucked, but it was better than walking.

He saw workers in the fields, but no cars or trucks other than those parked at the occasional house or barn. Dust coated his sweaty skin, and he could taste the grit on his teeth. Several kilometers later, he came to a T in the road and turned south. He pedaled to where the road stopped at a long line of trees, which he had guessed correctly bordered a river.

Dropping the bike in the brush, he staggered to the bank and fell into the water. The muddy river washed away his sweat and dirt. He wanted to take long drinks but was afraid of getting a parasite that would make him shit out his insides. As he wallowed in the water, he took in his surroundings. Beached on the other side of the river was a wooden pirogue with an outboard motor.

The river had to go to the Gulf of Paria, he reasoned, and from there it was a quick ride across the gulf to Chaguaramas and his sailboat. Billy Ron swam across the river and crawled through the mud onto dry ground. He stayed low in the brush, scanning for the owner before inspecting the boat. Music drifted on the breeze, and through the bushes, he could see a white, ramshackle house surrounded by trees. Two ancient pickup trucks sat in front of the building.

He turned his attention back to the boat. The little red gas tank was half full, and the owner had taken good care of the motor. He checked the starter fob and found it in place. A small cooler sat near the bow, containing several bottles of water and a cold Carib beer.

Billy Ron pushed the boat into the river and climbed aboard, letting the languid current carry it downstream. Several minutes later, he tugged the starter rope, and the engine roared to life. He engaged the drive, twisted open the throttle, and shot down river.

When the motor sputtered, Billy Ron cursed. He'd already made it out of the meandering river, saw the building-studded shores of Port-a-Spain to the west, and charted a course across the bay toward Pointe Gourde peninsula. The motor fell silent and the boat drifted in the hot afternoon sun. At least his clothes had dried. Not long after boarding, he'd kicked off his shoes, and even they were almost dry.

Turning in the seat, he spotted six islands to the starboard side. A group of kayakers in bright red and banana yellow boats floated just above the water, crossing from island to island, their paddles flashing. He could practically see the keyhole cove from here. Freedom was so close, yet the current was carrying him farther away.

He grabbed the short paddle jammed under the thwart, but no matter how hard he paddled, he couldn't make any headway. Disgusted, he slammed the paddle into the bottom of the boat and hunched over with his chin on his hands, elbows on knees.

Dusk closed on him, and his spirits dropped. He stretched out and stared at the stars. He'd escaped, but now he was drifting out to sea in this piece of shit boat.

———

Billy Ron struggled to come awake and at first, he couldn't figure out where he was. Then his boat bumped into something, and a voice said harshly, "Watch the boat."

He sat up and looked around. Barely visible in the darkness were two men in a boat similar to his. One of them clicked on a flashlight and pointed it at the bottom of Billy's.

"Wuz de scene?" a Trini voice asked.

"I ran out of gas," Billy Ron confessed.

The two men laughed.

"No problems. We get you back to shore. Where you go, boy?"

"Five Islands Yacht Club in Chaguaramas."

The main speaker let out a whistle. "Ya a long way from home, boy."

"Can you help me?" Billy Ron asked, feeling the prickling heat build at the base of his skull.

"Yeah," the flashlight holder said. He tossed a line to Billy Ron. "Ties that to de bow."

Billy Ron went forward and tied off the line. Then the other boat pulled him toward shore. The heat had subsided just enough to become comfortable.

"You got any water?" Billy Ron shouted.

A bottle arced through the air, bounced off the gunnel, and landed between his legs. Billy Ron scrambled for it and opened the cap before savoring the sweet water.

They were almost to Pointe Gourde peninsula when Billy Ron tied his shoes together and slung them over his neck. He waited until the men were smoking a joint, the cherry glowing bright with each toke, and rolled out of the boat. The cool water invigorated his tired body, and he used a slow side stroke to swim the quarter mile to shore. The high, tree-covered limestone hills were a darker black against the night sky. To his right were the lights of Five Islands Yacht Club, and to the left, open water. He quickened his pace, trying not to think about the current carrying him offshore.

He noticed the darker blackness had moved to his right, and he swam hard, reaching the shore moments later. He crawled onto a rock and caught his breath. The first wave of mosquitoes dive-bombed him while he put on his shoes. He stumbled up the rocky beach, reasoning he could walk along the beach to the keyhole.

Partway there, the rocky shore forced him to return to the water. This time, he stayed against the limestone cliffs, wading or swimming until the land bent inward to form the cove. A partial moon had risen, and he could see *Barefoot* and two other sailboats riding at anchor behind the sunken hulk of an old freighter. He cursed. So much for a clean getaway. He'd just have to chance being spotted.

He swam to the boat and hung on the boarding ladder, listening. He could hear no movement, so he climbed aboard. The door lock was still intact. He was thankful he'd stowed the keys under the starboard cockpit bench before going ashore. He dug them out, thrust the engine key into the pedestal-mounted ignition switch, then unlocked the cabin door. Inside, he changed from his wet clothes into dry shorts and drenched himself in bug spray. Finally, he drained a beer and carried another out to the cockpit, where he started the diesel.

The anchor chain clattering into the chair locker seemed like the loudest thing he'd ever heard. He watched the other boats for movement but saw none. As soon as the anchor had snubbed up to the bow roller, he threw the transmission into gear and motored out of the cove.

CHAPTER TWENTY-THREE

The smell from inside *Alamo* made Ryan want to burn the boat to the waterline. But he'd promised to sail her to Trinidad, and he was a man of his word. He'd dipped a rag into the diesel jug and held it under his nose every time he went below.

St. Vincent and the Grenadines police had removed the bodies of Mike Walcott and Archie Darling but left the blood. It had dried, and he wondered if they could ever get out the stench. Somehow, the flies had found their way into the locked cabin and spawned massive hordes. Before leaving Union Island, where the police had towed the boat after they'd completed their investigation, Ryan had purchased lemons and cloves. He'd sliced the lemons in half, put the cloves in them, and set the citrus around the cabin to act as a fly repellent. While the flies hadn't gone away completely, most had left the cabin through the open windows and door.

Ryan maneuvered the boat through the Dragon's Mouth —named by Christopher Columbus when he'd first sailed through the region—and hailed Five Islands Yacht Club on the radio. They told him to come straight to the lift dock.

After he started the motor, he dropped the sails, the diesel chugging perfectly as he made his approach. Glancing to his left, he saw a small key holed-shaped cove with several sailboats anchored near the hulk of a sunken freighter. He wondered if the police had found *Barefoot*.

Ten minutes later, with the help of a dock boy, he had the steel-hulled Amazon tied to the pier. Ryan stepped ashore, feeling his sea legs wobble as he headed for the office.

Ramesh came out to greet him, extending his hand as he approached. "Come, we go to da bar for a drink."

Ryan let the man lead the way, and they took seats on stools. Ramesh ordered two Caribs, and a strikingly attractive Asian bartender set the sweating bottles before them. She and Ramesh conferred in low tones for a minute, and Ryan got the impression they were in a relationship.

"Ya wanna get her hauled out?" Ramesh asked, turning away from Bridgid.

"Yeah, the bottom needs scraped and painted, the running gear needs repair, and the interior needs cleaned."

"What's wrong with da insides?" Ramesh asked.

"There's blood everywhere. I flushed as much out as I could with a hose through the bilge, but there's still a lot left."

"Why is there blood in de boat?"

"You heard of the Sailboat Slasher?" Ryan asked, then took a drink of the icy amber beer.

Ramesh exchanged glances with the bartender. "We have."

"He killed two men on the boat."

"This is your boat?" Ramesh asked in surprise.

"No, my friends'. When Billy Ron stole this one, they bought a new boat in Martinique. They're sailing it here."

Ramesh frowned. "Dis bad scene, boy."

"Yeah, but we want to get it fixed up and sold."

"Nobody buy sailboat was people killed on."

Ryan shrugged. "Everything sells at the right price. Let's get it on the hard."

The boatyard owner drained his beer and set the bottle on the counter. "Okay."

They spent the next hour getting *Alamo* out of the water and set into a cradle. Then Ramesh leaned a ladder against her hull, and he and Ryan went up to the cockpit. The flies had found the blood again, despite the lemons and cloves. Ramesh waved a hand to dispel them as he glanced around at the carnage.

"De boy who did dis, they caught him at my bar."

Ryan glanced up at the larger man. "This is where they caught Billy Ron Sorenson?"

"De boy wanted a ho and we held him until de police arrived."

"At least he's in jail."

Ramesh laughed. "Dat boy escape. No one's seen him."

"What?" Ryan shook his head in disbelief, "How?"

"He knocked over de policemans and stole a car."

"Holy shit," Ryan muttered, waving his hand to shoo away flies before asking, "Do you have someone to clean this up?"

"Yeah, we make dis rell bess ting."

"Great," Ryan said. "When can they start?"

"Tomorrow."

"Where can I stay around here?"

Ramesh gave him several suggestions for hotels. Ryan pulled the folding bicycle off the front of the sailboat where it had been strapped to the safety rail and rode to the nearest hotel. After checking in, he went to the bar for a drink.

He couldn't believe the police had let Billy Ron escape. Where had he gone? More importantly, why did he care? He'd helped Mango find his boat, purchase a new one, and now he was taking care of *Alamo*. Pammie had disappeared and Billy Ron was on the loose, but that wasn't his problem.

He sipped the beer and watched a young mother swim in the pool with her toddler, holding the child under the arms while it kicked its legs. It made him smile, thinking of his nieces and nephews in North Carolina. He hadn't seen them since he'd left to take the job at Dark Water almost two years ago. His life had been one quest after another since then. After he helped Mango get *Alamo* prepped for sale and the couple headed west, he'd hop a plane and see his family.

It wasn't unusual for him to be gone for long periods. He'd left when he was eighteen to sail around the world, and when he'd returned, he'd joined the Navy. Ten years of constant deployments and workups had left little time for family as he traveled the globe.

After he'd gotten out of the Navy with two bullet wounds, he'd settled back in Wilmington with his folks and worked for his father's construction firm, but it hadn't been the same. He'd missed the adventure and excitement. There was something about disarming bombs while under fire that sharpened the senses and honed the reflexes. During that short period, life hadn't been a bang, and then Greg Olsen had come calling. Now, he was a commercial diver and a troubleshooter with more bang than he'd bargained for.

The waitress set a fresh beer on the table, and Ryan ordered a steak, medium rare, with rice and sautéed vegetables. When she left, he thought about the work ahead of him. It wouldn't take long to do the repairs on *Alamo*; then, after a quick trip home, he could rejoin the crew on *Peggy Lynn*. Ramesh seemed like a competent man, but Ryan had heard stories about how notoriously difficult it was to get work done at the marinas in Trinidad. If a customer left the boat and expected the boatyard to complete the work, they often returned to find a bill double the original estimate and the repairs shoddily done or incomplete. Ryan would have to stay on top of Ramesh's workers.

His cell phone rang, interrupting his thoughts.

"What's up, Greg?" he answered.

"Where are you?"

"Eating dinner in the Search Light in Dolphin Cove Hotel and Marina, in Chaguaramas, Trinidad."

"Good, stay there," Greg instructed.

"Why?" Ryan asked, glancing around the room. The other restaurant patrons didn't seem to notice he was on the phone, but he felt his hackles rise. He crossed his left arm over his chest and tucked his hand under his right elbow as if subconsciously protecting himself.

"I'm sending a guy to talk to you. Just listen to what he has to say then make your own decision."

Ryan's jaw clenched and his brow furrowed. With a sigh of disgust, he asked, "What's this about?"

"Just do it," Greg said, matching Ryan's exasperation.

"Fine." Ryan punched the *end* button and put the phone on the table. He had a good idea who was about to join him.

The waitress came past the table, and he told her he was stepping out for a minute. She nodded and smiled. He carried his beer to the small veranda off the dining room and lit a cigarette.

This was not what he needed. He wanted to complete the work on *Alamo*, go to North Carolina, then back to commercial diving, but how could he face his family knowing he'd left another human being to live in slavery? If this was one of his nieces, he would leave no stone unturned until he had her back. He had to do the same for Pammie Walcott. As soon as Mango and Jennifer arrived, he'd start the hunt for her in earnest.

He finished his smoke and went back to his table. The waitress brought his food a minute later, and he dug into the perfectly cooked ribeye. The juice oozed with every cut of the knife, the meat practically melting in his mouth.

A man approached the table and sat. Ryan glanced up, annoyed the stranger didn't have the decency to ask if he could join him during his meal. He continued to eat while studying the interloper. He was mid-fifties with black hair graying at the temples and receding to a widow's peak. His eyes were green and his face clean shaven, thickening at the cheeks and neck with age and the extra weight that also strained his midsection. The bags under his eyes told Ryan the man was experiencing difficulties in life despite his manicured fingernails and expensive-looking charcoal suit and crisp white shirt.

"I'm sorry to interrupt your meal, Mr. Weller, but please hear me out."

Ryan nodded.

"My name is Kent Walcott. My son, Mike, was murdered, and my daughter is missing."

Ryan forked another chunk of meat into his mouth and chewed as he glanced around the room. A medium height man with short brown hair and a square jaw stood near the entrance. He wore jeans and a polo shirt, the sleeves tight around his muscular arms.

"That's Jeremy," Kent explained. "My bodyguard."

"What do you need, Mr. Walcott?" Ryan asked after washing down his steak with a drink of water.

"I'm told that you are a man who can find things."

"I can find a cold beer and a bathroom."

Kent leaned forward. "Don't be flippant, Mr. Weller. I need your help. My daughter is missing. I want you to find her." He pulled a four-by-six Kodak print of Pammie from his jacket pocket and laid it on the table.

"Why not have Jeremy do it?"

"Jeremy is good at many things, but not this." Kent nodded to Ryan. "I need a professional."

"How did you get my name?"

"I made a few calls, and to make a long story short, you have friends who speak very highly of you and what you can do."

Ryan laid his knife and fork on his plate and wiped his mouth with a napkin. "Mr. Walcott, I'm in the middle of another job right now."

"I'll pay. How much do you want?"

Ryan chuckled.

"This isn't a laughing matter," Kent said through clenched teeth.

"I'm not laughing at the situation, Mr. Walcott. I'm laughing at you for thinking you can just throw money around and get whatever you want. If that's the case, put up a reward."

"I have," Kent exclaimed. "I just want to find my daughter, and I was told that you would help me."

"How do you think I can help? Pammie could be a thousand miles from here by now. We don't know who that sick bastard sold her to."

A vein pulsed in Kent's neck. He clenched his teeth and balled and relaxed his right fist several times before leaning forward and tapping the table with his finger. "But *you* can find out."

Ryan stared into the man's pleading eyes. "Okay, Kent, I'll help." He was already trying to figure out how to find the girl, so he didn't know why he was busting Kent's balls, maybe it was the instant dislike he felt for the man or the way he cavalierly threw around money, thinking it would get his daughter back.

The older man nodded and sat back. "Just get her back."

"I have a few commitments to take care of when my friends arrive."

Kent leveled a finger at him. "You better not be partying."

Ryan shook his head. "My friends own the boat your son

was murdered on. It's sitting in dry dock at Five Islands Yacht Club. I'm helping them move their things, so his wife doesn't have to go back aboard."

Kent closed his eyes. Ryan thought the man might vomit on the table.

Tentatively, he asked, "Would you like to see the boat?"

Kent nodded.

Ryan waved the waitress over and asked her for the bill. She returned a moment later and handed it to Ryan, who pushed it across the table to Kent. "Business expense."

The real estate mogul paid with a wad of TTDs—Trinidadian and Tobago dollars.

The three men walked to the parking lot. Ryan packed his bicycle into the trunk of Kent's car, and they drove the short distance to Five Islands. Once Jeremy parked the car, they went through the gate with Ryan pushing his bicycle and walked to where *Alamo* sat in her keel blocks and stands.

Kent went up the ladder, and Ryan followed. Jeremy stayed at the base; hands clasped in front of him.

Ryan unlocked the cabin door. He glanced back at Kent. The color had already drained from the man's face, and he looked again like he would vomit. "I cleaned most of it up, but it's bad, Kent. Are you sure you want to do this?"

Kent pushed past Ryan and went down the stairs. Ryan followed close behind.

Kent stood rooted to the deck, looking at the blood-spattered cabin. When he turned, Ryan saw the tears on his cheeks. His heart went out to the man. While Ryan had held men as they'd died in battle and had lost close friends, he'd never known the pain of losing a child. He'd heard it said that it was the worst of all pains.

Feeling sorry for the man, Ryan stepped to Kent and put his arms around him. "We'll find her," he whispered.

Kent trembled as he let out a sob.

After a moment, Ryan urged him up the steps. Kent stumbled to the starboard cockpit bench and dropped onto it. He wiped his eyes with a handkerchief and blew his nose while Ryan locked the door.

"You going to be okay?" Ryan asked.

Kent shook his head. "This is all my fault."

"Don't take the blame for this, man. It's not your fault."

"You don't understand. I was always harsh with the kids, and I didn't spend much time with them when they were young. Pammie and I argued about everything. Then she cashed out her college savings and bought a boat. She was always a wild child, and now ..." He let out another sob, pressing the handkerchief to his face.

Ryan sat down across from him and fished the last two beers from the cooler. They were lukewarm. He popped the tops and handed one to Kent.

Kent took a long pull, then glanced at Ryan. After a moment's hesitation, he asked, "Can I have one of your cigarettes?"

They drank and smoked in silence. Behind Kent, the sun set in shades of gold and red over tree-covered hills and a forest of sailboat masts.

CHAPTER TWENTY-FOUR

Early the following morning, Ryan found Ramesh in his office. The boatyard owner offered him a cup of coffee, which he gratefully accepted.

"Those are local beans," Ramesh said before drinking from his own cup.

Ryan sipped his and nodded in approval. Strong and black, just the way he liked it.

"Ah have bad news," Ramesh said.

Ryan raised his eyebrows.

"My men won't work on your murder boat. They think it's a bad sign."

"Not even to do the hull painting?"

"Maybe." Ramesh waggled his hand. "But not de inside."

Ryan groaned. This meant he'd have to do the job himself or wait until Mango arrived and let him do it, which at this point sounded like a better choice. "I came to ask you about the Sailboat Slasher."

"Dat monkey?" Ramesh slapped the desk. "What'd ya wanna know?

Ryan was getting used to the wild arm gestures the Trinis used while talking. "I'm looking for the woman he sold."

Ramesh shook his head. "No good come of dat, boy."

"You said they captured him here. Who was the arresting officer?"

Ramesh smiled now. "Winston Carlo."

"You know him?"

"He come eat in my kitchen. Ah call him." He dialed his ancient rotary phone and spoke to Winston. When he set down the receiver, he said, "He come to talk to you."

"Thanks. Now, about the work on the boat."

"I can get da workers, but it'll cost double what I told you."

Ryan snorted. Of course, it would—what else had he expected? "I'll let you know."

"They do best work on de island. Rell bess ting, boy," Ramesh assured him.

"I'm not paying your people to lime."

The yard owner gave him a look of annoyance.

"Thanks for the coffee." Ryan set the half-empty cup on the desk and left the office. He crossed to where *Alamo* sat, not wanting to return to the cabin and see the blood and breathe the stench. He would have liked to leave the cabin doors and windows open, but there were too many valuable items still stored inside, and this area was rife with thieves and opportunists.

Ryan opened the forward hatch in the V-berth and left the cabin door open to allow the breeze to remove the heat and stink from the cabin. He planned a stop at the market to pick up more lemons and cloves.

Before Mango had left for Martinique, he'd given Ryan a checklist of items to do in order to prepare the boat for sale. Ryan sat on the cockpit bench and smoked a cigarette while he read through it. Most of it was manual labor: polishing the brightwork and cleaning the fiberglass deck; staining the teak; checking the bearing box, packing, shaft, and prop; changing the engine oil and sanitizing the interior. Ryan tossed the list on the seat and climbed down to the ground. He strolled to the bar, got a large cup of coffee, then went back to the boat.

When he arrived, Superintendent Carlo was waiting for him. Carlo went up the ladder to study the murder scene while Ryan examined the prop shaft. There was corrosion on the bearing box, and it needed to be repacked. He was studying the shaft configuration to determine the best way to remove it when Winston came down the ladder.

"That's bad," he said.

Ryan agreed, noticing the man enunciated his words to sound more professional.

"Ramesh said you wanted to talk."

"Pammie Walcott's dad asked me to look for her," Ryan said.

Winston shook his head sadly.

"Can you give me any information?"

"It is police business."

"The guy wants his kid back, Superintendent. Let's work together on this."

Winston scoffed.

Ryan lit a cigarette and leaned against the ladder. "I can do this with or without you, Winston. I'd rather have your help."

The superintendent rubbed his hair and sighed.

"I have connections in the Department of Homeland Security, if that helps," Ryan offered.

A man in loose fitting coveralls and flip-flops walked up, towing a pressure washer. He ignored the two men and turned the machine on before aiming the wand at *Alamo*'s hull. The noise made it hard to carry on their conversation.

Winston motioned Ryan to follow him. Ryan stubbed out his cigarette and flicked the butt under the sailboat. He'd pick it up later. They walked across the boatyard to the parking lot. Winston opened the passenger door and removed a file from a briefcase, handing it to Ryan.

Ryan flipped open the cover. It was Billy Ron's arrest record and transcripts of the interrogation.

"Everything I know is in there," Winston said. "If you need something, call me." He handed Ryan a business card, which he shoved in his pocket.

"Thanks, Superintendent."

"I don't know what you're going to do to find her, but I think they'll move her off the island, if they haven't already. You better hurry."

CHAPTER TWENTY-FIVE

A rat ran along the brick foundation of Pammie's tiny room, its paws scratching the dirt as it sniffed for food. She watched it in horror and fascination. The single bare bulb in a metal cage cast its weak light across the room, leaving the corners in shadows. Age and water damage had taken its toll on the brick walls, causing them to flake. In places, the mortar had fallen out, loosening the bricks enough for Pammie to wiggle them out of their holes. There was nothing behind them but dirt. She didn't have the strength or endurance to tunnel her way out.

She lay on a stained mattress that smelled of vomit and sweat, much of it her own. She had to pee in a bucket, making the whole basement smell of acrid, dehydrated piss. The rat didn't seem to mind, though, and after two days underground, Pammie no longer smelled the bucket's contents, either.

The door opened and Gita ambled down the rickety wooden stairs, holding the handrail loosely attached to the wall. She set a metal plate on a rotten stool. Pammie watched her with hooded eyes, keeping her knees pulled to her chest and her thin wool blanket around her shoulders. She shivered as Gita knelt beside her.

"There is no need to fear me, child," the woman said.

Pammie returned her gaze to her feet. She remembered what Gita had said about keeping her eyes downcast. She'd looked at one of her kidnappers when they were moving her into the basement, and he had come unglued, screaming and cursing at her. Her cheek still stung from his slap, the inside raw. Then he had tried to rape her on the tiny mattress, but the man with the dreadlocks had dragged him away.

She could still smell her attacker's breath, sour from whiskey, and she wondered how long it had been since he'd changed his clothes or even showered. Teenage boys didn't smell that bad, and she'd been in many of their rooms when she was in high school and college. Sex was nothing new to her, but she was an adult, and it had always been by her choosing. More than one jealous woman had called her a slut or a whore.

"You must gain your strength," Gita said, handing her the plate.

Pammie let her eyes shift from her grimy bare feet to the metal plate containing a macaroni dish. Yesterday, Gita had brought what she'd called 'curry goat,' but it hadn't agreed with Pammie's stomach, and Gita had been forced to empty and clean the bucket Pammie had filled several times. Her bowels still rumbled.

"This will make your stomach better. Lots of cheese and dairy. Bind it up *gut*," she promised, mixing English and German.

Pammie took the plate and shoveled the food into her mouth with her fingers. It was bland compared to the spicy curry. She gobbled it down quickly, then took the bottle of water Gita handed to her.

The minder stood and stepped over to look in the bucket. "What is this?"

"I got my period."

"*Oh, Scheiße,*" Gita muttered. *Oh, shit.*

"What?" Pammie asked, forgetting her lesson and looking up at Gita.

"It is shit!"

"No, I got my period."

Gita rolled her eyes and stormed up the stairs.

Ten minutes later, she came back with feminine hygiene products and a clean pair of underwear, which she threw at Pammie before carrying the bucket outside and cleaning it. She stood at the top of the stairs and tossed it into the darkness, the metal handle clanging as the bucket bounced.

Pammie listened to a man berate Gita for being so careless. They needed Pammie healthy and uninjured to get the most money for her. She curled up into a ball again, trying to be strong, but terrified at the same time. What were they going to do with her? Why were they keeping her in this basement? They wanted her to be healthy. Maybe they would ransom her to her father.

Pammie felt a flicker of hope at that thought. She latched onto it and held the flame close to her heart. Her father had to come to get her. He loved her, didn't he?

Footsteps vibrated overhead, and a breathless Trini voice shouted, "Linford!"

She cocked her head to hear better. More footsteps crossed the floor. She heard Linford's distinct voice, "Wah yuh wa?"

"De buyer call. He say he be here tomorrow for de gyuls."

Pammie's flame of hope wavered as tears ran down her cheeks.

There was no way out.

CHAPTER TWENTY-SIX

The phone rang several times before Superintendent Carlo answered. After Ryan told him who he was, he asked, "Were there security cameras at the hotel where you were attacked?"

"There are, but not in the alley."

"That seems strange," Ryan said.

"Nah," Winston replied. "They're protecting their clients."

"So, no one saw this guy?" Ryan asked incredulously.

Winston sighed. "I think he came in through the alley and left with Billy Ron."

"How did he know you were posing as Junior Botus?"

"Someone told him," he conceded.

"Then you need to pressure every employee until you find the person who fingered you as the buyer."

"We did, Mr. Weller; they didn't talk."

Ryan sighed. How had cops done it in the days before cell phones and security cameras? "Do you know who Billy Ron talked to before he went to the massage parlor?"

"Ah, yes. My friend Chalk, the barman."

"Your report says he called you and you posed as Junior."

"Correct, and then somebody struck me on the head."

"Nothing else? You didn't hear or smell anything?"

"Nah, Mr. Weller. I don't remember much, and that frustrates me just as much as you."

"Thanks, Winston. I'll call if I have more questions."

Ryan ended the call. The worker was still pressure washing the hull. Ryan climbed up the ladder and tossed all the cushions to the ground—they needed to be burned—then went into the engine room, opened the seacocks, and turned on the bilge pumps. He piled everything he didn't want to get wet from the salon in the V-berth.

After opening all the hatches and windows, he called down to the guy power washing and had him send up the wand. He spent the next thirty minutes spraying the dried blood from the floors, walls, and cabinets. Then he pulled up parts of the cabin sole and sprayed the bloody water back to flush out the bilges and seacocks.

When the job was complete, Ryan was just as soaked as the boat. He dropped the wand to the ground, seeing the worker had disappeared, and went down the ladder. Standing in the sunshine, his clothes steamed. The inside of the boat would take a while to dry, so he went to get lunch. He found Ramesh doing paperwork and the lovely Bridgid mixing drinks at the bar.

After ordering a margarita on the rocks, Ryan settled into a seat beside Ramesh. "Do you know Chalk at The Peninsula Hotel?"

The man nodded, not looking up from his calculations.

"He called Winston to tell him that the Sailboat Slasher was trying to sell a girl."

"Yuh?"

"Think you could ask Chalk if he saw someone leaving with Billy Ron?"

Ramesh looked up now. "Dat boy gave Winston a good lick."

"Yeah, I want to find out who hit him. It may be the same guy who bought Pammie Walcott."

Ramesh tapped his pencil on the bar top, then glanced at Bridgid. "Call Judith."

Judith arrived fifteen minutes later. She was a good-looking woman of twenty, maybe older, with skin the color of nutmeg, almond-shaped eyes, and arched brows.

"Yuh take Judith to The Peninsula," Ramesh said. "Yuh get a room and yuh wait for her to ask around."

"Why not just send her?" Ryan asked. "Why do I need to get a room?"

"You be da john. Less suspicion."

Ryan cocked his head. He leaned close so only the big Trini could hear him. "Are you the pimp?"

Ramesh chuckled. "Ah no pimp. Ah run a clean business. We jus' make you look like a john."

Ryan nodded. "I sprayed out the blood, and I need to leave the boat open. Can you make sure nothing gets stolen?"

A look of disappointment crossed the yard owner's face. "You need not worry 'bout dat." Then he nodded to Judith, and Ryan followed the petite woman to the base of *Alamo*'s cradle.

Judith tied her frizzy black hair into a ponytail. "Do you have a car?"

"No," Ryan answered.

"We take mine." Judith led him to the parking lot. She pulled off her polo shirt with the bar logo. Under it she wore a tight yellow camisole. Standing beside her, the top of her head came to Ryan's chest on his six-foot frame.

Judith tossed her polo shirt into the backseat with a pile of others before driving them to Dolphin Cove. Judith waited in the car while Ryan went to his room to change clothes, when he came back, she drove them to The Peninsula Hotel.

"You wait here," she told him when they were in the room Ryan had rented. "Git me two rum and cokes."

Ryan ordered the drinks from room service and had a bottle of water and a margarita sent up for himself. He pulled the curtains back just enough to see into the courtyard, where Chalk was serving drinks at the small bar. Wrought-iron railings protected the balconies, and flowering vines snaked up trellises attached to the walls, winding their way through the railing. Large flagstone pavers made paths through dense stands of vegetation in the courtyard. In one corner, a fountain babbled.

Ryan watched as Judith approached the bar and ordered a drink. She spoke to Chalk for a few moments, then carried her drink out of the courtyard. Chalk glanced up at the room, and for a moment, he and Ryan made eye contact.

Reflexively, Ryan jerked back, letting the curtain swing into place. There was nothing to do now but wait. He stretched out on the bed and put his hands behind his head. Why hadn't Winston gotten any leads? Were the Trinis scared of the police?

His cell phone rang, startling him from his nap. Glancing at the time, he realized he'd slept for an hour. "Hello?"

"You sleeping on the job, bro?" Mango asked.

"Just taking a nap."

"Well, get your ass up. Jennifer and I are here. Speaking of that, where the hell are you?"

"Following a lead."

"While taking a nap?"

"I'm waiting for Judith to ..." Ryan stopped himself. "Never mind. I'll be there in a bit. Introduce yourself to Ramesh; he's the yard owner and a good guy."

"Will do."

Ryan ended the call as the door to the room opened. Judith came in and closed the door behind her. She picked up a drink from the room service tray. The ice had melted, but she still sipped it.

"Well?"

She motioned for him to wait while she drank more.

Ryan rolled onto his side. "What happened?"

Judith set the drink on the cabinet. "Ramesh said you pay for information."

"What did you find out?"

"How much you pay?"

Ryan sighed. "Tell me something so I know what it's worth."

"I give you name and description of man who hit de superintendent."

"One hundred American."

Judith shook her head. "No have sex for one hundred."

"I don't want to have sex," Ryan said. "I want the information."

Judith picked up her drink and motioned upward with a thumb.

"Two hundred."

"This gyrul's life not worth much?"

Ryan rolled his head. This was irritating. "Three hundred."

Judith drained the first drink and started on the second. "I take three hundred American dollars and give you a massage."

"I don't want a massage," Ryan growled.

"You need relax." She motioned for him to roll over. "Take off shirt."

"Just tell me what you learned."

"Leave money on the stand."

Ryan pulled out three hundred dollars and set the money

beside the drinks, close enough that the condensation from the drinks soak into the bills.

"You leave the extra hundred," Judith said, eyeing the last hundred-dollar bill in his hand.

With a sigh, Ryan left it with the others, feeling thoroughly fleeced.

Judith went to the door and let in a diminutive young black woman with close-cropped hair. She wore a gray uniform shirt and shorts and flip-flops. The woman stared at the floor as she described Linford to Ryan. Judith handed the four hundred-dollar bills to the girl, who slipped them into her bra.

When the woman left, Ryan headed for the door.

Judith caught him by the arm. "Ah told her yuh pay. Yuh give her almost one-month salary. Yuh help other gyul, yuh help her, too."

CHAPTER TWENTY-SEVEN

Two hours later, Ryan met Jennifer and Mango on their new, luxurious catamaran. Mango stood on the back deck with a beer in his hand. Jennifer lounged on one of the sofas.

"What's up, RoboCop?" Ryan asked.

Mango held up his artificial leg. "Couldn't be better. Where have you been?"

"I found the guy that whacked our cop in the alley before buying Pammie."

"Leave it to you, Ryan. You're the one."

Ryan shrugged. "Just doing my job."

"You're awful cheery," Jennifer said. "If I didn't know better ..."

Ryan waggled his eyebrows. "Just a nice massage."

She laughed.

"I sprayed out the inside of *Alamo*," he added, turning back to Mango.

Mango nodded. "I looked at it."

"You'll need to stay on top of Ramesh's guys. They don't want to work on a murder boat."

"I can't blame them, bro."

"I need to go talk to the cop in charge of Pammie's case," Ryan said. "I'll meet you back here for dinner."

"No worries, bro." Mango held out a fist, and Ryan bumped it.

Ryan rode the bicycle to his hotel. He called Winston and asked him to meet him at the bar, then went to his room to shower.

Winston was in the bar when he came down the stairs. They walked out on the dock where no one could overhear them.

"The name of the guy who hit you is Linford. He's a Jamaican with long dreadlocks."

"How'd you learn this?" Winston demanded.

"I have my ways," Ryan replied, wanting to remain vague. "Do you know Linford?"

"We know of him. He's been supplying women to the local massage parlors and selling them internationally for several years."

"Do you know where he lives?"

Winston shook his head. "No."

Ryan turned away and watched as a large yacht cruised through the bay. He recognized it as a Benetti Oasis 135. He'd seen another one like it in the Virgin Islands. Benetti yachts were custom designed, costing the owners tens of millions of dollars to build. This one had an infinity swimming pool on the aft deck and a bevy of beauties clad in white bikinis acting as crew. From the rear, its multiple decks reminded Ryan of a pagoda.

"Do you have a picture of Linford?" he asked Winston.

"We have a sketch," the policeman offered.

"I guess it will do."

"I'll have it sent to Ramesh's office."

Ryan watched the yacht and wondered how much money

the owner spent each month to fuel it and pay the crew. "Have you tried running facial recognition on the sketch?"

"We have limited capabilities and resources for that."

Ryan took out his cell and called Ashlee Calvo, a computer specialist at Dark Water Research. When she came on the line, Ryan asked, "If I send you a sketch can you build a model to run facial recog?"

"We can try. Why?"

"I have a lead on Pam Walcott."

"Oh, yeah," Ashlee said enthusiastically. "She's been all over the news. Send it to me now, and I'll jump on it."

"Thanks." Ryan finished the call and thumbed a text message to Winston's cell phone. "Have your people email the sketch to this address. Title it 'Pam Walcott.'"

Winston's phone chimed with Ryan's incoming text, and he passed on the message to a tech in his office, then called and ordered them to send the sketch right away.

"Are the security cameras around the waterfront tied to a central system or are they privately owned?"

"They're privately owned," Winston said.

Ryan nodded. "See if we can access their footage. Maybe we can spot him."

"I don't have the manpower for that."

"Okay," he sighed. "Get me the footage, and I'll have my girl at Dark Water run it through the facial recog scanner after she gets it set up."

Winston nodded and extended his hand. As the two men shook, the inspector said, "We'll continue to look for Pammie as well, but call me if you get a lead."

CHAPTER TWENTY-EIGHT

Mark Silverman leaned over the railing of his Benetti Oasis 135, watching his bikini-clad crew of women place the fenders over the starboard rub rail. He ran a hand through his thick white hair, then stood and straightened his suit coat. Normally, he wore only a Speedo, and many times not even that, but today, he'd chosen his black suit without a tie. He wanted to make the right impression when he and his entourage arrived in port.

At sixty, he was tan and fit, and felt like he had made it in life. He had a custom-built yacht, more money than he knew what to do with, and he'd surrounded himself with scantily clad women every hour of the day. His boyhood dream had come true, and by chartering out his yacht, someone else was paying for it.

Svetlana, the blonde Norwegian in charge of the girls, called out orders. Mark watched her, the long limbs of her six-foot-tall frame moving with grace and efficiency. Each woman wore either a white bikini or one-piece bathing suit, the uniform he'd designated. He had twelve women onboard, down from the normal fifteen, meaning he needed to refill his stable for the next cruise. Five businessmen from Brazil were coming aboard tomorrow, and they expected the full complement of Mark's quality entertainment.

The Oasis—Mark thought there was no better name, and he couldn't call it *Money Maker* at the risk of offending his clients—was truly an oasis for businessmen of a certain discretion. They rented the boat for a million dollars per week, expecting a cruise through tropical waters, exotic ports of call, and a woman on each arm. Along with a well-stocked bar and a two-star Michelin chef for their dining delight, Mark kept the men and women plied with cocaine and marijuana. Those who chose to partake did. This was a party, after all; a place for them to try new things and release their inhibitions.

Not all the young women on his ship wanted to be there, but most did. He provided them with a job and the ability to live what he thought was an amazing life. Sure, they had to lie on their backs to make their money, but, he mused, weren't *all* women just lying on their backs to make money?

Mark glanced back at Andrew, his head of security, a thirty-two-year-old former British SAS officer with spiked blond hair. His head continuously swiveled as the captain maneuvered the ship to the dock. Timothy, a South African with a fair completion, buzz-cut brown hair, and arms the size of sewer pipes stood beside Andrew. He carried a FN SCAR-H short barrel rifle on a sling, keeping it below the railing and out of sight.

There were many dangers for a ship as lavish as *The Oasis*. Some saw her opulence as a target of opportunity, and the guards had repelled boarders on several occasions. Then there was the Ukrainian who'd gotten so high on the meth he'd snuck aboard that he'd gone berserk, injuring the girl who'd been with him. After that incident, Mark instructed his security to always carry concealed pistols. He couldn't have the clients damaging his merchandise or his beloved ship. And, he had to admit, the guns and guards were also there to intimidate the girls and keep them in line.

As the yacht came alongside the pier, Mark saw the Jamaican, Linford, his dreadlocks making him easily recognizable. He smiled in anticipation of what Linford had for him. When the captain had shut off the engines and the crew secured the gangplank in place, the girls lined up along the rail, standing at attention as he stepped off the ship.

Andrew trailed him down the ramp, and they walked to the customs office to register his ship and crew. Mark slipped a large stack of TTD into his passport and slid it to the customs officer. For a nominal donation—Mark liked the word more than bribe—the man stamped the passports and did the paperwork for the ship without a formal inspection or having everyone present.

Once the paperwork was complete, Mark and Andrew climbed into a Toyota minivan with Linford and another black man. They drove along the edge of the sea, then turned north on Diego Martin Highway. The road ran through a valley to the far side of the island with houses crowded into the narrow space between the mountains. Thirty minutes later, the driver pulled into the yard of a small house at the top of a mountain. Tall trees surrounded the home, and someone had planted a vegetable garden behind the place.

As Mark stepped from the van, he glanced at Andrew, who nodded. They had been here before to purchase women, and neither of them liked the isolated location. While Linford had never threatened them or put them in danger, both men carried concealed pistols.

Linford led the men into the house, where ten women in short red robes barely covering their bottoms had gathered in the small living room under the watchful eyes of Gita and several men. Mark glanced at them with an appraising eye. In one corner was a girl who couldn't have been over fourteen. The oldest was perhaps twenty.

Mark sat on a plush sofa while Andrew took a position behind him. One by one, the women paraded past, disrobing and turning in place for the buyer. Mark selected three: a blonde, a brunette, and a woman with onyx skin.

Linford's men herded the unchosen women to a waiting van. Mark heard the vehicle start and drive away. Andrew took the newest members of their stable to their van, where a Trini with a pistol on his hip handed over forged passports. They stayed with the women while his employer settled the bill with Linford.

While Mark liked to have willing women join his crew, and he recruited them at every port, he needed women to complete his roster and would pay Linford handsomely for the choice of his stable. Mark removed a packet of money from his inside jacket pocket. Linford counted the hundred-dollar bills as Mark laid each on the table. When Mark finished, he put his remaining money back in his pocket and stood.

"I have special treat for yuh, mon," Linford said.

Mark raised his eyebrows.

Linford stepped across the room and opened a door. "Gita."

The German woman led another girl out of what Mark assumed was another room.

"This be a special gyul," Linford said in his mingled Trini slang.

Mark liked what he saw. The girl appeared to be in her twenties, with a tangle of shoulder-length blonde hair. She wore only white cotton panties. Gita had bound her hands and hobbled her feet with a short length of rope. Even from ten feet away, Mark could see the raw skin where the ropes had rubbed her wrists. She was beautiful and well-proportioned. The lack of food had trimmed the fat from her frame.

He walked up to her, put his hand on her chin, and raised her head. Her green eyes shifted to anywhere else in the room but Mark's face. Her body language told Mark that they had seasoned her.

He grinned like a kid in a candy store. This was a truly exquisite specimen, and he would pay handsomely to have her.

CHAPTER TWENTY-NINE

Pammie trembled even though the humid air had to be above eighty-five degrees. The white man examined her, turning her face side to side. Then he lifted the corner of her lips to look at her teeth. She remembered the hell of having braces and the weekly visits to the orthodontist to get her crooked teeth to become the straight white pickets they now were. The man ran a hand over her body, and she tried to think of anything other than how his touch made her skin crawl.

"What am I looking at?" the white man asked.

Linford said. "I kept her just for yuh."

"She's beautiful. Where did you get her?"

"I buy her, same as other gyul."

"She got a passport?" Mark asked.

Linford handed it to Andrew. Pammie wondered where he'd gotten it and decided Billy Ron must have given it to him.

The new man took the passport and opened it to her picture. "Pamela Rachel Walcott."

"Twenty-five," Linford said.

The buyer snorted. "Ten, like the others."

What others? Pammie wondered. *How many times will I be bought and sold?* At least only Billy Ron had forced her to have sex with him. She had thanked Linford for saving her from being raped on the mattress by the man she'd accidentally looked at earlier. Linford had told her to shut up and Gita had smacked her.

"Twenty," Linford bargained.

Was this what slaves felt like on the auction block, stripped naked and made to parade for buyers before being sold into bondage?

Her examiner dipped his hand into his jacket and retrieved the packet of bills. He counted the money out onto the counter. "Fifteen grand. My final offer."

Linford stroked his chin for a moment while appraising Pammie. Finally, he nodded and gathered the cash.

Her life had gone up in value.

"Get her a robe and cut off the ropes," Mark ordered.

Pammie stood stock still as Gita sliced off the ropes.

"Do not move," the older woman warned in a whisper. Then she returned a moment later with a robe and slipped it over Pammie's shoulders. "Put your arms through and knot the strap."

Pammie did so, grateful to cover her body. Gita held out a plastic bag filled with hygiene products to the white man in the suit.

"Put that shit somewhere else," he barked. "I'm not carrying it."

Gita stuffed it into a pocket on Pammie's robe, and the four of them walked out of the house. Pammie squinted. Her eyes had adjusted from the dark basement to the dimly lit house, but this was the first time she'd seen sunshine in several days. Gita herded her into the van with several other women, all staring sullenly out the windows, any place but at her or the men. She sat beside another blonde girl with a slack face. They all wore matching robes. Had the buyer examined them, too, treating them like pieces of meat on display at a market? Where were they going now? She wiped at a tear forming in her eye.

Linford climbed into the van and backed around to pull onto the road. Pammie inspected the man who'd bought her for fifteen thousand dollars. He looked in good shape for an older man, but there was something sinister about the way he'd laughed. What did he want with all these girls? She turned her head and stared out the window, watching the passing cars and houses. Her eyes saw the beauty of the island, but it didn't register in her mind.

Linford stopped the van in a no-parking zone beside the docks and climbed out, leaving the motor running. A security guard for the marina approached, and the Jamaican handed him a wad of cash. The man turned away without a glance inside the van. Pammie watched as the other men exited the van, and the shorter, well-built guy with the spiked blond hair opened the sliding door.

"Out," he commanded.

One by one, the girls dismounted. When they were standing beside the van, Spiked Hair slammed the door closed.

"We're going to that yacht." He pointed at a vessel that reminded Pammie of a small cruise ship. "Line up single file."

They walked in a row to the yacht and boarded it. A tall blonde woman in a white one-piece swimsuit waited for them at the top of the gangplank. She led them through an opulent salon and down a flight of stairs. She assigned them to small bunkrooms. Pammie shuffled inside hers. A girl with bra-length chestnut hair leaned against the bunks, wearing a skimpy white bikini that barely contained her large breasts. When she straightened, Pammie saw the woman was about three inches shorter than her five-foot-six height.

"I'm Teya," the girl said, her voice heavy with a Tennessee twang. "You got the top bunk, sugar."

Pammie nodded.

"Hey, look at me."

Pammie lifted her eyes.

"You don't have to be afraid no more. Mr. Silverman takes real good care of us 'cause we make a lot of money for him. Pretty good money for us, too."

"What do you mean?" a bewildered Pammie asked.

"Mr. Silverman takes us out on this here yacht with a group of guys. We have sex with them, and Mr. Silverman puts money into an account for us. We each have one, and we get paid according to what we do for the guy. There's a list with prices."

Pammie, still confused, sank to the bunk.

"Hey, that's my bunk."

Pammie put her face in her hands and sobbed.

"It's all right, sugar. We're one big happy family." Teya sat beside her and put an arm around her shoulders.

"I don't want to be a prostitute," Pammie sobbed.

"Oh, sugar."

There was a knock at the door, and a man Pammie hadn't seen before opened it without waiting for an invitation. "Mr. Silverman says to get her cleaned up and in uniform. He wants to see her in his cabin."

Teya agreed, and he closed the door.

She pulled Pammie to her feet and led her to the bathroom. "Come on, you need to get fixed up."

Pammie stepped into the shower. The blast of hot water was the first she'd felt since the morning before Billy Ron had killed Mike. To her, it seemed like a decade ago. She washed her body and hair under Teya's supervision.

When she stepped out, Teya handed her a towel, and they blow-dried her hair. Teya used a curling iron to put a wave in Pammie's long locks, then Pammie pulled on a white one-piece swimsuit. Before Teya let her leave the bathroom, she applied salve to Pammie's rope marks and wrapped her raw wrists in gauze.

"Mr. Silverman is a good man. Be good to him."

How can I be good to someone who bought me? Pammie wondered.

Teya took Pammie by the hand and led her up the steps to Mr. Silverman's master suite. She knocked, and they went inside when the man told them to enter. Teya left Pammie standing in the middle of the room and backed out, closing the door behind her. Once again, Pammie felt powerless. At one time, she would have relished the challenge of seducing an older man like Mr. Silverman and taking as much money as he'd give her. Now, all she wanted to do was curl into a ball and disappear.

Silverman still wore his slacks and white shirt, but his jacket lay on the bed. He sat in a chair with a snifter of amber liquid in his hand. His smile wasn't unpleasant, but Billy Ron had had a similar smile. The fact he had paid the Jamaican for her made her hate him even more.

"Tomorrow, five businessmen from Brazil will board my boat," he began. "I expect you to entertain them like the rest of the girls. Everything you need will be provided for you. It will take two years for you to earn back what I paid for you. So, you have a job to do, and I expect you to do it with the utmost of your ability. There are recourses I can take if you do not perform. I don't want to do that, so please don't force me."

Pammie stared at the floor. She had to be a sex slave for two years. Did he think he was her savior by buying her from Linford? He was just as depraved.

"Look at me, girl."

She looked up at his command.

"I know who you are and what has happened to you. Every girl here has a similar story. Your parents think you're dead. They aren't looking for you. I am your father now; think of me as such."

Pammie nodded, fighting back tears.

"Your period should be over in two or three days, according to Gita. Until then, you will assist the crew and act as a waitress."

Silverman nudged a silver platter on the desk blotter. Pammie eyed the thin lines of cocaine.

"Help yourself," he said.

She stepped forward, eager to dull her mind and senses with the drug. Picking up the small tube, she fit it to her nostril, pushed the other shut with her finger, and inhaled two lines of powder. The buzz was immediate as she straightened.

Silverman smiled. "Good. Now get some rest." With a louder voice, he called for Teya.

She entered the room and did a line of coke before guiding Pammie back to their bunkroom. The drug gave Pammie confidence, and she held her head high.

Maybe this would all work out, but how much coke would she have to do to make her forget everything?

CHAPTER THIRTY

Mango and Ryan piled the Hulseys' belongings in *Alamo*'s cockpit, then bundled them into a cargo net and lowered them to Jennifer, who had procured several wheelbarrows to move everything across the boatyard. Jennifer pushed one and the men took turns pushing the other cart to *Margarita*.

On the latest return trip, Ryan and Jennifer ducked behind the giant wooden hull of an old fishing boat. The planks were rotting, the paint flaking off, and weeds had sprouted between the timbers. Ryan doubted it would ever see the water again. He fished out a pack of Marlboro Golds, because the local store didn't carry his favored Camels, and handed a cigarette to Jennifer. She took a long drag while he lit his.

Ryan had his shirt off and wore just board shorts and flip-flops. She had her hair in a ponytail and was wearing her green-and-white, one-piece swimsuit with terry cloth shorts. Perspiration had soaked the white diamond around her navel, making it translucent, and her nipples were hard. It was hard not to notice.

"You need to come up with a different name for the boat," he said, distracting himself.

"Yeah." She leaned against an old sawhorse. "We talked about it but haven't had any good ideas."

They finished their smokes and walked back to *Alamo*.

"Where have you guys been?" Mango demanded. He had several loads on the ground and was on his way up the ladder for another.

"Ryan took a smoke break."

"One-handed worker," Mango grumbled.

"I can go find something else to do," Ryan replied.

"One hand is better than no hands. Now get your ass up here."

Ryan scrambled up the ladder.

Mango lowered his voice. "I need to figure out how to get two items to the cat that aren't exactly legal here, know what I mean?"

In the cabin, Mango pulled out a Springfield SOCOM M1A rifle with a large scope, bipod, and a precision adjustable stock. He laid it on the sofa, then retrieved a Mossberg Marine shotgun. "That bastard stole my Glock."

"What about breaking them down?" Ryan asked.

"That works for the shotgun, but the rifle doesn't come apart as easily, and you're still stuck with the length of the barrel and the stock."

"We'll figure something out. Put it back in the hole for now."

Mango slid the guns back into their hiding spot beneath a false bottom of the settee seat.

Ryan watched with curiosity. "Where are you going to stick those in the new boat?"

"For now, under the tub. No one's going to tear it apart to look for contraband."

Ryan's phone rang, and he climbed out of the hot, stinky cabin to answer it.

Ashlee Calvo was on the other end of the line. "Hey, Ryan, guess what?"

"You got a hit on my mystery sketch and the feds are closing in to arrest him."

"Close," she said. "You know, Don and I set our wedding date. Next May at his parents' house on Buchanan Lake outside of Austin. They have a little beach in their backyard where we'll have the ceremony and we're going to set up tents for the reception. I found this awesome white dress, and Don is going to wear cargo shorts and a white shirt. The bridesmaids and groomsmen are wearing blue. What size dress shirt do you wear? Do you have khaki cargo shorts? Of course, you do. This is going to be so freaking great, Ry!"

"That does sound great, Ash," he said, wishing she would get to the point.

"Anyway, I know you don't care about my wedding plans. Your sketch artist did a good job. I got a hit right away without doing much computer modeling. Partly because I searched for guys named Linford and the sex trade. His full name is David Linford, and he's from Jamaica. He's been involved with sex trafficking for the better part of ten years, and he fled Jamaica when they convicted him and tried to send him to prison."

"He's doing the same thing now, in Trinidad?"

"Yes. The police sent me the security cam footage, but there's so much of it I didn't know where to start, so I programmed an algorithm." She went into detail about her programming process.

"What's important, Ashlee?"

"Oh, yeah, I was rambling, wasn't I?" She sighed, and he heard computer keys clicking. "Well, I'm working through it. Have them send more footage as they get it."

"Roger that. Anything else? I'm a little busy."

"Nope. I'll let you know." She ended the call.

"Good news?" Mango asked as Ryan pocketed his phone.

"Yeah, I get to be a groomsman at Don and Ashlee's wedding."

"Don't sound so overjoyed," Mango said. "Nothing on your boy?"

"Not yet." Ryan dropped down the ladder and helped push another load to the catamaran.

On the way back, he detoured to the old fishing boat again, this time rummaging through a pile of junk in the weeds. He found a section of hollow aluminum tube long enough to slip the rifle inside. He set it on the wheelbarrow, then pushed it to *Alamo*. He jogged up the ladder with the tube on his shoulder, then passed it through the cabin door to Mango.

Mango knew what the tube was for right away. He took the rifle and shotgun from their hiding place and removed the scope. They fit easily inside the tube. The men packed the ends with rags and dish towels, then wrapped the tube in the old canvas dinghy cover.

"Perfect," Mango said. He took it out to the cockpit and lowered it to Jennifer.

It was dark when the trio finished their work. Alamo was now devoid of the Hulseys' possessions and ready for a serious cleaning. They walked to the bar for dinner, taking a table overlooking the harbor, and placed their orders.

When Ryan finished eating, he approached Judith. "Can I take you for a drink later?"

She smiled shyly. "Maybe."

"I'll be at the bar at Dolphin Cove Marina if you want to stop by."

She shrugged again and walked away.

"Striking out right and left," Jennifer said as Ryan walked to *Alamo* to get the bicycle.

He grinned. "All the good ones are taken—or I've already dated them."

"I'm sure you'll find the right one someday," she replied.

He passed her a cigarette.

"You're a bad influence."

He smirked. "I just do it to piss off your husband."

"Keep it up and you won't die from natural causes," Mango said, stepping out of the darkness.

"Damn, RoboCop, aren't you supposed to say, 'Warning, warning,' when you're sneaking up on people?"

"Not when you're being secretive with my wife."

Jennifer took a drag of her cigarette and flicked her ashes.

"Well, I'm out of here," Ryan said. "I'm catching a flight to Union Island tomorrow so I can get my boat."

"Aren't you supposed to be looking for a girl?" Mango asked.

"Yeah, but there's not much I can do right now. While Ashlee's shifting through data, I'm going to move my boat."

Mango shrugged. "What about beating the bushes?"

"Nobody wants to talk to a white American. They all think we're CIA or some shit."

"I'd ask if you need a hand," Mango said, "but we're pretty busy."

"And after all I've done for you," Ryan scoffed. "Maybe I'll just take Jennifer. She's a better sailor than you are."

"She is," Mango acknowledged, then added, "If I didn't trust you, I'd think you were trying to steal my wife."

"Okay, boys," Jennifer cut in. "Stop trying to see who can pee the farthest. You've already staked your territory, Mango."

Ryan smirked at his friend. "Gee, and she's such a sweet talker, too." He grabbed the bicycle and headed for the gate.

CHAPTER THIRTY-ONE

The flight to Union Island was uneventful. His previous night had been uneventful as well. Judith hadn't shown up, and after several beers at the bar, he'd gone to bed. He stood as the plane came to a stop, pulled his backpack from the overhead bin, and shuffled off the plane with the other passengers.

Ryan shouldered his pack, made his way through customs, and chose to walk to the harbor, which was visible from across the runway. The road took him along the chain-link fence bordering the airport, his feet kicking up dust on the narrow berm. Motor scooters, minivans, and taxis whizzed past him, honking and inviting him aboard. He declined and continued to The Waterfront, where he, Mango, and Jennifer had once enjoyed a meal.

He stepped out on the dock and scanned the boats riding at anchor or on mooring balls. *Windseeker* gleamed in the morning sun. A boat boy came alongside the dock, and Ryan hopped into the overpowered skiff for a ride to his sailboat.

Everything seemed in order as they approached, but once he was standing in *Windseeker*'s cockpit, he noticed that someone had tampered with the cabin door lock. He dropped his pack and bent to examine the wood around the latch. There were several gouges from either a slipped pick or a screwdriver. He ran a finger over the lock, feeling the deep groove carved through the chrome.

He unlocked the door, the pins grinding as his key turned. The interior smelled musty from being closed.

Ryan went through the cabin, opening windows. When he came to the V-berth, he spread out on the bed and stared up through the hatch. He put his hands behind his head and rested there, content to be home. He closed his eyes and drifted off to sleep.

When he awoke, the sun had moved into the western sky, and the cabin had warmed even more. He reached up to open the hatch, but he paused, his gaze catching on a tiny black box no bigger than his pinky nail with two wires snaking into the ceiling.

Ryan climbed to his knees to get a closer look. Upon examination, the box became two separate boxes stacked one on top of the other with tiny screws fixing the lower section to the hatch frame and the upper half to the hatch. A wire snaked away from each side of what he surmised was a circuit. As long as the circuit remained closed, electricity flowed from one box to the other, but if he opened the hatch, the circuit would break, and trigger ... what? The setup reminded him of a magnetic window sensor for a house alarm.

He let his eyes travel around the plastic hatch combing, searching for clues as to where the wires went. They had to be attached to a power source that would activate either a detonator or an alarm. Why would someone need to know when he opened the hatch? It made more sense for the circuit to connect to a bomb, but why the hatch? Why not the cabin door, so as soon as he stepped inside, the bomb would blow, and he had no chance of seeing the wires or the circuit?

The boat builder had finished the ceiling with white panels, and a thin strip of edging covered the seam. He used his pocketknife to pry the edging back and saw the wires tucked into the seam. Ryan continued to peel back the edging until the wires disappeared into the bulkhead. He went into the head on the other side of the wall.

After a quick search of the room, he found the wires led under the deck beneath the toilet. Opening the small access hatch, he saw what he had feared: a block of C-4 plastic explosive with a detonator shoved into it and a nine-volt battery held to the contraption with electrical tape. He'd seen many makeshift bombs during his years with EOD but seeing one on his own boat took his breath away. He studied the bomb, trying to calm his nagging fear.

Ryan crouched on his knees, mentally reviewing the bomb disposal checklist he'd memorized more than a decade ago. He followed the explosive train. When the hatch circuit broke, the battery would ignite the detonator, causing the C-4 to explode. It seemed straight forward, but he continued to study the bomb, looking for remote triggers or booby traps.

Certain the circuit was as straight forward as it looked, he gathered a few tools from this toolbox and carried them to the head. He knelt by the toilet again. This time, he plucked the detonator out of the C-4, rendering the bomb safe, and clipped the wires six inches back from the detonator with a pair of wire cutters.

The whole operation was anticlimactic. He put the detonator in the chart table drawer, sliced the tape to remove the battery from the C-4, and left the plastic in the hole under the toilet. The battery, he tossed into a junk drawer for later. After putting away his tools, he went topside and looked in the lazarette. The mystery GPS unit was still operating.

Ryan replaced the cover and did a careful three-hundred-and-sixty-degree scan of the mooring field. He couldn't see anyone or anything unusual, but someone was watching his boat, and now they'd tried to kill him.

He locked the cabin, leaving the pothole windows open, as they were too small for someone to enter through, and hailed a boat boy. There were a few things he needed from town. While he was there, he figured he might as well see if anyone was following him on foot as well as electronically. When he stepped onto the dock, he watched to see if any boats had shadowed him. After five minutes, he saw none, and moved to the bar to surveil the patrons while sipping a beer.

Afterward, he spent several hours walking around the waterfront, buying supplies and arranging for their delivery so he could leave for Trinidad in the morning. As he browsed the meager supplies at a mini mart, Ryan spotted a woman standing near a restaurant across the street. He'd seen her at another stop. It was hard not to notice her in short, black, spandex shorts and a dark-gray tank top, the tie straps of her blue bikini top knotted behind her neck. He judged her to be near the five-and-a-half-foot mark.

Ryan tried to hide behind a shelf loaded with canned goods and stare at her through the store's front window, but she must have felt his eyes on her. She turned, swinging long, straight black hair over her shoulder. Her complexion suggested she was Latina. Her gaze bored through him, and he looked away, reaching for his wallet to pay the cashier. When he checked over his shoulder, she was gone.

The plastic handles of the grocery bags were cutting into his fingers by the time he made the five-minute walk to the dock. His supplies had been delivered, and he loaded them into a boat and rode to *Windseeker*. After he stored his purchases, he caught a ride back to shore.

Stepping onto the dock, he took a moment to survey his surroundings as he bent to pay the driver. On the western horizon, the sun had turned the sky vibrant shades of red, pink, and orange. Where the ocean and sky met had deepened to a dark purple. A fresh breeze carried the sounds of music and laughter. As always, the ever-present smell of salt air pervaded his nostrils, mixed with diesel smoke and cooking food. His stomach growled.

As he straightened, he saw her again. This time she wore a loose blue dress that fell to her sandal-clad feet. She looked dressed for a party on the beach. Ryan jogged down the dock and slowed to walk when his feet hit dry land.

She turned and walked away. He hurried to catch up, but she turned a corner and disappeared.

He ran to the corner, scanning the crowd for her head of dark hair. He spotted it as she rounded another corner, and as people walked past, he lost her. Ryan pushed through the throng of people, thinking she couldn't have gone far. Soon, he spotted her again, the dress swirling around her legs.

As they passed another bar, he wondered why he was following this woman at all. He was about to say nuts to it and get a drink when she glanced over her shoulder and smiled at him. Their eyes met, and he quickened his pace.

Then she turned right into a hotel courtyard where a band was playing at the open-air bar. He followed her between teal-colored buildings and along the pebbled walkway through lush vegetation. Where was she leading him? Was this a trap?

Ryan paused at the corner of a building and watched as the woman walked to a small shack and ordered a drink. She leaned against the counter under the large shutters that covered the sides of the building when the bar closed. The whole thing couldn't have been bigger than ten feet by ten feet, with just enough room for the bartender to walk around a center stand that held stacks of liquor bottles.

Ryan approached, checking the other patrons for signs of hostility or aggression but only saw happy locals and tourists. He stopped next to the mysterious woman, shoving his body between her and a woman in a red dress who chatted in the native Creole with her two friends.

The bartender, a tall, thin man with a fringe of dark hair around his high-polished dome and a short, neatly trimmed salt-and-pepper beard, asked Ryan what he wanted to drink.

"I'll have what she's having," he replied, nodding to the mystery woman. "And put hers on my bill."

The bartender grinned and turned around to mix the drink.

"What are you drinking?" Ryan asked as he turned his head to look at her.

"Rum punch," she replied.

"I'm Ryan."

"I know." She took a drink through the straw.

Ryan's eyebrows rose a fraction. "Then you have me at a disadvantage. What's your name?"

"Kendra," she replied, turning to face him. "Kendra Diaz."

"Nice to meet you, Kendra. Can I ask how you know my name?"

The bartender set his drink on the counter.

Kendra said, "Word gets around when you pilot the ship of the dead."

That made him take his eyes from his drink. "Is that why you're following me?"

"I could say it was you who was following me." She smiled coyly.

"True." He sipped his drink. The rum was strong in the fruit concoction. "What brings you to the island, Kendra?"

"Business."

"Really? What do you do?"

"Waste disposal."

Ryan sipped his drink again, not sure what to say.

Kendra placed a hand on his arm and looked into his eyes. "I'd love to say it's been a blast, but you must have found the bomb."

Ryan's mouth fell open.

She smirked, then walked away. He jammed his hand into his pocket and pulled out the wad of euros. He tossed several on the counter and went after her. She knew about the bomb on his boat. Was she the one who'd planted it there?

Before he could reach her, she entered the lobby and went up the stairs to the rooms on the second floor.

The man at the counter stopped him from following by saying, "Guests only, suh."

Thinking quickly, Ryan said, "The lady invited me."

The clerk gave him a patronizing smile. "No, suh, she no invite you."

Ryan sighed in defeat and left the lobby. He circled the building, looking for another way to the second floor. Even if he could get up there, what then? Knock on every door until she opened it? What would he say or do?

He had to get away from this "waste disposal" expert. He didn't want to be taken out like the garbage. At the end of the hotel's dock, he found a boat boy sitting with his feet dangling over the edge.

"Take me to my boat," Ryan instructed, stepping into a garishly painted runabout.

The lights of the buildings clustered around the bay reflected off the dark water, no longer holding gaiety and mystique. The music no longer made his body throb. He needed to get away from this island and from Kendra.

"How hard would it be to leave the harbor at night?" Ryan asked his driver.

"I'd advise against it. The reefs be tricky, and the tide be low. Best wait for mornin'."

Ryan paid the man his fare and climbed aboard his boat. He unlocked the cabin door, feeling the groove in the lock. Had it been intentional, or had she been clumsy? Something told him she was very methodical about her work, and the fact he'd found the bomb at all had been dumb luck. Normally, he'd have just cranked open the hatch, and they'd placed the switch in such a location he might not have noticed it. But he'd taken a nap on the V-berth bunk, something he rarely did.

Fortune had smiled on him once again. He didn't wish to tempt fate by trying to escape during the night and wind up on a reef. The boat boy was right; it was better to wait for high tide.

He turned on his computer and looked at the tide tables. High tide would occur just after dawn. Ryan put fresh grounds in the coffeemaker and set the timer for five-thirty. He made a quick pass through the cabin, stowing any gear that might come adrift, and fixed himself a sandwich.

Finally, he accessed the hidey hole where he kept his Walther PPQ. He screwed on the suppressor and settled down to wait for dawn.

CHAPTER THIRTY-TWO

Ryan was awake a half hour before his alarm sounded or the coffeemaker started. It was still dark. He lay on the bunk, listening to the sounds of the water against the hull and the creaks and groans the old boat made as she moved at anchor. He rose, pulling board shorts and a T-shirt on over his naked body to ward off the chill. He flicked on the coffeemaker and went topside.

A few lights still shone in the town, but most of the curving bay was dark, the mountains providing a shadowy contrast against the starlit sky. A light breeze ruffled the water, promising a stiffening wind as the sun rose; perfect for sailing south to Trinidad. He surveyed the surrounding boats, wondering how Kendra had found him and if she were watching him now. Had she planted the GPS tracker?

The sun was just peeking above the eastern horizon as he finished his first cup of coffee. He poured another, and as the light grew, he started the engine, then went forward and released the mooring ball bridle. Back at the helm, he guided *Windseeker* to the channel. The coral heads were easily visible in the clear water, and farther out, a line of breaking white caps marked the reef line. The wind had picked up, showing eight knots on the anemometer.

As he cleared the small harbor, motoring toward the final channel through the reef into open ocean, Ryan turned to see a sleek craft muscling its way toward him. There were two people in the boat: a man in the stern crouched low, one hand on the outboard tiller; the other, a woman in the bow. Her dark hair streamed behind her, and as the boat came alongside, she stood.

Ryan recognized Kendra wearing white shorts and a striped tank top. He reached for the throttle, thinking she meant to come aboard, but the motorboat stayed twenty feet off his port side. She stood, feet braced against the bouncing of the boat, and extended her right arm. Kendra pointed a finger pistol at him, thumbing the trigger twice. She sat, and the boat veered away, heading back toward Clifton.

"What the hell?" Ryan muttered, watching the boat recede into the distance.

Just past the final reef line, he set the sails and cut the engine. *Windseeker* heeled in the wind, her bow pointed toward Trinidad. He set the autopilot and ran to the toolbox. He grabbed the wire cutters and returned to the cockpit. Throwing open the lazarette, he knelt and cut the wires to the ghost GPS. He jerked on the sending unit until the epoxy let loose and he flung it over the rail.

"That'll fix your wagon," he muttered.

The voyage to Trinidad went smoothly, and he was glad to tie up beside Mango's giant catamaran. He found the Hulseys preparing to leave.

"What's going on?" he asked.

"Haven't you heard the news?" Jennifer asked.

"No. What happened?"

"Last night, a guy broke into a shop owner's house and tied up the daughter with duct tape. When the parents got home, he did the same to them, then set the house on fire."

"What?" Ryan asked incredulously.

"Yeah, bro," Mango replied. "The dude took off and the people escaped with minor burns, but their place was torched."

"Here in Chaguaramas? This is supposed to be the safest place on the island."

"Right up the road," Mango said. "It's too much bad shit in one place. We're out of here."

"What about *Alamo*?"

Mango paused his work and moved to the side on the catamaran. "I got it cleaned up as best I could. Ramesh will sell her cheap and let someone else do the work."

"Okay." Ryan shrugged. "Where you headed?"

"The ABCs."

Ryan nodded and glanced around the harbor. The ABCs were the former Dutch territories of Aruba, Bonaire, and Curaçao, roughly five hundred miles to their west.

"How soon are you leaving?"

"Tomorrow," Mango replied. "I'd say tonight, but the customs office closes soon."

"Let me buy you dinner before you leave," Ryan suggested.

Mango slapped him on the back. "No worries, bro, I'll drink your beer."

"Yeah," Ryan muttered. He shoved his hands in his pockets and headed for the customs office. He felt like he was chasing his tail, moving boats from one island to another just to have his friends leave. There were other members of the sailing community who would arrive, and those who he'd met during his stay here, but it wasn't the same as being with good friends. The three of them had been through a lot of shit together.

After he cleared customs and spoke to Ramesh about a mooring ball, Ryan fueled his boat and topped off the freshwater tanks before moving to a mooring ball. Then he met Mango and Jennifer for supper at the marina's small restaurant.

"Are you going to keep looking for Pammie?" Jennifer asked.

"I've got Winston sending security camera footage to Ashlee, but I haven't heard anything from her."

"Maybe you need to put on your gumshoes and hit the bricks," Mango prodded.

"The police have more pressing issues than kidnapped women," Jennifer added.

Ryan nodded, took a sip of ice water, and ran a hand through his hair. He'd become reliant on technology, and so far, their leads hadn't panned out.

Mango said, "You should recruit your friend Judith to show Pammie's picture around at the marinas and hotels, see if she rings any bells."

"Maybe."

"Don't sound so defeated," Mango said.

"I know you're doing everything you can, Ryan," Jennifer said. "If I was missing, I know you'd do everything in your power to help Mango find me. Do the same for this girl."

"Have you talked to her father recently?" Mango asked.

"No, he went back to California after I agreed to look for Pammie. He said he had business he needed to take care of."

"I'd be here tearing my hair out looking for her if I were her mother," Jennifer said.

Ryan nodded. Was he really doing everything to find this girl? No. To be honest, he'd mailed it in so far. Other than finding out their mystery buyer, Linford, he'd done little to move the search forward. Then there was the woman on Union Island. What the hell was that about, standing in the boat's bow and mock shooting him?

He ate little of his meal, excused himself before the others finished, and went to his boat to formulate a new plan.

CHAPTER THIRTY-THREE

Ryan lit a cigarette and sat in the dark, feeling the shift as the tide rose and swung the boat around on the mooring ball. Darkness had long fallen, and the night had cooled with the breeze sweeping off the mountains. Lights danced along the shore where people partied, and he could hear laughter and music. The carefree life continued despite the horrible acts committed by men. He wondered if Pammie could return to that carefree life if he rescued her.

Literally, he'd been phoning in his search. He'd asked Ashlee to do the leg work with her computers. Tomorrow, he would pound the pavement. Before, he'd always had a team, be it the buddy system while scuba diving, an EOD team in the Navy, or partners during his missions for Dark Water Research. Yes, as an EOD tech, he made the long walk alone; when he dove commercially, he was alone in the water, but there was always a team, another EOD tech nearby, or a tender ensuring his umbilical was clear and his gas blends were correct. Now, he was a singleton asset, pointed and fired at the bad guys.

Ryan snorted. No one was truly a singleton asset. There

was always someone helping them. The greatest singleton of modern times had M directing him, Q building custom gadgets, and always, always a gorgeous woman. Ryan snorted again. He was no James Bond. Where was his beautiful woman on his lonely sailboat?

The hunt for Pammie Walcott had been the first job he'd taken as a singleton. He needed to apply the skills he'd learned as a member of a team.

When dawn came, Ryan awoke to a light rain, and mist shrouded the mountains. He fixed himself a breakfast of eggs, toast, and coffee. He called Ashlee Calvo from his settee while he sipped a second cup of java.

"I haven't found her," she answered when he asked for an update on the search.

"Are the police sending you more camera footage?"

"No, and when I talked to Inspector Carlo, he said the priorities have shifted and he'll send footage if he could get it."

Ryan blew out a breath through puffed-up cheeks and closed his eyes in frustration. "Okay," he said.

It was up to him now.

"If you get something, let me know," Ashlee said. "I still have everything set up for the search."

"Thanks, Ashlee. Tell Don I said hi."

"I will. Bye."

Ryan ended the call and sipped his coffee. There was only one thing left to do, and that was to beat the bushes and see what fell out. He put his mug in the sink and grabbed a windbreaker, slipping his phone and the picture of Pammie into his pocket. As he climbed in his dinghy and motored toward shore, he noticed Jennifer on the back of *Margarita*. He detoured over to the catamaran and shut off the dinghy's engine when he arrived at the stern.

"When are you leaving?" Ryan asked over the waves.

"Mango says we're going to stay another day and wait out the weather."

Ryan nodded.

She gestured to the salon. "Want a cup of coffee?"

"No, I'm going to show Pammie's picture around the docks, see if anything shakes out."

"Want some company?"

"Nah. You guys need to get ready to sail."

"We're all set. I want to come with you." She disappeared into the cabin and returned a moment later holding a windbreaker. "Mango's busy hiding his toys."

Ryan started the Honda outboard, and they chugged across the mooring field to Five Islands Yacht Club. Jennifer tied the painter to the dinghy dock post, and Ryan shut off and locked the motor. He climbed onto the dock, and they walked to the restaurant.

Ryan pulled Pammie's photo from his pocket. "Let's start here. I know Ramesh said she wasn't here, but maybe one of the workers saw her someplace else."

Jennifer motioned with her fingers. "Let me have it. Women will talk to a woman easier than a man."

He shrugged and handed over the photo.

"Can you get me a latte?"

Ryan hooked a thumb over his shoulder. "There's a coffee place down the road that's much better."

Jennifer nodded before walking over to a group of Trini women huddled near the bar, wearing polo shirts with the restaurant logo. She showed them the picture. They all shook their heads no.

Ryan and Jennifer walked to the main road. They had loaded the bicycles on *Margarita,* so they hailed a Maxi Taxi as it passed. Ryan didn't want to run the dinghy the three miles around Pointe Gourde in the rain. They got out of the van a mile down the road at the turn-off for Dolphin Cove

Hotel and Marina, where Ryan had stayed before flying to Union Island to retrieve his sailboat.

Their first stop was the coffee shop. They shed their rain jackets as the sun broke through the clouds and the rain stopped. Between the heat and humidity trapped in his jacket, Ryan felt like he was wearing a portable sauna. Still, they ordered hot coffee and sat in the shade of the café's awning, watching the shimmering water. Fisherman, water taxis, and pleasure boats of all kinds cruised along the waterfront, heading in and out to sea.

"Do you think you can find this girl?" Jennifer asked.

"Honestly, I don't know." Ryan sipped his coffee. He'd ordered it black like his soul, and the girl behind the counter had looked at him as if he were the Devil himself. "Her old man asked me to look, and I was going to anyway."

Jennifer smiled, putting her hand on his. "You're a good guy, Ryan."

He raised his eyebrows and leaned back, withdrawing his hand.

She squirmed in her seat, then said, "There have to be clues. What about the Linford guy?"

"No one knows where he is or has seen him."

"He's not a ghost. Someone has to know who he is."

Ryan nodded and sipped his coffee. A young couple, the only other customers on the patio, left. Ryan passed Jennifer a cigarette. They smoked and drank coffee while watching the passing boats. When the waitress asked if they needed anything, Jennifer showed her the picture. The waitress shook her head and walked away.

"What about a picture of Linford?" she asked.

"I can have Ashlee send me one."

"Maybe we could show it around, too; kill two birds with one stone."

Ryan looked up from dialing his phone. "You sure you

aren't a private investigator?"

"Just a nurse. We think differently than other people." She picked up his smokes.

"Mango is going to kill me," Ryan said as he pressed his phone to his ear, watching her light the cigarette.

"Why?" Ashlee Calvo asked. Ryan almost jumped—he hadn't noticed that she had picked up.

"Nothing," he replied. "Do you have a recent picture of Linford?"

"Just his mugshot from five years ago when he was in Jamaica. He looks a lot different in the sketch. Why, what's up?"

"Never mind, I still have the sketch in my email. I'll show it around to see if we can drum up some clues."

"I can clean it up, add some details from his mugshot, then colorize it just for fun."

"You have too much time on your hands."

Ashlee laughed. "Give me a few minutes and I'll send it."

"Thanks. Did you get anything from the camera footage yet?"

Hurriedly, she said, "Nope. I'll call you if I do. Gotta go."

Ryan put the phone on the table. A few minutes later, it dinged, and he opened his email. Ashlee had rendered a lifelike image of their bogeyman. He downloaded the picture to his phone and spun the screen so Jennifer could see.

"That dude just looks sketchy."

"Well, it is a sketch," Ryan replied sardonically.

When the waitress came by to ask if Ryan needed a refill, he told her no and showed her the sketch of Linford. She regarded it for a moment, brows furrowed, then shook her head, the beads in her braids clicking together.

"Thanks," Ryan said. He tucked away his phone and paid the tab.

The two friends worked their way along the waterfront,

showing the pictures to anyone they could get to look at them. By lunchtime, they'd walked several miles and only made it halfway to the western edge of Chaguaramas. Ryan had determined that they would canvas the entire waterfront to where the Coast Guard had gated the road, blocking access to the station, and ask at every bar, shop, and marina between here and there. They ate a quick lunch and rested their feet before returning to their mission.

It was late in the afternoon when they came to the Coast Guard's gate. Ryan had gained a new layer of sunburn on his bare arms and neck. There was one last hotel to check, and Ryan told Jennifer they'd take a water taxi back to Five Islands Yacht Club. They moved through the hotel, showing photos and talking to guests before finally arriving at the dock. No one had seen either of their missing persons.

They had a splendid view of the Caribbean Dockyard's massive dry docks. The high steel walls contained a white offshore utility vessel used to service the many oil rigs around Trinidad and Tobago. To Ryan's right was Gasparillo Island, a tree-covered rock compared to its big brother, Gaspar Grande, just a little farther out. As the water taxi motored through the blue waters of the Gulf of Paria, Ryan glanced over at Dolphin Cove Hotel and Marina. He had the sudden memory of standing on the dock beside Superintendent Carlo and watching the Benetti Oasis 135 come into port.

Ryan leaned forward so the driver—a thin kid with an afro, blue jeans, and two different colored Nike shoes—could hear him and he pointed across the bay at Dolphin Cove. "Can you take us over there first?"

The driver nodded and turned toward the marina.

Jennifer, using one hand to hold her hair out of her face, asked, "Where are we going?"

"I want to stop at Dolphin Cove again."

"We already asked there. I'm ready to go home."

"Just give me a few minutes, okay?"

She sighed and slid lower in her seat to get out of the wind.

A few minutes later, the driver pulled alongside Dolphin Cove's dock, and Ryan climbed onto the dock. Jennifer remained seated in the boat; arms crossed.

"You coming?" Ryan extended his hand to help her.

"Fine." She clamored to her feet and took his hand to help step onto the dock.

"Will you wait a few minutes?" Ryan asked the driver. "I'll pay for the time."

The driver nodded.

"We'll be right back."

He turned, scrutinizing the marina. He spotted a heavy-set security guard in his mid-thirties standing near the fence separating Dolphin Cove from the shipyard next to it and moved toward him.

Reaching back, Ryan took Jennifer's hand in his. "Let's go chat up the guard."

She responded by leaning into his arm and nudging him with her shoulder. When he glanced at her again, she had a goofy smile on her face.

"We make the sweetest couple," she said with a giggle.

"Cut it out." Before he could say anything else, they came abreast of the guard and stopped. He counted two oil service vessels along the concrete quay.

"Mind if we walk down there?" Ryan asked.

The guard shrugged. "I work for the hotel."

"Thanks." Ryan and Jennifer strolled the length of the eight-hundred-foot quay, looking at the large ships and stopping to show their pictures to workers and crewmen. They headed back to the water taxi.

This time, when they passed the guard, Ryan said, "Hey, man, have you seen this guy?" and showed him the picture of

Linford. Like always, Ryan watched his face for clues. The man's nostrils flared, and his eyes widened, but he shook his head.

"What about this one?" Jennifer showed him the picture of Pammie, and again, he declined to answer.

However, this time, the corner of his mouth turned down, and his eyes darted away before flicking back to the picture. He took a shallow breath before saying, "I'm sorry. I haven't seen those people."

Ryan was positive the man was lying, but he let it go. "You work nights?"

The guard adjusted his baseball cap bearing the security company logo. "I come on at three and work until midnight.

"Thanks," Ryan said.

He and Jennifer boarded the water taxi for the ride to Five Islands Yacht Club. Neither searcher said a word until they were in Ryan's dinghy.

"I had fun today," Jennifer said.

"Yeah, me, too."

"Too bad we didn't learn anything."

"I'll just have to keep looking." He started the outboard and steered them to *Margarita*.

Mango had stretched out on the aft deck sofa with a beer in his hand. When Ryan pulled up to the stern, he said, "I thought you'd stolen my wife."

"You wish," Ryan retorted.

Mango grinned at her, then said, "Don't run off with this squid. He's got a woman in every port."

"Don't be jealous." Ryan smirked. "You could have blisters on your feet from walking all day. Well, one of them, anyway."

Mango held up his middle finger.

"I'll see you in the morning before you take off," Ryan said and headed for his boat. The new plan was a bust, but he'd formulated a plan B.

CHAPTER THIRTY-FOUR

At eleven p.m., Ryan was hunched in the bucking dinghy, racing around Point Gourde. He kept the dark shape of the mountainous peninsula to his right, the Carrera Island Prison lights to his left, and dead ahead, Bombshell Port on Gaspar Grande. When he passed the peninsula and saw the lights of Chaguaramas to the right, he swung the outboard, and the dinghy's nose skipped toward them.

Five minutes later, he tied the dinghy under Dolphin Cove docks and made his way to the fence where he and Jennifer had seen the guard earlier. Dressed in black BDU pants, a black long sleeve T-shirt, and black boots, Ryan blended into the shadows. He cinched the straps of his backpack as he ran. The guard wasn't where he had expected, so Ryan moved along Dolphin Cove's perimeter fence toward the guard shack at the resort's entrance. Lively steel drum music floated on the night breeze, and he heard the high-pitched laugh of a woman who sounded intoxicated.

He spotted the portly guard talking with two other men in uniforms. Ryan guessed they were the man's evening relief. The men walked into the guard shack, and the guard Ryan was stalking walked along the fence before disappearing around the corner into an employee parking lot.

Ryan jogged to the corner and peered around it. The guard had the rear driver's side door of a four-door sedan open. He tossed his hat in and placed his lunchbox beside it. Moving fast, Ryan circled around to come up behind the guard. He took the final steps at a run and smashed his shoulder into the guard's lower back.

The man fell forward, slamming into the car. His head bounced off the roof. Ryan kept pushing him into the car, but his knees buckled, and the upper half of his limp body landed on the seat.

The guard didn't stir, and Ryan guessed the blow to the head had knocked him out. He patted the man's pants pockets, found the car keys, then shoved the guard's wobbly legs into the backseat. Uncertain how long the man would be out, Ryan wasted no time starting the car and driving away.

A few minutes later, he turned onto a road leading into the mountains. The pavement narrowed, switching back and forth in long loops as it rose through the hills. Except for the sweep of the car's headlights, there was no other light. At a small dirt pull-off, Ryan stopped the car and shut off the engine.

Before Ryan pulled the unconscious man from the vehicle, he pulled on a balaclava. Then he duct-taped the guard's hands behind his back and wrapped more tape around his ankles. In the low light provided by the car's interior lamps, Ryan frisked his prisoner again and removed a wallet, cell phone, and a handful of coins.

Except for the driver's permit, Ryan tossed everything onto the driver's seat. Turning the license to catch the light, he read, 'Dwight Atwell.' Ryan snapped a photo of the permit with his phone, then pulled a water bottle from his backpack.

He splashed water on Dwight's face while observing the bruising on the side of the man's face.

Dwight slowly came around, shaking his head to clear away the water and the cobwebs. "Wuz de scene?" he mumbled.

"Look at me, Dwight."

He looked up at the masked man with fear in his eyes.

"What do you know about Linford and this girl?" He held up Pammie's picture, visible in the interior light from the open car door.

Dwight turned his head so he couldn't see the picture.

"I know you've seen her. Tell me where."

He shook his head.

Ryan was thankful the man's English was understandable. He figured it had to be to answer questions for the resort guests. "We can do this the easy way or the hard way, Dwight." Ryan snapped open his CRKT tactical folding knife.

Dwight's eyes widened. The only sounds around them were the ticking car engine and the buzzing of insects in the humid night air.

Ryan ran the knife's tanto point along Dwight's jaw. "Where did you see the girl?"

Tears formed in the guard's eyes, and one rolled down his dark cheek, sparkling in the low light.

"Are you afraid of Linford?" Ryan asked.

"Yes."

"Then you should be afraid of me, too." This shit sickened Ryan. He hated torturing people for information, but if it put an end to Linford's business and helped him find Pammie, then he would.

Dwight regarded him silently.

Ryan pulled the knife away and held up the driver's permit. "Do you have children?"

Dwight nodded.

"Do you want them to disappear?"

The man's jaw trembled. "No," he gasped.

In a cold, hard voice, Ryan said, "I know where they live, and if you don't tell me what I need to know, I'll take them from you. I promise you'll never see them again."

Dwight shook his head. "No, please, don't take my children."

Ryan held up the photo. "Tell me where you saw the girl."

"Linford brought her to the dock at Dolphin Cove."

"What happened after he brought her to the docks?"

Dwight stared into the darkness and sniffed.

"What are your kids' names?" Ryan asked.

"Sade and Angelika."

"How old are they?"

Dwight buried his chin in his chest, refusing to look at his tormentor.

Ryan shoved the spine of the knife blade against Dwight's throat, and growled, "How old are they?"

"Fifteen and twelve," he sobbed.

It sickened him to have to involve the man's children, but he needed the information and they were the greatest leverage he had. "That's the perfect age. Nice and young. I can get a good price for them."

"No!" Dwight thrust out his feet.

Ryan sidestepped the kick and shouted, "Did this woman get on a boat?"

The prisoner nodded.

"Stop being so coy, Dwight." Ryan squatted beside him, pressing the knife point against Dwight's chest, his shirt dimpling with the pressure. "Just tell me what I want to know. Don't drag this out." When Dwight didn't respond right away, he turned on the phone and pulled up Mango's number. "All I have to do is make a call and you'll never see your girls again."

Dwight squeezed his eyes tight and grimaced. "De got on dat real big boat couple days ago."

"What big boat?"

"De yacht. She come in one day, go out the next."

Ryan racked his brain, trying to remember if he'd seen a big yacht. There were always several in the sheltered waters off Chaguaramas. "What's the boat's name?"

"*De Oasis*."

Sweat had soaked Ryan's tactical balaclava, and it ran through his eyebrows and dripped off him as he leaned over his prisoner. Had he seen a boat named *Oasis*? Wait, it wasn't the boat's name, but the make. "Was it that Oasis 135? A big superyacht that looked like a spaceship?"

Dwight nodded. "That one."

"Good," Ryan said soothingly. "What day did it leave?"

"Two days ago."

"Okay. Now tell me where to find Linford."

"He come and go. That boy be jumbie."

Ryan didn't know what a jumbie was and didn't ask for a translation. "Where does he live?"

"I don't know."

Ryan hit the dial button. It rang twice before Mango answered. Ryan said, "Write down this address. There are two girls there. Go get them."

Dwight's eyes widened, and his nostrils flared as he heard Mango affirm the message. "No," he screamed. "Please." He struggled against his bonds, tugging at the tape on his wrists. The jerking of his legs caused dust to rise and drift in the flashlight's beam.

Ryan slapped Dwight hard across the face to get his attention. "Tell me where I can find Linford."

Dwight jerked away, falling over onto his left side. He stared into the dirt. "He has a house near Cameron."

"Have you been there?"

Dwight nodded.

"Dwight, will you take the police there?"

He shook his head.

Ryan kept the phone to his ear. "My man is on his way to your house, Dwight. Do you want to listen while he rapes your daughters?"

Tears flowed freely over Dwight's cheeks and snot bubbled at his nose. He dropped his head to the dirt, twisting it back and forth as if he could dig his own grave with it, and pleaded, "No, please, no."

Using the point of his knife to raise Dwight's chin, Ryan asked, "Will you take the police there?"

The distraught father remained motionless under the knife point. Ryan backed the knife away, and Dwight nodded his head. "Yes. Yes. I take whoever you want, just don't hurt my girls."

Ryan shut off the phone and put it in his pocket. He sat Dwight up duct taped his mouth shut then ran more duct tape around his waist to keep his wrist tight to his back, then helped him stand and forced him into the backseat again. Ryan slammed the door and climbed into the driver's seat. He hauled the car around in a tight U-turn and headed down the mountain.

At the intersection where the tiny road joined the main coast road, Ryan parked the car under the canopy of trees and switched off the ignition. Dwight kicked the door and screamed into his gag.

Ryan walked away. As he did, he pulled off his balaclava, reveling in the breeze fanning his uncovered face. He drew in several deep breaths as he put distance between himself and the car.

He dialed Superintendent Winston Carlo's number.

Winston answered in a sleepy voice. "Aye?"

"This is Ryan Weller. I found a guy who will tell you where Linford's house is."

"Eh?"

"He promised me he'd take you to Linford's house. Now, get out of bed and come get him."

"Where?"

"I left him in his car parked in the trees off Tucker Valley Road right where it joins Western Main Road."

"What makes yuh think he won't leave?"

"'Cause I wrapped him up with duct tape. He thinks I'm going to kidnap his daughters if he doesn't help you." Ryan ended the call, powered off the phone, and jogged toward the marina.

He glanced at his watch. The luminous hands told him it was half past midnight. The customs office wouldn't open for another eight hours, and he was sure the police wouldn't be happy when they found Dwight. He could always leave and claim ignorance at his next port of call when they asked him for his Trinidad exit stamp. Linford wasn't his priority; Pammie was, and now he had a lead.

Ryan covered the mile to Five Islands Yacht Club in eight minutes. He felt the burning in his lungs from too many cigarettes and the lactic acid build up in his muscles from his lack of exercise. He rounded the gate to the yacht club and slowed to a walk, putting his hands on his head. Then, he remembered he'd left his dinghy at Dolphin Cove.

Reluctantly, he turned around, jogged to the marina, and retrieved his dinghy. By the time he'd started the motor and was idling through the mooring field, the moon had risen, leaving a long silver trail on the black water. Ryan bent low before the tiller to avoid the spray coming off the bow as he bounced through the waves.

When he got back to *Windseeker*, he tied off the dinghy, stepped into the cockpit, and unlocked the cabin door. He swung down the ladder and turned to go forward to the galley.

The weighted leather sap fell silently through the air, giving Ryan no reason to think something was about to smack him across the temple until it crashed into his head and he sank to his knees. Blackness clouded his vision as he lost consciousness and fell face first onto the cabin floor.

CHAPTER THIRTY-FIVE

Six thin lines of cocaine stretched along the mirror like snowy mountain ranges on a flat plain. Pammie Walcott fitted the rolled up one-hundred-dollar bill into her nostril, bent to place it at the beginning of the first mountain, then inhaled while watching the white powder disappear up the Benjamin. Almost instantly, the cocaine found its way through the thin mucus membranes and into her blood stream. Pumping faster now, the heart pushed the drug to her brain where it crossed through the blood-brain barrier and stimulated her dopamine neurotransmitters, giving her a euphoric high.

She had been serving the men drinks and had been solicited several times. When one man began chopping coke, she'd eagerly sat beside him. After two lines, she put the money on the table and reclined on the couch. A pleasant smile crossed her face as the drug took full effect, dilating her pupils and making her dizzy.

This was why she loved cocaine and why she'd become hooked on it as a teenager. A stint in rehab had interrupted high school; that was when she'd formulated her plan to sail around the Caribbean. A fellow rehabber, Mary, had told her stories about sailing the azure waters of the Caribbean, the parties, and the guys she'd met.

The drug had fully kicked in, now, swamping her inhibitions and pushing away thoughts of anything but seeking the next pleasurable high. The coke gave her energy. Glancing around the salon at the Brazilian men, she felt both a strong repulsion for them and a desire to party all at once.

She stood, reeling on her shaky legs for a minute as she waited for her head to clear then made her way aft to where the youngest Brazilian lay stretched out in the sun in nothing but a blue Speedo. She hated herself for inhaling the blow and for what she was about to do, but she needed the drug to force herself to do anything. As she stumbled to the aft deck, she let herself go to the drug, pushing out the anxiety and paranoia.

CHAPTER THIRTY-SIX

The sudden jolt of *Windseeker*'s shaft drive being engaged brought Ryan Weller from unconsciousness. His head ached and blood pounded in his skull. Rapidly blinking his eyes, he tried to bring his swimming vision back into focus. He rolled his head side to side, then brought his fingers up to touch his temple where the sap had landed. To probe the goose egg, he had to bend the fingers of his left hand and extend his right. It was then that he realized his hands were bound together at the wrists.

Fear rippled through him as his memory returned. Who had hit him on the head and who the hell was driving his boat?

Other than the intense pain in his skull, his body seemed fine. His leg muscles ached from his midnight jog, and he'd scraped his knee when he'd toppled into oblivion. Forcing himself upright, he leaned back against the settee and stretched his legs out under the table.

He listened to the sounds of rushing water. The drone of the Westerbeke diesel drowned out any sound coming from topside. If he could figure out the number and position of his assailants, he could formulate a plan to retake the boat. They couldn't have found all his weapons stashed around the boat, although they would have looked in the obvious places like under the settee table, where he'd taped a kitchen carving knife.

Ryan stared up at the empty cardboard sheath. He rolled to the right, fingers probing the wood under the built-in couch opposite the table until they found the tiny depression in the paneling. He pressed inward, and the magnetic latch clicked open. A razor-sharp Spyderco Aqua Salt sprung out. He used it to slice the ropes binding his wrists, then crept to the navigation table. Lifting the lid, he saw someone had removed his Walther pistol. He gently reseated the lid and moved to grab his secondary gun, a Glock 17.

Ryan plucked it from behind another recessed panel. No country would allow him to pass customs if they knew how much firepower he carried on his boat. Besides the two 9mm pistols, he had a Remington V3 semi-auto shotgun, and a KRISS Vector short barrel rifle which used Glock magazines. When he went into battle, it was nice to have magazines that interchanged with rifle and handgun. It was the only reason he owned a Glock. He knew the gun had a full magazine and a hollow point in the chamber, but he pressed the slide back just enough to see the twinkle of brass in the ejector port, then pushed the slide back into place.

Armed with a knife and gun, Ryan moved to the aft hatch. It was open to the cockpit, and he guessed someone was behind the wheel or in the cockpit. He'd developed a theory that only one person was aboard, reasoning if there were more, one would have been standing guard over him. At least, that's how he'd have worked it.

Just as he started up the ladder, he saw movement, and two feet slammed into his chest. He flew backward, crashing into a cabinet door. The wood splintered beneath him as the breath was expelled from his chest in a whoosh.

Ryan lost his grip on the gun as his right hand and arm went numb from the elbow to his fingers. Before he could bring the knife up or even catch his breath, his attacker delivered a series of blows to his midsection. He grunted with each impact, doubling over. His lungs burned from the lack of oxygen.

Struggling against the smaller assailant, Ryan looked up into Kendra Diaz's face, his hand clutching the smooth skin of her leg. On instinct, he looped his right hand around her glossy black hair and jerked as hard as he could.

His attacker let out a scream, and Ryan jammed the knife forward as she clawed at his face. He felt the blade slice through her flesh, then her hands clamped on his wrist, fighting to keep him from shoving the knife to its hilt. Blood coated his hand as he worked the blade deeper. In a desperate move, the woman shrieked and drove her leg upward, delivering a vicious blow to his testicles.

With a loud moan, he sank to his knees. The woman backed away, pushing his hand and knife from her belly. As she drew her leg back to knee him in the face, Ryan jerked on the woman's hair, still balled in his fist. She let out another scream and toppled over, her knee buckling under her.

Outside, an air horn blared, followed by another long blast.

A bright light swept over the cabin, stabbing through the port holes in thick shafts. Kendra lay on her side, clutching her stomach wound, blood seeping between her fingers. Ryan scooped up the gun, keeping a tight grasp on the blood-soaked knife as he staggered up the stairs. For a moment, the light blinded him, and he pressed his hands over his ears to block the deafening blasts of the horn. He glanced up to see the sharp prowl of a freighter bearing down on *Windseeker*.

Forgetting about the pain in his groin, Ryan sprang to the helm, dropping the knife and pistol. Not bothering to face the bow, he ripped the throttle forward and spun the big wheel to starboard. The boat began a slow turn to the right.

He couldn't bear to look at the high steel walls of the freighter looming over them. The rush of the massive vessel's bow wave shoved *Windseeker* over, driving the little sailboat's bow a few more points to starboard. Ryan braced his legs against the pulpit, his knuckles white on the wheel, and the blinding spotlight illuminating the inside of his shut eyelids. He scrunched them tighter, cringing as the freighter's air horn pierced the night once again. He would go deaf if they didn't shut the damn thing off or die if his boat capsized in the turbulent water rushing past the freight.

Sensing a change in the spotlight's glare, he glanced up at what he guessed was fifty feet of freeboard between the waterline and the freighter's deck. *Windseeker* was a mere fifteen feet away from a collision with the charging freighter. If they collided, the big freighter would run *Windseeker* over, and she'd be chopped to bits by the propeller.

He took a deep breath as the freighter steamed past. *Windseeker* bobbed and wallowed in the cavitated water left by the freighter's wake. Ryan swung the wheel amidships.

Just as he turned to round the pulpit and determine their course, he heard a sound behind him and instinctively ducked. The assassin's sap smacked the compass built into the pulpit and shattered the glass cover. Ryan fired straight upward, his shoulder catching Kendra in her wounded midsection. The impact drove the air from her lungs with a gasping hiss.

Spinning to face her, Ryan took a glancing blow from the sap to his shoulder. His arm stung, and his fingers went numb again. She backed away, swinging the sap in front of her to keep him at bay. The knife and gun were somewhere on the deck, forgotten in his plight to save his boat. He crouched into a fighting stance, bringing his hands up to shield his face. They squared off in the three-foot-wide gap between the benches, his back to the pulpit, her feet against the step up to the cabin ladder. There was barely enough room between them to throw a decent punch.

Kendra brought the sap back and sprang forward at the same instant, driving herself and the sap toward Ryan. He dodged to the right, missing the crashing blow of the lead weight covered in leather, and jammed a fist into her gut. He felt the slick blood pouring from her wound cover his knuckles and heard her scream of pain. Out of reflex, he brought his knee up and smashed it into her face.

She slumped forward, the sap falling from her hand.

As Ryan recovered from the fight, he felt the urge to kneel beside her and tend to her wounds. Why did women always bring out the protector in him? This crazy woman had attacked him from behind, tied him up, then attacked him again, and almost destroyed his boat. Why did he care what happened to her? He'd have no trouble stomping her into a bloody mess if she were a dude, but she was the fairer sex, wasn't she?

His hesitation cost him.

Kendra braced her feet against the step and launched herself upward. Her shoulder drove into Ryan's stomach and slammed him into the pulpit.

A piece of shattered compass glass sliced open his back, and he let out a scream. She brought her knee up hard and hit the inside of his thigh. The blow sent ripples of pain cascading up and down his leg, spasming and cramping the muscle into a hard knot where the blow had landed. She tried again, but he avoided the strike as he shook his leg. Her driving knee strikes kept him pinned against the wheel, the glass lacerating his skin with each grinding movement.

Ryan locked Kendra's head to his side and squeezed, trying to tighten his grip around her neck. Now, she thrashed against him to free her head. She slammed her foot down on top of his, then tried to do it again, but as she raised her leg, Ryan grabbed her by the seat of her pants and picked her off the ground. In one violent twist, he threw her to the right.

Kendra hit the high back of the bench and the mainsail winch and plummeted to the hard-wooden bench surface. Both combatants breathed heavily through gritted teeth, staring at each other with narrowed eyes. Blood ran down the bench and pooled in the cockpit walkway. She amazed him with her fortitude to move, let alone her ability to continue to fight, and she was gathering herself for another strike. She leaped at him with the ferocity of a tiger, lashing at his face with her fingernails.

The narrow cockpit provided little room to maneuver, but Ryan sidestepped her assault by stepping into the opening between the cockpit bench and the rear lazarette seat behind the wheel. The narrow space provided just enough room for him to squeeze between the hull and the wheel. As he stepped back, Ryan's gaze flicked to the chart plotter mounted beside the cracked compass. Oil had leaked out of the case and splashed across the electronic screen, which had a horizontal crack across it. Their autopilot corrected course would take them through the Dragon's Mouth and into the Caribbean.

He lashed out with his bare foot and caught Kendra in the stomach. From the way she screamed, he knew he'd hit the knife wound. Out here in the utter blackness of night, there was no one to hear her cries of pain. Or his.

She had to be losing strength, but she fought valiantly, pummeling his stomach and ribcage with hard punches. He grabbed her hair and twisted violently. His Krav Maga instructor had always said if you're going to fight, fight to win, and win at any costs. Old men play dirty. He wasn't old, but he was tired of taking abuse from this woman. He forced her against the rail, grabbed a handful of her pants, and shoved her over the lifeline.

Kendra screamed as she fell. Then, the boat was moving away from her, leaving her to sink into the pitch-black water. Ryan disengaged the autopilot and spun the wheel hard to port. He kept his eyes where he'd last seen her thrashing in the water and brought the boat around.

When he neared the spot where he thought she was, there was no sign of his female assailant. Ryan cut the motor and let *Windseeker* coast in silence. He snapped on a spotlight and swept it across the water's choppy surface. There was no sign of her.

"Kendra," he shouted. "Kendra!"

After a half hour of sporadic motoring and stopping, Ryan gave up looking. The chart plotter had taken a shit moments after he'd started the search, and the compass ball flopped lazily in its half-empty cup. He retrieved a handheld compass from the chart table and used it to plot his return course to the mooring ball at Five Islands Yacht Club.

CHAPTER THIRTY-SEVEN

It was dawn by the time Ryan finished clipping his bridle to the barnacle-covered ball and made his way aft to the cockpit. With the sailboat finally tethered, he grabbed a bucket to rinse the blood from the bench and scrub the decks. With the job done, he could finally relax, and his weary muscles demanded sleep. First, he tried to keep his hands steady as he held the lighter and shielded the flame to light his cigarette.

He'd just had an all-out battle with a woman he'd dumped into the ocean, and he had no clue why. Ryan exhaled a long plume of smoke, which drifted away in the morning breeze. The sunlight turned the surrounding hills from black to gray, and finally, to their normal shades of green, hovering above the pale grays of the limestone and dark sand beaches washed by azure seas. He breathed deeply and let out a long exhale. His eyelids fluttered, and when his head lolled forward to touch his chin to his chest, he snapped awake, jerking so hard it hurt his spine. Pressure was building behind his eyes and in the frontal lobe, signaling the worsening of his headache. He needed water and rest.

As he stubbed out the cigarette, he heard an engine kick over, and glanced up to see Jennifer wave from the bow of *Margarita*. He waved back, thinking of yesterday's excursion to find someone who'd seen Pammie Walcott. Had it only been twenty-four hours ago? He remembered times when he'd stayed awake for days, either solo sailing or during combat missions, and he couldn't recall ever feeling this tired —but he'd also been a younger man.

Ryan stumbled down the ladder to the cabin, found his sat phone, and dialed Ashlee Calvo's number. She could work on the video surveillance scans while he took a nap.

A male voice answered with a sleepy, "Hello."

"I hope this is Don Williams."

Don chuckled. "What's happening, Ryan?"

"I need to talk to your better half."

"Lucky for you, I am the better half."

Ryan snorted. "Okay, how about the better-looking half?"

"Are you trying to butter me up with all these compliments?"

"Dude, just put Ashlee on the phone."

"All right, calm down."

Ryan could hear Don laughing as he passed the phone to Ashlee.

After a moment, she said, "Hi, Ryan. What do you need?"

"Did you get any hits for our missing persons?"

"No."

"Did you have footage from Dolphin Cove Hotel and Marina from two days ago?"

"Maybe." She sighed. "I'll have to look."

"An eyewitness told me Pammie boarded an Oasis 135 super yacht. Can you run the footage through your program and see if you can find her?"

"Sure, but if you have an eyewitness, why do I need to waste my time?"

"Because I need confirmation before I assault a multimillion-dollar boat."

"Okay. I'll call you in a couple of hours."

"Make it fast, Ash," Ryan snapped. "This girl is getting farther away by the minute."

"Do you know what the name of the boat is?"

"My informant said *The Oasis*, but I don't know if he meant the name or the model because I saw an Oasis 135 enter port three days ago and now, she's gone."

"Look it up on marinetracker.com."

"Good idea." He yawned. "I need some shuteye. Call me as soon as you have something."

"I will," she promised.

Ryan tossed the phone on his bunk and went topside again. He wanted to say goodbye to Mango and Jennifer. When he stepped into the cockpit, he found Mango motoring toward him in a dinghy. Ryan lit another cigarette and sat on the bench.

When Mango came alongside, he tied off the dinghy and climbed over the rail. "What happened to you last night? I saw you take off in your dinghy and then your sailboat disappeared."

Ryan fingered the goose egg on his temple.

"That looks painful, bro," Mango said when Ryan dropped his hand.

"I came back from my midnight run and got the shit kicked out of me."

"By whom?"

"A crazy chick I met on Union Island." He described his encounter with Kendra and the strange scene of her miming shooting him as he motored out of the bay. Finally, he told Mango about dumping her overboard to end their epic battle.

"You have the worst luck with women, bro."

"What do you think it means? What was she doing?"

Mango shrugged. "Based on your description of her, and your hunch that she was Latina, I'd say it's a safe bet she was trying to collect the bounty."

"I disabled the mystery tracker, but she was still able to follow me here."

"If she had any connections, she could have easily found out you were on your way back here. That wasn't a secret."

Ryan nodded and took a final draw on his smoke before stubbing it out. "I've got Ashlee looking at video from Dolphin's Cove to verify Pammie got on a super yacht called *The Oasis*."

"I saw her come in and go out. She's a beautiful ship."

"Yes, she is," Ryan agreed.

"What if Pammie's on *The Oasis*?"

"We go get her."

"Who's we?" Mango asked.

"I don't know." Ryan rubbed his face with both hands. He just wanted to go to sleep. "I need a team of shooters to take down the boat. Want to help?"

Mango tapped his fingernail against the fiberglass and stared across the water at his catamaran. After a moment he said, "You love this shit, don't you?"

"Kinda."

"Why didn't you stay in the Navy? You could have had your fill of it there."

"I've got my fill of it here, too. Besides, I wouldn't have gotten to meet you, stop a Mexican gunrunning ship, and steal millions of dollars."

"We wouldn't have a two-million-dollar bounty on us, either."

"Yeah, but you gotta admit, you had just as much fun as I did."

Mango tilted his head, a smile lifting one corner of his lips. "Yeah, bro, I did."

"So, help me with *The Oasis*."

Mango tapped the boat hull again. "You know I made a promise to my wife."

"I think she'd understand if you helped rescue a kidnapped woman."

Mango pursed his lips and snorted, causing his head to bob slightly. "Okay."

"You go clear it with her. I'm going to take a nap." Halfway down the ladder, Ryan stopped and said, "Oh, and look up *The Oasis* on Marine Tracker and see if you can locate her. A ship like that has to have a tracking system."

"Roger that, boss."

"And keep an eye out for Winston Carlo and the police. If they head for my boat, call me."

"What else did you do on this 'midnight run?'" Mango asked, using air quotes.

Ryan held a finger to his lips. "Plausible deniability."

CHAPTER THIRTY-EIGHT

Windseeker shifted unnaturally as someone climbed aboard. Ryan's eyes snapped open, and his hand reached for the pistol under his pillow. When Mango stuck his head in the hatch, Ryan had his forehead centered in the sights of the Walther PPQ 9mm, which he'd found in the cockpit last night.

"Glad to see you, too," Mango said.

Ryan stowed the pistol and laid his head back. Mango slipped down the ladder and sat on the bench across from him.

"What time is it?" Ryan asked.

"Four o'clock. I let you sleep, like, nine hours."

Ryan rubbed his face, groggy from being woken from a heavy sleep.

"I found *The Oasis*."

"Good." Ryan rolled onto his side to face his friend. "Where is she?"

"Island hopping toward the U.S. Virgin Islands. The owner, Mark Silverman, has a set route for his guests. He picks them up either here in Chaguaramas and sails north or in St. Thomas and sails south to here."

"Nice that he keeps a schedule for us."

"He runs a sex cruise."

Ryan shook his head.

"I also talked to Ashlee. She found a video of what we think is Pammie and three other girls getting out of a van and onto the boat."

"What do you mean *think*?"

"All she could find was the back of her head and a blurred side view of her." Mango handed Ryan several photographs.

He sat up and sifted through them. A camera had captured four women being led onto the yacht. An older white-haired man preceded them down the dock, followed by a muscular younger man. One picture was a facial shot of the muscle. A third zoomed in on a blonde, and the fourth pic showed a side view of the same woman. The blonde had her chin to her chest, and her hair partially obscured her face.

"Ashlee says the old guy is Silverman. The bodyguard is Andrew Gauge, former British SAS." Mango tapped the photo of the brunette. "This girl right here is Andrea Rodriguez, reported missing from Aruba in January of 2016."

"Nothing definitive about Pammie?"

"Based on height, weight, and hair color, Ashlee is seventy percent positive the blonde is Pammie."

Ryan held the picture Kent Walcott had given him beside Ashlee's surveillance footage. "Seventy is better than fifty."

"If he has one bodyguard, you can bet there's more on the boat."

Getting up, Ryan went to the galley, where he started coffee brewing. He leaned against the counter and sifted through the photographs again. "We're going to need a few more shooters to take a ship of this size."

Mango moved to the settee. "I spoke to Greg. He'll have Chuck fly a team to the U.S.V.I. with all the gear we need."

"When?"

"Silverman's boat is due in port in four days."

"What did Jennifer say about you tagging along?"

"Green light, bro."

Ryan raised his eyebrows.

"She said something along the lines of keeping you out of trouble. I don't know what happened between you two, but she's taken a real shine to you."

"Huh," Ryan muttered.

"She used to hate your guts for getting us into the bounty thing."

Ryan shrugged one shoulder. "We buried the hatchet."

"I'm glad."

Ryan turned to pour a cup of coffee into his U.S. Navy mug. "Who is Greg sending?"

"I know Rick for sure. He said he'd round up a few more guys."

"Guess we need to figure out a plan of attack." Ryan took a sip of coffee.

"The only plan that got planned was dinner, then my wife sidetracked me." He waggled his eyebrows.

"Good for you," Ryan huffed. He took another drink. "You see or hear from Winston?"

"Nope."

"No news is good news, I guess."

Mango peered at him pointedly. "Did this have something to do with that phone call last night?"

"Yeah. I was extorting information from a Dolphin Cove security guard. The guy knows where Linford is living. I left him bound and gagged in his car with the belief that if he didn't cooperate, I'd steal his kids. I called Winston and told him where to find the guy."

"You're hoping Winston used the guy's information to get Linford?"

"Exactly." Ryan sipped again. "I wore a mask, but Winston is getting tired of me running roughshod over his investigations."

"Then let's clear out of here tomorrow and go to Grenada. We can leave the boats there and hop a flight to the U.S.V.I."

"Sounds good," Ryan agreed.

"First, let's go have dinner. Jenn is waiting on us."

The two men went topside, and Ryan locked his boat before climbing into the dinghy with Mango and idling to *Margarita*. They picked up Jennifer and cruised to Five Islands Yacht Club.

The trio had just sat down at a table when Ramesh approached, a big grin on his face. "You hear the news?"

Ryan shook his head.

"Winston capture dat boy Linford."

"That's great news," Jennifer exclaimed.

"Yeah, it tis," Ramesh agreed, then nodded to Ryan. "You do it?"

Ryan shook his head. "I don't know anything about it."

"Come on, boy, you be askin' all over de docks an you know nothing?"

"Haven't a clue."

Ramesh smiled. "I know yuh helped. Dinner is on me tonight."

"Thanks," all three said. Ryan added, "But you don't have to do that."

The big Trini gave him a wink and waved Bridgid over to the table and instructed her to get them whatever they wanted on the house. She gave him a sharp look, but he returned it with one of his own that said for her to mind her own business.

"You want de usual?" she asked the group.

"Yes, please," Ryan replied, knowing the usual meant a version of the tasty Trinidad rum punch.

When she left to get the drinks, Mango informed his wife of their decision to sail for Grenada in the morning. She nodded her approval.

"Thanks for letting Mango go play," Ryan told her.

"Oh, I'm coming with you."

Ryan and Mango glanced at each other, and Mango shrugged to indicate he didn't know this was her plan but said, "Are you sure?"

Jennifer nodded before taking a drink.

"All right, mother hen," Ryan said, "are you sniper overwatch or the boat driver?"

She smiled. "Seeing as how I drove the boat so well the last time we saved your ass, I'll do it again."

"So now you're both in on this saving my ass joke?" On every mission he and Mango had been on together, Mango had used a sniper rifle to take out a man about to harm Ryan, and it had become a running joke.

"Absolutely," Jennifer said, then high-fived her husband. "You need all the help you can get."

CHAPTER THIRTY-NINE

Ryan sat in a Chevy Suburban at the far end of the runway at Cyril E. King Airport on St. Thomas, watching the Beechcraft King Air B200C taxi to a stop. When the propellers of the twin turbojet engines stopped spinning, Ryan drove across the concrete pad of the fixed operator base and backed up to the plane's cargo door.

He slid out of the driver's seat and flashed a thumbs-up to the pilot, Chuck Newland. Ten seconds later, the passenger door opened, and a woman in tan shorts and a red DWR polo shirt came down the steps, blonde ponytail swishing back and forth in time with her movements. She stood at the base of the steps as the passengers disembarked.

The first man out of the plane wore cargo shorts and a garish Hawaiian print shirt. Rick Hayes stood just five-feet-five and three-quarters of an inch tall—every fraction mattered—and his shaved head reminded Ryan of the television police detective Kojak. All he needed was a lollipop. They bro hugged, and Ryan slapped him on the back.

Following him was another man from Ryan's past. Roland "Jinks" Jenkins had been a Navy SEAL, serving with the secretive DEVGRU, formerly SEAL Team Six. He had been with the team who'd helped Ryan and Mango take down Arturo Guerrero's pirate ship in the Gulf of Mexico. Jinks and Rick could have been brothers, with similar stocky builds and shaved head, but Jinks was two inches taller, and his darker complexion indicated Samoan descent. Dressed in tan cargo pants, combat boots, and a blue Columbia fishing shirt, he slung a green flight bag over his shoulder and put on his Wiley X tactical sunglasses before descending to the tarmac.

Jinks and Ryan shook hands as a third man Ryan didn't recognize exited the fuselage. The tall African American had close-cropped hair and wore dark wash jeans, brown square-toed dress shoes, a crisp white dress shirt, and a blue blazer. He shifted a messenger bag in one hand and adjusted his aviator shades, flashing a million-dollar smile at the blonde woman, who blushed beneath her deep tan.

Rick said, "By the way, this overdressed seaman is Aston Dent. He was DEVGRU with Jinks."

"Nice to meet you, Aston," Ryan said. After they shook hands, Ryan turned to Jinks. "I didn't expect to see you. Did the Navy give you leave?"

"I'm on permanent leave to the U.S.S. *Backyard*."

"Congrats, man." Ryan fist bumped Jinks's.

"After twenty-two years, I decided it was time to retire and let those young guys do the heavy lifting. Now I'm sipping sweet tea and doing consulting work. Aston decided not to reenlist about the same time I retired, and we went into business together."

Chuck Newland descended the steps, squaring away his white Stetson. He wore jeans, a DWR polo, and scuffed cowboy boots. He gave Ryan a high-five.

"So, all you guys are hanging around DWR?" Mango asked. "See what we started, Ryan?"

Aston said, "We're consultants. We work for ourselves."

Ryan placed the man's accent somewhere in New England, maybe Connecticut.

"Well, let's get the show on the road," Jinks said. "I hear we have limited time to plan this op."

While Chuck and the woman, who Ryan assumed was the copilot, chocked the wheels of the sleek, white airplane, the men formed a line to move black duffle bags from the plane's cargo bay to the rear of the SUV. Then they piled in, and Ryan drove them away from the airport.

Chuck leaned forward to speak to the blonde, who'd hopped into the passenger seat beside Ryan. "We got busy back there and I didn't have time to introduce you two. Ryan, Erica Opsal. Erica, you better stay away from this guy."

Ryan glanced into the rearview mirror. "Chuck, you know I'm an angel."

Rick snorted. "The only reason your halo is straight is because your horns hold it in place."

Ryan flipped him the bird. "Welcome to the club, Erica. I'm sure you've heard your share of stories."

She smiled warmly. "The whole trip here."

Ryan glanced in the mirror at Aston, who stared silently out the window.

Fifteen minutes later, Ryan backed the Suburban down a driveway and bumped the garage door opener to lift the door. While it rose with a squeal, the team disembarked. Once again, they formed up in a line to move their gear from the SUV into the garage. As soon as they had passed the last bag, Jinks pressed the wall-mounted button, and the garage door rattled closed.

They walked up the stairs to the main house and found Mango in the kitchen. He handed beers to each member of the team as they filed through to the pool deck where they had a stunning view of Charlotte Amalie and Long Bay.

Mango handed a beer to his wife, who lay beside the pool on a chaise lounge.

"Nice digs," Rick said.

"They are," Ryan replied. "You can thank Jennifer. She's friends with the people who own this place, so let's treat it nicely."

"Thanks, Jennifer,"

Extending the hand holding his beer bottle, Ryan pointed at the yacht basin beside the cruise ship quay, where at least a dozen enormous private yachts were tied stern first to marina's finger piers. "Silverman usually docks down there with the other mega yachts. Did you guys have time to look at *The Oasis*'s deck plans?"

"We did," Jinks said. "We came up with a plan, but we wanted to hear what you had to say first."

Ryan stepped through the French doors and over to a kitchen table, where he unrolled the blueprints for the Benetti Oasis 135. He'd had a local print shop enlarge the ship's prints. From his research, he'd learned Benetti had customized the interior for Mark Silverman when they'd built the ship. Ryan had pretended to be a foreman at a local shipyard doing work on the yacht and called Benetti and asked them to email him the schematics. He overlaid them so they could easily see the three tiers of the ship.

The team gathered around the table.

Jinks said, "Let's hear it."

Ryan crossed his arms and leaned against the counter. "I called the number on Silverman's website and arranged for us to be his next charter. We're going to take a little trip on the love boat."

"Shit," Jinks said. "That's even better than the airborne assault we'd planned for when the boat was in international waters."

Aston, the newest team member, asked, "Have you confirmed that Pammie Walcott is on board?"

Ryan nodded. "We have video surveillance footage and an eyewitness that places her on the ship."

Rick frowned as he glanced over the plans. "What if she got off on one of the stops *Oasis* made on the way here?"

"I doubt Silverman lets any of the girls off the boat," Ryan said. "Especially a high-value asset like Pammie."

"We know Silverman has one bodyguard, that SAS dude," Jinks said. "Does he have more?"

"I bet he has several," Ryan said. "We'll count heads to see how many girls and guards are on board when the ship docks."

"What if he keeps them hidden?" Aston asked.

Ryan held up his hands. "We won't know the full details until we're on the ship."

"This doesn't sound like good operational tactics," Jinks added. "Right now, we're guessing."

"Let's get two guys on the boat then chopper in the rest after you get into international waters," Rick said. "Whoever is on *Oasis* will confirm the target is there, get an accurate head count on the girls and guards, then radio us with the information. We'll be able to come in with guns blazing."

Jinks ran a hand over his head, then rubbed his chin. "That's the best idea we've had yet."

"What about me?" Jennifer asked.

Ryan glanced at each of the people gathered in the room. Before he could speak, there was a knock on the door that echoed across the tiled room like a giant hammer beating on the door.

Mango strode over and opened it. He had to look up at the much taller man, who towered over his five-ten frame by almost a foot. "What's up, bro?"

"I'm looking for Ryan Weller," the man's voice boomed.

"Let him in, Mango," Ryan called.

Mango stepped back, and the hulk of a man stooped to enter the door. His chest and back were as wide as a yard stick and his hands could easily palm a dinner plate. He strode in, tossing a backpack on a sofa and whipping his head to the side to clear his shoulder-length brown hair from his bearded face. He lifted Ryan off his feet in a bear hug that Ryan believed would crack his ribs.

When the big man set him down, Ryan croaked, "Everyone, this is Steve Bishop. Steve, this is everyone."

Steve lifted his chin by way of greeting, stepped to the fridge, retrieved a beer, and then examined the blueprints.

Ryan continued, "Chuck is going to rent us a helicopter. Mango and Jennifer will rent a boat and trail us as a secondary means of escape and a sniper platform for Mango. Aston and I will go aboard *The Oasis*, since he looks more like a professional businessman than the rest of you shitbirds."

"Now that we have a plan, let's look at the party poppers," Jinks said.

The men trooped down the stairs to the garage. They found a plastic folding table and set it up before laying out Heckler & Koch MP5 submachine guns, and a variety of pistols tailored to their individual tastes. More bags held body armor, black battle dress uniforms, boots, chest rigs, and a sundry list of other items the men needed in a combat situation.

Ryan held up a Walther PPQ, his preferred side arm. "Aston and I will need our pistols in case the shit goes pear-shaped before you guys show up."

"You can hide them in your bags and hope they don't find them," Mango suggested.

"You think they'll search your bags before letting you on board?" Jennifer asked, sitting on the bottom stair step, holding her beer. She'd pulled a sundress over her white bikini.

Jinks replied, "Anything is possible when you're dealing with a pimp of this caliber."

"Let's wait," Aston said. He'd shed his sport coat, leaving it on a chair upstairs, and had rolled up the sleeves of his dress shirt before examining his rifle. "No need to arouse suspicion if we don't need to. Besides, those SAS guys can smell a rat."

"Okay," Ryan agreed. "We wait."

The men checked their firearms and separated their battle kits before retreating upstairs to find Chuck and Erica lounging in the pool.

Standing on the pool deck with fresh beers, the men talked about past missions, old friends, and new adventures. Ryan hoped Pammie's dad wouldn't be too shocked when he got the bill for feeding and outfitting the rough crew of former special operators he'd thrown together to rescue his daughter. He didn't know what Jinks and Aston's consulting fee would be, but he knew Steven Bishop charged ten thousand dollars for his services. Mercenaries gotta get paid.

Ryan had first met Steve at EOD school in Florida. The man had been in the Air Force and was one of the few Chair Force guys Ryan didn't give any shit to. Now, he ran a two-hundred-man private security firm with U.S. government contracts. He'd based his operational headquarters in Fort Pierce, Florida, and had been happy to help Ryan free a few hostages.

Ryan took a swig of beer as he watched the team. Tomorrow, they'd know where things stood. Silverman would arrive in port, and their operation would begin in earnest.

He walked to where Chuck and Erica sat at the edge of the pool and squatted beside them. "Think you can get us a bird?"

"Oh, ye of little faith. I made one call and have an Airbus EC120 Colibri at our disposal." At Ryan's questioning look, Chuck continued, "She's a five-seater, single engine. Should do everything you need."

"Now we need a boat," Ryan mused.

Chuck said, "The helo wasn't cheap. I can't imagine what a boat will cost."

"Hey, Ryan."

Ryan looked up to see Jennifer motioning for him. He walked to where she sat at a patio table with Mango.

"Pammie's dad might know someone here who has one of those super yachts we could borrow."

"That's a good idea."

"I'm not driving a center console past the twelve-mile limit, especially if he goes to St. Croix first," Jennifer said. "That's, like, forty miles away."

Ryan nodded in thought.

"We need to do this in U.S. territory," Aston interjected. "If Silverman goes south along the islands, he'll cross into St. Kitts and Nevis's territory, but if he heads east, he'll be in Venezuelan waters."

"How the hell does that work?" Rick asked.

"Venezuela has a navy base and research station on Aves Island one hundred and sixty-three miles from St. Croix. According to the 1980 U.S.-Venezuela Maritime Boundary Treaty, Venezuela controls the Caribbean right up to the U.S.V.I.'s limits."

"Aren't you a font of information?" Rick said.

Aston lowered his beer bottle. "DEVGRU worked with Fourth Fleet when they were getting operational. It was my job to know this stuff, especially with all the hostilities in Venezuela."

"Then we'll take him before he leaves U.S. waters," Ryan decided.

CHAPTER FORTY

The morning sun rose over the low hills of St. Thomas, awakening a new day. Around the island, people welcomed the first orange and red rays that pushed back the darkness and illuminated the sparkling blue harbors, lush green trees, and blue seas.

Ryan chugged up the hill, sweat pouring off his body as he tried to keep up with the long strides of the running Steve Bishop. He stopped and put his hands on his knees, sucking in deep breaths of moisture laden air. Somewhere over the Atlantic, a storm was brewing, pushing bands of rain ahead of it. The slick streets and damp palms were evidence of the rain that had fallen overnight.

"Come on, squid," Steve shouted from the top of the hill.

Ryan straightened and jogged again; his long legs carried him quickly up the hill. He went straight to the outdoor shower and doused himself with hot water. Glancing over at the pool, he saw Jennifer and Erica enjoying the first cups of coffee of the morning. They had on bikini tops and shorts, prepared to meet the yacht captain Kent Walcott had arranged for them last night after Ryan had called him.

He shut off the water and wrapped a towel around his waist before going inside to change. His wardrobe consisted of shorts and T-shirts, and he needed clothes befitting a man of wealth and leisure looking for a sex cruise.

Making his way to the kitchen, he found most of the team gathered there, sipping coffee. Aston manned the stove, slinging scrambled eggs and bacon onto plates. He had a towel draped over his left shoulder and wore a frilly apron Ryan guessed he'd found somewhere in the kitchen to protect his light pink dress shirt and dark gray slacks. Ryan wasn't a man for wearing pink, but the outfit looked good on Aston.

Ryan took a plate and carried it out to the patio table where the girls and Mango sat. "Where's Chuck?"

"He's probably still in bed," Erica said. "I heard him come in late last night."

Ryan finished chewing the crisp bacon. "The man knows how to party."

Erica's blue eyes met his. "I want you to know that I can fly the Airbus in case Chuck is under the weather."

"Good to know."

Erica's lips curled in a tight smile. "DWR didn't hire me to be a babysitter, but I spend a lot of my time making sure Chuck gets where he needs to be."

This surprised Ryan, and his face must have showed it.

In response, she said, "He's a good pilot, but he's been a little wild lately."

"Why?"

"He lost his dad two months ago, and it's been hard on him."

Ryan nodded sympathetically. During one of their flights together, Chuck had told him stories about his dad's time in Vietnam as a Cobra pilot, then working for the CIA's Air America in Laos. The man was Chuck's hero, and he'd joined the Air Force to be a pilot like his father. Chuck had qualified for jets but chose to fly helicopters to support the Air Force's special operations forces.

"It's thrown him off the rails," Erica added.

"Has it affected his flying?"

"Not one damned bit," Chuck growled.

Ryan had to twist around to see Chuck standing behind him, holding a cup of coffee. "Sorry to hear about your dad."

"Everyone dies, Weller."

"You good to go?" Ryan asked.

Chuck sipped from the mug. "Ready to pull chocks."

Ryan gave him a mock salute. "Roger that. Carry on."

"I'm headed for the airfield to check on the helicopter. Erica, you're welcome to join me."

She glanced at Ryan, who shrugged. "I think I'll go with Mango and Jennifer to the yacht," she said.

"Suit yourself." Chuck spun on his heels and headed for the door, cowboy boots clicking on the terracotta tile.

By the time breakfast was over and the dishes put away, it was past ten o'clock. Jennifer, Ryan, Mango, and Erica walked down the hill to find a clothing store. They spent half an hour wandering through the shops before they spotted a small men's clothing boutique. Ryan purchased a pair of slacks, dress shirt, and a suit jacket after receiving the women's approval. While he owned a Brookes Brothers suit, packed away at his parents' home in North Carolina, he liked to joke that he only owned two suits—a wet suit and a dry suit, both for diving and neither were for formal wear.

After leaving the shop, they caught a cab to the marina. Mango and Jennifer met with the captain of the Sunseeker Predator 82; a sleek yacht capable of fifty knots with her high-performance motors. It also had a hard top over the main cabin, perfect for a shooting platform.

An hour later, Mango and Jennifer joined Ryan and Erica

at a barbeque restaurant with a view of the docks. They didn't have to wait long for *The Oasis* to arrive as they sipped their ice teas and chewed on pulled pork sandwiches.

Ryan pulled out his digital camera with telephoto lens to snap pictures of the ship and her crew. He captured Silverman leaning over the rail as the captain backed the yacht alongside the dock. The large vessel took two slips, and when the bikini-clad crew of women had secured the lines, they folded down the aft rails of the vessel, allowing for more room on the stern around the built-in infinity swimming pool. He took pictures of every crew member he saw, searching for Pammie. He didn't see her during his many sweeps of the ship.

"I guess you'll just have to get aboard to find out if she's there," Mango said.

Ryan put the camera back to his eye. "With all the press she's gotten lately, I wouldn't let her out of her cabin while in port."

"What happens if you get on the ship and she's not there?" Erica asked.

"Then you and Chuckles got to vacation in St. Thomas for a few days, and you'll fly everyone back tomorrow."

She giggled at the joke Ryan made from the pilot's name.

"The clients are disembarking," Mango said. "Do we care about them?"

"No. They're Brazilian citizens, and as much as I hate to let them go, they're not our priority."

"Someone should lop off their nuts," Erica muttered.

"I agree," Jennifer added.

"We all do," Ryan said.

They watched the Brazilians march off the pier, laughing and staggering as they made their way to a waiting cab.

Ryan's sat phone rang. "Maritime Recovery, Bob Parker speaking."

"Mr. Parker, this is Mark Silverman. I'll be ready for you to embark at four o'clock if that's satisfactory to you?"

"Yes." Ryan glanced at his wristwatch. "Oh, by the way, the rest of our gang was delayed at the airport in New York—something about electronics on the airplane. They'll join us via helicopter after we're underway."

"Perfect," Silverman purred. "I'll have the crew prepare for a landing on the forward deck."

"There will be two of us this evening. We'll inspect the goods before we get underway."

Silverman chuckled. "I would expect nothing less."

"See you soon."

Ryan paid the bill, and they piled into a cab for the ride to the rental house. When they arrived, Ryan attached the camera to a laptop and downloaded the pictures. Then he attempted to cast them to the home's large flat screen television but couldn't figure out the connections. Steve Bishop stepped in and deftly fixed the problem. His giant hands made the computer's keyboard look like one of those old sliding cell phone keyboards.

As they watched the pictures in a slide show, the former special forces operators took notes and examined everything in detail.

"I count three security personnel," Jinks said when they'd run the slide show multiple times.

"I counted fifteen women," Rick said.

"None of them were our target," Aston added.

"I told Silverman we'd inspect the women before we left the dock," Ryan said. "If she's not there, we throw a fit and storm off the boat."

Aston grinned. "I'm good at that."

At four o'clock, Ryan and Aston changed clothes and packed bags. Mango and Jennifer had left for the yacht basin to board the Predator, which they agreed was an apt name for a boat used to stalk their prey.

In the garage, while the team kitted up in BDUs, chest rigs, and checked firearms, Ryan pulled out his Walther, several extra magazines, and a large fixed blade knife. Aston retrieved his Glock and a similar kit, then he wrapped it in a waterproof bag and handed it to Jinks.

"What am I doing with this?" the retired senior chief asked.

Ryan coiled a length of paracord around his hand before stuffing it into his pocket. "If we have the opportunity before we leave port, I'll signal you and you bring the bag to the ship. I'll lower the paracord for you to attach it."

"How am I supposed to do that?" Jinks asked.

"You're a SEAL. I'm sure you can figure it out. If I don't signal you, just bring the bag with you on the helicopter."

Jinks looked at him dubiously, then smiled. "I think I can figure it out."

They did one more bag drag to load the SUV then, with Erica behind the wheel, headed for the airfield to meet Chuck. Ryan, Aston, and Jinks climbed into another cab.

When they arrived at the docks, Aston straightened his suit coat as he stepped out of the car.

"You ready for this?" Ryan glanced over his shoulder at Jinks, who disappeared into a scuba rental shop.

"To act like a pretentious asshole? Not a problem. I'm a real-life trust fund baby. I've had a silver spoon in my mouth since the day I was born."

Ryan shouldered his garment bag. "I'd have never guessed."

Aston laughed.

"What made you become a SEAL?"

"You never rebelled against your parents?"

The former SAS officer, Andrew, met the two men at the marina gate. He introduced himself, not giving his last name, and pointed at a nearby cart. "I'll wheel your luggage to the boat."

Both men dropped their luggage into the cart. Andrew hefted the cart handles and led the way to *The Oasis*.

CHAPTER FORTY-ONE

As a man of action, Ryan had been in many difficult situations each requiring him to become a chameleon, adapting to his surroundings and relying on his wits to get him through safely. Stepping onto the party boat required a different skin from any he'd previously used. He shed his rough-and-tumble, commercial-diver-beach-bum persona for that of dress clothes which were his shell, reflecting that of a high-end businessman.

"Welcome aboard, gentlemen." Silverman shook hands with Ryan and Aston. "Svetlana will show you to your staterooms."

They followed the statuesque blonde to the lower deck, Ryan carefully surveying their new surroundings, cataloging threats, and mapping the ship in his mind.

After stowing their baggage, the men returned to the main salon where Svetlana was pouring glasses of champagne at a coffee table in the middle of a round sofa, the centerpiece of the salon. Large sliding glass doors curved around the rear of the room and against the forward bulkhead was a well-stocked bar.

Silverman picked up a flute and gestured to their server. "Svetlana takes care of the girls and is my right hand. If I'm not available, she can assist you with any issues."

Aston gave her an appraising gaze. "Are you one of the party girls?"

Svetlana fixed him with a hard stare. "I am here to ensure you have a good time."

"Is that a yes or a no?" He glanced at Silverman.

"Please refrain from aggravating my hostess, gentlemen. I'm sure you will find everything satisfactory."

Ryan sipped the champagne and wanted to spit it out. The bubbling wine juice was disgusting, no matter the vintage. "Svetlana, can you grab me a beer? Presidente, if you have it."

She smiled pleasantly and stepped around the bar to a refrigerator, where she retrieved a glass bottle with the distinctive green-and-white label. After opening it, she handed it to Ryan.

"Thanks, dear." He gave her a wink. "Champagne always gives me a headache."

Silverman sat on the leather sofa and held his drink out. Svetlana refilled both his and Aston's champagne flutes. She drank Ryan's champagne for him.

Silverman motioned to Svetlana. "Get the girls. We don't want to keep our guests waiting."

"We're paying for them; bring 'em out," Ryan encouraged.

"Yeah, our loser friends can catch up when they get here," Aston added.

Silverman leaned forward. "Before we get started, I want you to know that this is your home for the week. Please don't get too wild and respect the girls. I have security guards who will gladly constrain you if you get out of line."

Aston sat forward, reaching for the bottle of champagne. "How many do you have?"

"Four."

The two mercenaries shared a glance as Svetlana disappeared down the steps and returned several minutes later with a parade of women in tow, all wearing swimsuits and smiles. Several were topless. Ryan tried to keep his gaze on their faces, searching for the subject of their rescue attempt. Silverman had promised there would be fifteen women, and Ryan counted sixteen. Pammie Walcott came out last.

They stood in a line across the salon like contestants in a beauty pageant, each striking a pose with her right leg forward and hands on hips. Ryan stepped forward, casually looking them up and down. The young women would not meet his gaze, staring at the floor or somewhere far in the distance.

He tried to remain hard and objective, but his heart went out to the poor girls.

He'd once asked a stripper what she thought about while she gave lap dances. She'd said she made a mental list of chores, pictured doing laundry, or thought about going on vacation somewhere with the money she was earning from her customers—anything but sex and the job she had chosen for herself. Now, he wondered what these girls were thinking.

As he passed one brunette, she sniffed, and he saw white powder residue around her nostrils. She'd done a bump before being subjected to the next round of guffawing men who would paw and use her.

Aston carried his champagne flute and sipped it as he examined the women, casually stopping to caress a face. Ryan thought he was really selling their image, but he couldn't bring himself to do the same. These were women, not objects to be used and controlled.

Aston stopped in front of Pammie. "You're very pretty. I like you." He pushed a lock of her blonde hair out of her face and behind her ear.

Pammie bowed her head even lower.

Ryan watched Aston use a finger to raise Pammie's chin. When she lifted her head, she averted her gaze. Her green eyes locked on Ryan for just a moment, then flitted away. He had planned to get close to Pammie, but if Aston wanted the role, he could have it.

"Which one strikes your fancy, Mr. Weller?" Silverman asked.

Ryan grabbed another beer from the bar fridge to maintain his image as a hard-partying business executive. He had a view of their backsides from this angle. "I'm glad I have a whole week," he said.

He sipped his beer as he walked around to face them, running his gaze across the row of poised women once again, and settled on a well-proportioned woman of medium height. Her dark hair fell to mid back, and she seemed to stand a little straighter than the other girls, her chin held high.

Ryan went to stand in front of her. "What's your name?"

"Maggie." Her voice was low.

"I'm Bob. Care to join me on the aft deck for a smoke?"

She smiled, her brown eyes meeting his. "I'd love that."

He extended his elbow, and she looped an arm through it before marching past Silverman and onto the rear deck.

Once they were outside, Maggie stretched out on a chaise lounge positioned on the port wing platform facing the small pool. The whole yacht was overkill; if Ryan could afford it, he'd for damn sure own one. But even with his small fortune saved in a Cayman bank, he probably didn't have enough to fill the fuel tank. He handed a cigarette and lighter to Maggie. She lit hers and handed the lighter back.

Ryan sparked his and took the cigarette from his mouth. "Another nail in the coffin."

Maggie snuggled into the chaise. She stretched her long

legs and wiggled her painted blue toes. "Gotta die of something."

"Do you guys make small talk or just get down to business?"

"The guests mostly talk to each other. We're the eye candy and playthings. Do you want to play?" She reached her foot out and rubbed it along the inside of his leg, toward his crotch.

Ryan ignored her and scanned the harbor. He saw a familiar figure perched on the stern of a pontoon-style dive boat, wearing a scuba rig. The swim was an easy one hundred yards, but the diver would be visible in the clear water, his bubbles giving away his position. Ryan turned and looked around the ship for any sign of a guard. The four Silverman had mentioned blended into the scenery. Ryan had only seen Andrew, who had disappeared after escorting them back upstairs.

Now, however, Andrew stood in one corner of the salon. On the upper deck, another guard lingered near the rail. Where were the other two?

Ryan finished his beer and handed the bottle to Maggie. "Get me another."

She pushed herself out of the chaise and went into the salon.

He walked forward to the recess in the hull, into which the platform folded. He sat in the chair positioned there and glanced around to ensure he wasn't being watched. He dropped the carabiner attached to the paracord overboard then knotted it around the leg of the chair.

With the rope in place, he motioned for Jinks to approach. When Jinks rolled into the water, Ryan stood and walked around to the pool. Maggie met him with a fresh beer and one of her own. Ryan glanced over at the dive boat, scanning the water for the telltale bubbles.

Stepping to the side of the ship, he glanced down to see Jinks hovering above the seafloor, tying the care package to the paracord. It only took him several seconds to clip the bag to the carabiner before he gripped an underwater scooter and zoomed off under the dock, away from the direction he'd come.

Aston walked out with a blonde on one side and a brunette on the other, both laughing at something he'd said as though it was the funniest joke they'd ever heard.

Ryan made a motion as if to pull in a line, and Aston nodded. He motioned for Maggie to join them on the fixed sun pad at the head of the pool. The girls dropped onto the cushions, and Aston distracted them while Ryan pulled in the bag. He tucked it behind the cushion of the chair he'd tied the line to and stood. When he picked up the chair to move it to the pool area, the loop of paracord slipped off the leg and over the side of the boat.

He pushed the chair over to the sun pad and settled into it. Maggie draped herself across his lap, fished out his cigarettes, and lit them both one. They chatted while Svetlana ordered the crew to prepare for getting underway, starting with retracting the folding platforms. They cast off ropes while the yacht's diesels snarled quietly, providing a barely noticeable hum throughout the hull.

Aston and Ryan lingered on the back deck with the girls as the ship negotiated the strait between Rupert Rock and Hassel Island. Off their starboard quarter, the sleek looking Sunseeker Predator shadowed them. They conferred in low tones about the girls and the guards before Ryan sent a text to Mango and Rick detailing the situation and letting them know that the operation was a go.

Two hours later, all traces of the lush green islands had faded over the eastern horizon. Ryan and Aston sat at the dining table on the middle deck with their chosen girls.

Maggie had a sharp wit, and she'd told him this was her job, and that Silverman was putting money into an account for her and the other girls so they could eventually leave.

This added a new twist to the puzzle. As the men ate steak and asparagus, a third man Ryan hadn't seen before approached the table. He was tall, lean, and capable looking, with a wicked scar running across his left cheek. Even though he had groomed a thick brown beard, the wide scar was easily visible, drawing the eye to the void in the hair. The man bent and whispered into Silverman's ear.

When the man straightened, Silverman wiped his mouth with a napkin and looked at Ryan. "Your friends are on the way. They should be here in ten minutes." He turned to Scar and asked, "Have you cleared the foredecks?"

"Yes, sir. Everything is set for their arrival."

"Excellent. Please continue with your meal, gentlemen. I will see to your friends." He folded his napkin and laid it on the chair seat.

Ryan glanced around the boat. Andrew hovered nearby, hands behind him at parade rest. Ryan excused himself and went down the steps to the pool deck. He lit a cigarette and watched the tiny black speck silhouetted against the towering cumulous clouds grow larger with each passing second. Dropping into the chair he had occupied earlier, he reached behind him for the bag, but it wasn't there.

CHAPTER FORTY-TWO

Ryan's pulse quickened as he frantically slid his hand under the cushions. What the hell had happened to the bag?

Maggie joined him and sat in his lap again. Ryan wanted to throw her off and strip the chair bare of its pillows and cushions but knew he wouldn't find the weapons.

Maggie nibbled on his neck, running a hand through his hair. She whispered, "I have your bag."

"Where is it?" he hissed.

"I moved it because Andrew was snooping around. Take me to your room and I'll show you where I put it."

Ryan stood, hefting her in his arms, and carried her into the salon. He set her on her feet at the stairs, and she led him, hand in hand, to his room.

When the stateroom door swung shut, Maggie opened the top drawer of the dresser. She removed the bag and set it on the bed. Ryan could see she'd opened it. She must have moved it when she'd excused herself to use the restroom before dinner.

"You know what's in here?" Ryan peeled open the top and

dumped the contents onto the bedspread. He seized his Walther, press-checked the slide, and stuffed magazines into his pocket and the knife behind his back.

"I looked. What are you going to do?"

"Take down the ship."

"Why?" she asked in dismay.

"I'm here for Pammie. She was kidnapped in St. Vincent after watching a lunatic kill her brother and another man right in front of her. Then, he sold her to a guy in Trinidad before your boss bought her."

Maggie covered her mouth with her hands.

"How many of you are here by choice?" He jammed his gun into his back pocket and checked Aston's Glock, making sure the silencer was tight and a round had been chambered. He left Aston's gear in the bag and carried the Glock, ready to use.

"A few," Maggie finally replied. Still, she sounded unsure.

"We're here to rescue all of you. Stay on this deck. If you see any of the other girls, let them know we're taking the boat. There will be gunfire."

Maggie threw her arms around him and kissed him hard. She broke away and whispered, "Good luck."

Before he let her go, Ryan squeezed her upper arms and focused on her eyes. They met his, flicking back and forth. "I'm counting on you, Maggie. Get those girls in one place. We're getting you out of here."

He released her and ran up the steps, keeping the Glock by his side as he continued to the second deck salon. Through the giant windows, Ryan saw the helicopter hovering just off the bow. Aston rose from the table.

The helicopter's door slid open. Without warning, Jinks leaned out and shot the bodyguard on the foredeck.

The men jumped from the chopper to the sun pads. Andrew turned at the sound of gunfire, reaching behind him, but Ryan brought the Glock up and drilled two rounds through his chest. Before the gun finished smoking, he tossed it sideways across the room to Aston, who had his hands up like an outfielder catching a line drive.

Ryan pulled his Walther free and aimed it at the captain. "Keep it steady."

"Yes, sir," he replied, never taking his eyes from the helicopter.

As soon as the men had deployed, the helicopter veered away from *The Oasis*. The shooters fanned out, moving through the ship. Jinks pushed a handcuffed Mark Silverman ahead of him.

"Two down. Two to go," Ryan said, and Jinks relayed it to the team via their wireless communications.

The women who'd been at the table with Aston were now cowering behind the sofa and sobbing. Somewhere a woman screamed.

"What do you want to do with him?" Jinks asked.

"Take him to his suite. Aston, round up the girls. Make sure Pammie is the first one off this boat." Ryan turned to the captain. "Shut her down."

The captain bumped the throttles into neutral and turned off the diesels, then went down the steps with Ryan.

Suddenly, the whole ship shook, and a ball of fire rose from the stern.

"What the hell!" Ryan charged toward the stern but couldn't get closer than the rear doors of the salon as a wicked conflagration engulfed the aft deck.

Jinks stumbled out of the master suite and stopped beside Ryan. "One of those assholes just set off a grenade in the engine room. Rick plugged him, but he'd already pulled the pin."

"Are the girls safe?"

"We're rounding them up now."

Maggie ran up the steps and tripped on the top one. She sprawled on the floor, and several girls trampled her before she could get back to her feet.

"Where the hell is Mango?" Ryan blurted.

"On the way," Jinks replied.

"Maggie, get the girls to the bow." Ryan sprinted to the master suite, where Jinks had left the yacht's owner. He came to a halt in the doorway when he saw Silverman pointing a pistol at him.

"This is your fault!" Silverman roared.

Ryan dove to his right as Silverman fired. He rolled and came up in a crouch, his Walther in a two-handed grip, and pulled the trigger. The bullet slammed into Silverman's leg, and he fell to the deck, dropping his gun.

Ryan came out of his crouch and ran to the fallen man, kicking away the pistol. Behind where Silverman had stood was an open safe. Ryan saw several thick packets of money, paperwork, and velvet boxes.

The ship shook again. Jinks screamed, and Ryan turned to see him trying to roll onto his back, clothes dark with sticky blood. A puddle was forming beneath him.

"Stay down," Ryan shouted. Before he could move, he saw Steve lumber into view. The private security contractor opened a medical blowout pack and knelt beside the fallen SEAL.

Ryan turned back to Silverman. The man writhed on the floor, clutching his leg with bloody hands. Hurriedly, Ryan ripped open dresser drawers and closet doors, looking for a bag. He found a small hardside suitcase and dumped the contents of the safe into it. Spotting a laptop on the desk, Ryan tossed it into the suitcase, too, then squatted over Silverman.

"Maggie said you started bank accounts for girls. I want to know how you access them."

Silverman glared up at him. Ryan could see the pain and anger in the man's hooded, gray eyes.

Ryan squeezed Silverman's thigh below the bullet wound and listened to the man scream. After a moment, he let go. "I want routing and account numbers."

"Please, stop." Tears streaked the man's cheeks. Through labored gasps, he said, "I told them I was doing it, but it was a lie to keep them working."

"You rat bastard," Ryan growled.

Steve joined Ryan. "We need to go. The girls are moving to the Predator right now."

"What about Jinks?"

"Aston and Rick are making a stretcher."

Ryan nodded. "Will he be okay?"

"He will be as soon as we get him on the helicopter."

"Take this to the Predator. Don't let it get wet." He shoved the suitcase into Steve's hand. "I'll be over in a minute."

"The ship is sinking."

Ryan spun to face the big man. "You take care of the girls and Jinks. I've got this covered."

Steve backed away, hands up with his palms out. "Handle your business."

"Don't leave me here with him," Silverman cried, staring at Steve.

"You made your own bed, jackass. Time to pay the piper."

Ryan squeezed Silverman's gunshot wound again, and the man bellowed. As he eased the pressure, Ryan said, "Routing and account numbers."

Silverman panted. "Will you get me off this yacht?"

"Right after you give me what I want."

Silverman whined, "You already took two hundred grand out of my safe."

"Don't get cheap on me, Mark."

"Okay. Okay. Just get me off this boat."

"Give me the money first."

The Oasis shuddered and rolled, settling into a heavy list to port. Ryan glanced over his shoulder at the stern. The Caribbean Sea lapped at the lip of the shattered infinity pool, and flames danced through a hole in the deck. Rick, Steve, and Aston were loading Jinks onto a makeshift litter.

He gave Silverman's leg another squeeze. "You need to tell me, now."

Silverman's indolent eyes tracked Ryan, then, in recognition of his fate, shifted away. "Why are you doing this?"

"For the girls. They deserve better than the way you treated them."

"Those worthless bitches don't deserve a penny."

"I want bank account numbers and passwords." Ryan applied more pressure to the wound, grinding his thumb into the puckered and bloody flesh left by the bullet. Strands of pant fiber protruded limply from the mutilated muscle. He had no qualms about torturing this mouth breather.

Tears and snot streamed down Silverman's face. His once well-coifed hair was now a tangled, disheveled mess, sticking out where he had gripped it tightly to help quell the pain.

"I have your computer," Ryan said, grinding his thumb into Silverman's leg. "I can hack it and get all the information I need."

"Let's go, Ryan," Rick shouted, appearing in the doorway. "Choppers inbound and the girls are safe."

"Hear that, Mark? Your little business venture is over. I've got the girls, the boat is on its way to Dave Jones's locker, and you're going with it. Do something good for once in your life and help those kids."

"Screw you." Silverman spat a glob of bloody saliva, but it lacked the desired force and dribbled down his chin and across his once pristine white shirt. "It's encrypted."

"Give me the password."

"We gotta *go*, Ryan," Rick shouted again. Outside, the helicopter rotors beat a steady tattoo. "Leave him. We got what we came for."

"Dead check," Ryan said, straightening and stepping away from Silverman.

Once he was clear, Rick Hayes put a bullet between Mark Silverman's eyes.

The two men ran toward the bow, the big yacht beginning a slow roll. They kept moving to starboard as the ship settled onto her side. Scrambling over the gunwales and along the slick surface of the hull, they tried to stay out of the sea. Then the boat rolled over completely, and they found themselves treading water.

Mango tossed a rope to them, and Rick and Ryan pulled themselves onto the Predator.

When they climbed onto the stern, they found Jinks lying in the bottom of the Predator's small runabout, a hastily wrapped bandage circling his abdomen. Above them, Chuck circled in the Airbus.

They helped push the runabout into the water. Aston, Rick, and Ryan climbed aboard and motored two hundred yards away from the Predator and the capsized Benetti before Aston signaled Chuck to come to a hover. He brought the helicopter straight down, keeping them in the hurricane's eye created by the rotor wash whipping the saltwater into a frenzy.

Ryan could see Erica giving Chuck verbal instructions while Aston used hand signals to guide them over the runabout. Once the skid of the helicopter came alongside the boat, the men transferred Jinks into the rear of the bird, then Aston scrambled aboard. Chuck added power, lifting into the sky and flashing away toward St. Thomas.

Rick and Ryan returned to the Predator and stowed the runabout.

"Where're the girls?" Ryan asked.

"They're in the cabin," Mango replied.

Ryan stepped into the salon and saw a mass of bedraggled women huddled on benches and the floor. They had towels and blankets wrapped around them, and Jennifer was playing nursemaid, handing out cups of steaming coffee and cocoa.

"Where'd you get all this stuff?" Ryan asked as he approached her.

"I had the captain pick up some supplies yesterday."

"Always a thinker." He smiled. "How's Pammie?"

"I think she's physically okay." Jennifer frowned. "This whole ordeal has taken a heavy toll on her."

Ryan spotted Pammie hunched under a blanket with a brunette girl, murmuring to her. He made his way through the cabin, steadying himself as the Predator turned around and came up on plane, heading toward St. Thomas.

He knelt on the deck beside the two girls. "Hi, Pammie, I'm Ryan. Your dad sent us to get you."

The girl broke into sobbing hysterics.

"Shh," the brunette purred into Pammie's ear, clutching her tightly.

"What's your name?" Ryan asked, his eyes meeting the brunette's glassy green ones.

"Teya," she replied.

"Where you from, Teya?"

"Nashville."

"We're going to get you guys home, okay?"

She nodded, tears streaking her smiling cheeks.

Ryan went topside and breathed the warm sea air. Mango and Rick were one deck up with the captain. Ryan sat on the sun-warmed bench, staring at the water rushing past the hull and forming a foaming V in their wake.

Maggie sat beside him and threw her arms around him. "Thank you," she whispered in his ear, her soft breath making him shiver.

He put an arm around her and pulled her close.

"You got any cigarettes?" she asked.

Ryan fished the soggy box from his pocket, and when he handed it to her, she scrunched up her face in disgust.

He laughed. "You asked if I had any, not if they were any good."

CHAPTER FORTY-THREE

Billy Ron Sorenson stared at the burned-out hull of *Barefoot*. The Island Packet 495 had caught fire, along with twenty other vessels at the Marina Venetur on Margarita Island off the northern coast of Venezuela. The yacht *Yeyo* had been set on fire and had its dock lines cut, freeing it from its moorings. A strong wind had pushed the boat into several others, and the flames had spread to other boats docked along the seawall.

The theory among the residents was that a local fisherman had set *Yeyo* ablaze because the yacht had hit and cut his trawling net. Billy Ron had also heard whispers that the boat had been torched to show the people's anger because it belonged to a government official.

Regardless, the shouts and clanging alarms had awakened Billy Ron. When he'd stumbled onto the deck, his main sail was on fire. He'd run back inside, grabbed a backpack, and stuffed it with his money, passports, clothes, and the Glock before beating a hasty retreat to land while the local fire department tried to contain the inferno. He could do nothing but watch helplessly as his home and means of escape turned into a raging inferno.

Barefoot's mast now lay across another boat in a tangle of guide wires and singed halyards. There was nothing left of the lavish interior. Only the engine remained, partially submerged in the hold.

He took a deep breath. The harbor stank of diesel fuel, and the water shimmered with oil. No matter which way he turned, the sunlight formed rainbows on the bay's surface. Standing on Marina Venetur's seawall, boat owners salvaged what they could with hooks and grapple lines. Others used small boats and dinghies to recover their possessions.

Desperation filled Billy Ron's soul.

He'd stopped on Margarita Island to visit friends, even though they had advised against it. With the deterioration of Venezuela's economy, crime had risen, and cruisers rarely visited the island. His plan had been to stay a few days at the marina to reprovision and then head out again. He wished he'd kept sailing for Panama.

Turning his back on the depressing scene, he walked off the seawall to find another boat to steal. As he walked along the beach, he saw little fishing vessels and rowboats, but no ocean-going sailboats. The island, which had once been a rich party scene and a retreat for wealthy people from around over the world, was now a ghost town. The marinas and harbors were empty, and the hotels shuttered or nearly vacant. Even though Venezuela produced large amounts of crude oil, fuel was scarce and expensive.

He found a bar and took a seat. Before coming into port, he'd done some research about the conditions on the island and had chanced landing there. Now, he regretted it with every fiber of his being. Sitting on the stool, swallowing big gulps of beer, he wondered if his friends would put him up for a few days. He had yet to see them, as he'd arrived late last night and gone to sleep shortly after docking.

If he weren't wearing flip-flops, he'd have kicked the bar. In his mind, he was doing plenty of mental ass kicking. Why had he come to this godforsaken island? There were a lot of islands that were infinitely safer than this one, and he'd still be on his way west. Billy Ron slammed the empty bottle onto the bar and motioned for another round, asking for a shot of tequila to go with the beer.

After tossing back the drinks and leaving a few dollars on the table, he headed out the door to find his friends' house. He remembered their house being surrounded by vibrant flowers and the backyard had been a garden full of vegetables. When he pushed open the gate and stepped into the courtyard, he found nothing but weeds and dead plants.

Billy Ron knocked on the door, and it was opened by a man who's smile quickly faded at the sight of the American.

"Raul, I need your help," Billy Ron implored.

"I told you on the phone, I cannot help you."

"Please, my boat burned up in the marina fire. I need a place to stay."

Raul shook his head. "My mother and father live with us and last week, my brother and his family moved in. We have no room and little food. Besides, it is dangerous for me. The police will think I am cooperating with the Americans and trying to start a coup. You need to leave."

The Venezuelan had once said his door would always be open to him, but that was no longer the case as Billy Ron stared at the door Raul had just slammed shut. He thrust his hands into his pockets and made his way to the street. His only choice was to find another boat to steal.

CHAPTER FORTY-FOUR

Ryan sank wearily into a seat by the pool and took a long swig of his beer. He'd spent most of the last three days on the phone, either speaking to tearful parents ready to reunite with their lost daughters or to U.S. Customs officials about getting passports for the girls. Most of them were not U.S. citizens, and arrangements were being made to return them to their home countries. For now, they were staying in the rented house above Charlotte Amalie, with Jennifer acting as den mother.

Several of the girls were in shock; others were showing signs of withdrawal from their daily cocaine habit, including Pammie.

Maggie joined him and lit a cigarette. "Thanks for everything you're doing. I just wish I could have gotten the money Silverman promised."

"I'm sorry he lied to you."

She shrugged. "Doesn't matter. Even if there were accounts, he's gone, and we can't access them. We have no idea what the passwords were or where he had the bank accounts."

"I did get two hundred thousand dollars from his safe. That's a twelve-thousand-five-hundred split sixteen ways."

Maggie's eyes lit up, and she threw her arms around him.

"And I took his computer. It's on its way to Texas to be analyzed."

"Where in Texas?" she asked, pulling away from him.

"Texas City, between Houston and Galveston."

"I know where it is. My daddy worked there when I was a kid. He's a pipefitter for the oil companies. We moved around a lot."

"How'd you get involved with Silverman?"

Maggie took long drags on her cigarette, letting the silence stretch out. "I wanted to be a model, and in Midland, there ain't shit, you know? So, I sent out headshots and did a few small jobs, then I got a call from this agency in Austin. Everything seemed legit, from the website to the lady on the phone. I even rode the bus over there and met with them in this fancy high-rise office."

She shook her head and was silent for a few more moments before continuing.

"They gave me an address for a photoshoot, and I went to this little theater. They had an office in the back, and when I went into the alley to find the entrance, I got jumped and tossed into a van."

Another long drag. Ryan waited as she blew out the smoke and ashed her cigarette.

"I had to turn tricks for this guy who demanded I make five hundred bucks a day. When he got tired of me, he sold me to another guy, who sold me to Silverman."

"I'm sorry, Maggie."

She shrugged. "Sorry doesn't get my life back."

"No, but it's a start."

"The only thing I know how to do is have sex and snort cocaine. You think going back to the States will make everything hunky dory? Hell no. Every time I go somewhere, people will stare at me and talk about me behind my back."

"What about your parents?" Ryan asked.

Maggie smiled. "I can't wait to see them, but I can't stay in Midland, not after seeing the Caribbean."

"Got any job skills?"

"Does laying on my back count?" She stubbed out her cigarette and lit a fresh one. "What pisses me off the most was that Silverman pretended to be all sweet and caring, but in reality, he was just another pimp making us think he was doing us a favor just to keep us happy."

Ryan wasn't sure what to say, so he just patted her hand.

"What am I supposed to do now? Get a job as somebody's secretary?"

"If you want a job, I can talk to some people," Ryan said.

"Thanks." She covered his hand. "Maybe we can finish what we started on the boat."

"I'm sure you're great, Maggie, but no thanks."

She jerked her hand back as if he were a snake, rubbed out her smoke, and stood. Emotionlessly, and with eyes downcast, she said, "If you change your mind, you know where to find me."

Ryan watched her walk away, wondering how different her life would be from now on. His ringing phone interrupted his thoughts. He answered with, "Hey, Ashlee, what's up?"

"I got your pimp's computer and I'm running a brute force attack to break the encryption. But here's some other news I didn't tell you because you were busy planning Pammie's rescue."

"What is it?"

"The day you got on the boat with Silverman, someone turned on Pammie Walcott's cell phone."

"It has to be Billy Ron."

"That's what I thought, too. I tracked the signal to a spot in the ocean off the coast of Margarita Island."

"What the hell is he doing in Venezuela?" Ryan asked incredulously.

"He called several numbers and spoke to one for about ten minutes."

"He knows someone there."

"That's my guess," Ashlee replied.

"Okay, let me know what you get off the computer."

"I will, but I wanted to let you know that he turned the phone on again today, and he's still on Margarita."

"Thanks, Ashlee. I'll talk to you later."

Mango sat beside Ryan. "What's that about, bro?"

"Billy Ron Sorenson is on Margarita Island."

"Must be getting fuel or provisions, but I wouldn't have put in there."

Ryan rubbed his chin.

"Oh, shit, I know that look. What are you planning?"

"Kent Walcott told me he'd pay to get *Barefoot* back. Maybe I can sneak in there and get the boat before anyone notices."

Mango shook his head. "That sounds like a bad idea, bro. We got Pammie. Forget about the boat."

Ryan leaned back in his chair and lit a cigarette. He couldn't forget about the boat because Billy Ron Sorenson was on it. As he had told Jim Kilroy not so long ago, some men just needed killing. Well, Billy Ron fit that category. "It's more than just the boat. You know he's going to kill again, and if you don't believe that, you're dumber than you look."

"I know this guy is a serial killer, but you're talking about Venezuela, bro. That country is in constant turmoil, and a civil war could break out at any minute. I mean, they're putting Americans in jail on all kinds of trumped-up charges.

Maybe they'll get Billy Ron or maybe they'll get you, and then what?"

"It's not as bad in Margarita," Ryan protested. "I can get in, get Billy Ron and the boat, and get out."

"Have you not read any cruiser posts in the last year? No one goes there anymore. It's a staging point for drug shipments and gang wars."

Rick came out of the house and joined them at the table. "What are you talking about?"

Mango pointed at Ryan with his thumb. "This idiot wants to go to Margarita Island and steal a sailboat."

"When are we going?" Rick asked.

Ryan shrugged.

"You can't be serious," Mango said incredulously. "He's probably traveling west, and this was a provisioning stop. Let's take him on another island."

"You know," Rick said, "if you catch him in Margarita, you could put a bullet in him, and no one would think anything about it. I hear that place is like the Wild West."

"Are you serious?" Mango shouted, throwing up his hands. "I can't listen to this anymore." He got up from the table and stormed into the house.

Rick leaned back in his chair and drummed his fingers on the chair's armrest for a few seconds before asking, "How are you going to get to Margarita?"

CHAPTER FORTY-FIVE

Ramesh pulled the throttles back, letting the Viking sportfisher come off plane and settle into the mounting swell. Ryan saw him glance over his shoulder. The man's face glowed red in the reflection of the instrument lights. They were abreast of El Farallón, a huge chunk of rock jutting out of the sea two miles off the coast of Margarita Island.

In the distance, the glow of Porlamar provided a beacon. Ryan jerked loose the ropes holding the fourteen-foot wooden pirogue across the cockpit and pushed it over the side. Ramesh jumped down from the bridge and manhandled the ancient Mercury engine to the Viking's swim platform. Ryan helped him fit the Mercury to the pirogue's stern—not an easy task with the two boats shifting in the waves. Once it hung on the transom, Ryan tightened the clamps and hooked up the gas line to a five-gallon tank. He squeezed the primer bulb until it was firm and set the choke. A few tugs on the starter rope, and the engine sputtered to life.

The big Trini smiled in the darkness. "Good luck."

"Thanks, Ramesh." Ryan extended his hand, and they shook.

Ramesh cast off the painter, and the two boats drifted apart. Once the bow was clear, Ryan twisted the Mercury's throttle. The little boat skimmed easily through the waters it had been designed for.

Two days ago, he had called Ramesh and asked him to drive him from Trinidad to Margarita. The marina owner had agreed for a price and sold Ryan the pirogue and motor. Pammie had given Ryan her login information for her cell phone account, and Ashlee had remotely turned on the phone's GPS. Billy Ron was still in Porlamar. The location kept moving along the city's coast, but always returned to the Hotel Venetur at night.

The pirogue's bow dipped, and water splashed over Ryan. Near the shore, he turned north, following the crescent of La Caracola Beach. The white foam of the breaking waves glistened in the city lights. He steered toward the opening in the breakwater for Marina Venetur. To port was a green-and-white navigational beacon tower that looked like a miniature lighthouse and, on the starboard, nothing but a small green light hovering over the dark seawall. The marina was well-lit, and as Ryan approached, he could see and smell the burned-out shells of former boats pulled up on the shore or still tied in their slips.

Once inside the concrete and stone breakwater, he tied the pirogue to the nearest cleat and stepped ashore. He shouldered a black backpack and strolled down the pier, looking for *Barefoot*.

He hadn't spotted the Island Packet 495 by the time he walked the U-shaped yacht basin and retraced his steps to where several of the burned yachts floated. After examining them closely, he saw the Island Packet's distinctive pulpit. It was the only thing left on the fiberglass hull other than the diesel engine and toppled aluminum mast and spar. He glanced around at the other burned boats, trying to figure out what had happened.

He wasn't sure who had the worst luck, him or Billy Ron.

Ramesh had begun his journey back to Trinidad, and Ryan had no way of contacting him. With *Barefoot* gone, he had to find another way off the island. Now it made sense why Billy Ron hadn't left.

Ryan snugged the straps of his pack. Straight off the pier was a small boat yard, and the twin helipads of the massive La Vela shopping center beyond, but Ryan turned right to go down the dirt path in the breakwater rocks to the beach.

In truth, Ryan had hoped to surprise Billy Ron aboard *Barefoot*, take him prisoner, and sail him to an extradition friendly country where he'd turn the serial killer over to U.S. officials for trial. But the best laid plans often went awry. Now, he had no plan other than to find Billy Ron, and when he finally laid eyes on the murdering bastard, he'd know what to do.

According to the last GPS coordinates Ashlee had given him earlier in the evening, Billy Ron had returned to the Hotel Venetur just up the beach from its namesake marina.

Fortunately, the beach was well-lit, and the hotel was a short walk, but as he moved up the dark strip of sand, he kept a careful watch on his surroundings. A white man walking alone in the dark would be easy prey for the numerous pickpockets and thieves, and tourists had been advised to stay in at night.

He reached the fourteen-story hotel, which had been a Hilton before the Venezuelan government had expropriated it and changed the name to Hotel Venetur Margarita. According to the news articles he'd read online, the island's tourist visits had fallen more than fifty percent in the last few years, and the government struggled to meet the island's infrastructure demands. Hotel owners had stopped providing meals because of food shortages, and the water ran sporadically, sometimes only every two weeks. Even Venezuelan President Nicolas Maduro had to import bottled water to use in the restrooms and to serve at meals when he'd recently stayed at the hotel Ryan was now approaching.

Sitting on a chaise lounge near the darkened pool, Ryan could smell the algae growing in the stagnant water. He fished out an energy bar from his backpack and munched on it while he waited for the sun to rise. There wasn't much in his backpack, and now he wished he'd brought a VHF radio to contact Ramesh. When his energy bars and water ran out, he'd have to fend for himself like the rest of the hungry locals.

Then the power went out, bathing everything in darkness.

Ryan clutched his backpack to his chest, unsure what to do for the moment. Then he realized that this was an opportunity. He shouldered the pack as he stood and walked into the hotel lobby. A woman behind the counter held a flashlight and shined it in his face as he approached.

Ryan held his hand up to shield his eyes. In Spanish, he said, "Turn that off. You're blinding me."

The light shifted away, leaving yellow spots swimming before Ryan's eyes. She set it on the counter, pointing at the lobby entrance.

"Can I help you?" she asked in her native tongue.

"I'm looking for an American. His name is either Billy Ron Sorenson or Archie Darling."

"You do not know his name?"

"He goes by both. He's tall, with long, blond hair."

Ryan's eyes were still adjusting to the light, but he saw a smile cross her lips. "So, you've seen him?"

She nodded. "He is here."

Placing an American hundred-dollar bill—almost two

months' salary—on the granite counter surface, he said, "That's yours if you tell me his room number."

Even in the low light, he could see her eyes brighten. "He is on the second floor. Room two fourteen. It faces the beach."

"*Gracias*," Ryan said, heading for the stairs.

He took the stairs two at a time under the watchful beam of the flashlight he'd pulled from his backpack. Carefully, he pushed open the second-floor landing door and closed it gently so it wouldn't slam shut. He covered the flashlight lens, barely allowing any light to shine through his fingers, and crept along the tiled hallway in darkness so complete it reminded Ryan of being inside a cave. Without the light, he would have been stumbling blindly.

Ryan froze when he heard a door latch click. He covered the light and pressed himself against the wall. His eyes searched the darkness, ears straining to pick up any sound beyond the ringing of his tinnitus.

Someone had just stepped into the hallway. The person carried a flashlight aimed at the ground. The cone of light reflected off the tiles and white walls, illuminating Billy Ron Sorenson's face. Ryan's rapidly beating heart seemed to double in speed, and he tried to keep his breathing slow and steady to quell the surge of adrenaline and anger.

Billy Ron let the door swing closed behind him, blocking it with his hand so it latched quietly. He wore a backpack, shorts, and T-shirt, and he'd pulled his long hair into a ponytail. In his right hand, he carried the light, and in the left, a pair of flip-flops. His bare feet didn't make a sound as he padded to the far stairs.

Once he was through the door, Ryan ran to the door he'd come through and jumped down the stairs, taking two hops to make the first landing and three to the second before he cautiously pushed the door open.

The clerk had lit candles and spaced them along the check-in counter. He could barely see her in the low light as he crossed the lobby and spotted the other entrance to the stairs. The door swung open and Billy Ron stepped through, being careful to conceal any noise he made. Ryan moved behind a pillar and tracked him as he headed for the exit to the swimming pool. Ryan followed him through the door.

A three-quarters moon provided illumination for the urban landscape. Ryan watched his quarry make his way along the beach, and when he passed the wall separating the once posh resort from the street which dead-ended at the beach, Ryan ran after him. This would be the perfect place to catch Billy Ron. If the locals found a dead American on a beach between the hotel and the marina, they'd assume a robbery had gone wrong.

Billy Ron must have heard Ryan coming, because he began to run, the flip-flops slapping against his feet.

Ryan lifted his knees higher and pumped his arms faster, speeding after the serial killer. Billy Ron stumbled and kicked away his left flip-flop. Ryan gained on him, his shoes sinking into the soft sand, his calves and lungs burning with exertion. Damn, he needed to quit smoking.

Ahead, the marina pier stretched out into the darkness, bordered by the rubble used to form the breakwater. Ryan remembered the two narrow paths leading through the stones, one on each side of the single-story concrete building he had assumed to be the marina office and store. The building was only a shadowy shape against the horizon as they sped toward it.

Billy Ron angled toward the path closer to the beach. It was the longer route up the breakwater, but they could run on the firm, water-soaked sand. When he reached the stones, he didn't stop, using his hands to aid him up the path.

Ryan closed the distance and bounced from rock to rock

on his toes, not slowing to use his hands. Billy Ron's stamina was flagging, and in the shadow the of the marina office, Ryan finally caught him.

He slammed into Billy Ron's back, tackling him to the ground. Billy Ron's breath exploded out of his chest as they landed. The hard contents of his backpack also knocked the breath from Ryan, and he struggled to breathe as he tried to pin a frantic serial killer to the ground. Before he could lock his legs around Billy Ron's waist and apply a choke hold, Billy Ron reached an arm under his belly and rolled to his right.

Ryan got his left leg under the man's waist and just started to snake his right arm around Billy Ron's neck when his eyes caught the glint of something black clutched in his opponent's left fist. Billy Ron aimed the pistol over his shoulder and pulled the trigger.

The boom of the pistol rolled across the beach, echoing off the boat hulls and concrete buildings. Ryan buried his face into Billy Ron's neck, trying to shield himself from the flash of orange fire. With his right arm, he squeezed Billy Ron's neck, and with the left, reached for the gun.

Before he could grab it, the pistol barked again, then a third time, the bullets whizzing just over his head and smacking into the block building behind them. His left ear rang so loudly that he was deaf. The right ear was only marginally better.

His hand clamped on the pistol slide and he gripped it with all his might, pushing up on the gun to raise the muzzle. The pistol fired again. Ryan let go of the gun, pushing himself to his knees over the prone man. Billy Ron pointed the pistol over his shoulder, right at Ryan, and pulled the trigger.

The gun did nothing but click, the firing pin falling uselessly onto the empty shell casing. By gripping the slide, Ryan had prevented the gun from cycling.

Ryan jerked his shirt up and pulled his own pistol from his

waistband. Without thinking, he put a bullet into the back of Billy Ron's head.

As the echoes of spent rounds died away, Ryan stood and worked the man's pack from his back to make the murder look like a robbery.

Suddenly, he was caught in the glare of bright lights. When he glanced up, shading his eyes with his forearm, he saw two men in green BDUs with *Policia* emblazoned across the chests of their brown bulletproof vests. They were aiming the tactical lights affixed to their AK-103s at him. The ringing in his ears had prevented him from hearing them approach.

Ryan let Billy Ron's backpack slide from his hands as he lifted them above his head.

Behind the policemen were three other men dressed in blue uniforms and holding pistols. Farther down the quay, more sailors poured from a Damen Stan 2606 high-speed patrol vessel belonging to the Venezuelan Navy. Had they been witnesses to his execution of Billy Ron Sorenson?

One policeman stepped forward, letting his gun dangle from the sling, and roughly searched Ryan. He tossed the pistol on the ground beside Billy Ron's, then liberated Ryan's folding knife and extra pistol magazines. The policeman stripped off the backpack before kicking Ryan in the back of the right knee.

Ryan's leg folded underneath him, and he flopped to his knees, falling voluntarily face down on the concrete, bringing his hand behind his back. The policeman straddled him and locked handcuffs around his wrists.

EPILOGUE

Six Months Later

THE SUN COMING through the small window flooded across Ryan Weller's face and bathed him in its warm glow. He rubbed his face with both hands then swung his feet to the floor and padded the two steps to the small cabinet fastened to the wall.

Splashing water from a plastic liter bottle into a bowl, he rubbed it across his cheeks and left them dripping while massaging in some soap. Quickly, he stropped the straight razor against a short length of leather belt cut down for just such a purpose and shaved while staring at himself in a piece of metal polished to mirrored perfection and mounted to the wall above the cabinet.

After washing away the leftover soap, he tucked the razor into his pocket. The tool might have been a shaving implement, but for Ryan, it doubled as a knife for cutting and self-protection. He pulled on his pants and T-shirt, having slept in his underwear. He slid his feet into his shoes and stepped outside his cell.

All around him, the prison was coming to life: inmates stirring from slumber, looking for food, performing their morning ablutions, and, like Ryan, preparing for the day. He stepped outside the cell and waited as the guards took the morning count.

Already he was sweating. Margarita Island might be the Pearl of the Caribbean, but it was hot and arid. Cactuses and scrub brush covered the lower elevations, reminding him of southern Arizona, and lush jungle carpeted the mountain peaks.

Soon he would be sweating in the tropical sun, laying block for the new prison barracks. If he stood high enough on the scaffold, he could smell the salt on the ocean breeze. He would close his eyes and picture himself in the cockpit of his sailboat with the crisp, white canvas spread overhead and the azure ocean rushing by. It was rarely the cockpit of his current boat, *Windseeker*, given to him by Joulie Lafitte, but rather his old Sabre 36, *Sweet T*, which he'd sailed around the world and had lost to pirates in the Gulf of Mexico. How he missed that boat and the adventures he'd had in her.

If he could get over the prison wall, past the double rows of concertina wire and the sharpshooters in the towers, he could make his way to the shore and find a boat to steal. He could escape this miserable existence and be free once again to roam the oceans. He could find *Windseeker* and disappear forever. He could get a forged passport, and he had enough money stashed in his Cayman Island bank account to never have to work again.

He licked his lips and scanned the guard towers, concentrating on the faces of the men on duty.

"You are thinking of escaping, *lucero?*" Tomás Navarro, the prison's *pran*—gang leader— asked as Ryan joined him on the walk to the outdoor bizarre.

"I'd miss your company."

Navarro laughed and slapped Ryan on the back. "You are my favorite gringo."

"Thanks."

"I'll buy you a cup of coffee. Come, before you work on rebuilding my glorious prison."

Ryan followed Navarro through the rows of concrete cell blocks to the bazaar, past the vendors hawking wares in the small market who stopped to call hello to the boss and his white lieutenant. Finally, the two men sat at a counter of a wooden booth where a young woman poured them two steaming cups of coffee.

"She likes you," Navarro whispered when Maria had turned her back to tend to her coffee machine.

Ryan shrugged.

"You need a little ..." He thrust his hips in a sexual motion. "She can spend the night in your cell."

"I don't think so."

"I know you're not ..." Navarro waggled his hand and lowered his voice. "*Pargo*."

Ryan scoffed, "Hell no, I'm not gay."

Navarro lifted his cup to his lips, then said out of the side of his mouth, "Then lay the pipe."

A short man interrupted their conversation by delivering two plates of *perico*—scrambled eggs with bell peppers, onions, and tomatoes. It was good to be a friend of the prison boss. They ate and drank in silence, Ryan considering the prospect of a conjugal visit.

When he finished his food, he sipped the second cup of coffee Maria had poured for him, watching her backside while listening to Navarro direct his men on the day's activities.

"What of you, Ryan?" Navarro asked, startling the man from his thoughts.

"We're finishing the south wall. Tomorrow, we'll put up the trusses." Ryan set his mug on the counter and stood to leave.

"Excellent. I will check on you this afternoon."

RYAN WALKED TOWARD HIS WORKSITE. Men were already mixing cement and preparing for the long day in the sun, laying concrete block. There was nothing like building one's own prison.

"Hey, *chamo*," an inmate named Herbert called from a picnic table. He sat with two other men in the shade of an acacia tree: Manuel, who blinked too much when he had a decent hand, and José, whose eyes were hidden behind wrap-around sunglasses. "Join us for a little five card stud?"

The American walked to the table, pulling off his shirt before sitting. Herbert grinned with his mouthful of jumbled and missing teeth. Teeth Ryan had knocked out.

Manuel dealt the cards, and Ryan picked them up. As head of the construction crew, he could take a break whenever he wanted. He nodded to Emmanuel, who acted as his foreman, and Emmanuel barked orders, putting the men to work.

Ryan tossed in his ante chips, which the prisoners used for everything from poker chips to payment of debts, into the pile and glanced at his cards again. Herbert was the hardest for Ryan to read. Since the fight, the two men had become friendly. Herbert tossed in his ante of plastic chips onto the pile.

In Spanish, José said, "You must have a good hand, Herbie."

"It's better than yours."

José grinned. "In that case, I'll call." With a laugh, he laid a pair of sevens, an ace, a two, and a queen on the table.

Manuel slapped his cards face up on the table. He had a pair of sixes. "I'm out."

Herbert grinned, and Ryan could see his tongue working through the gaps of the missing teeth. "Three of a kind, *hombre*."

"*Paja*," José muttered. *Bullshit*.

"Don't be angry." Herbert reached for the chips.

Before he could touch them, Ryan slapped his meaty paw and held up a finger to make him wait. He laid three nines, a king, and a queen.

Herbert leaned in close. "*Me cago en tu familia*."

Ryan stacked the chips. "Why are you shitting on my family? What did they do to you?"

"Your mother gave birth to you."

"How about another hand to see if your luck is any better?" Ryan glanced around the table.

The men nodded.

Herbert picked up the cards and shuffled them. "I will deal so you can't cheat."

Ryan shrugged and waited for him to pass the cards. He'd made money by playing poker, but he often fantasized about what he could do with the cash that had been in both his and Billy Ron's backpacks. No doubt the police had confiscated the American money for themselves.

Herbert finished doling out the cards and set the deck on the table. Ryan picked up his five worn cards and fanned them out, shifting them around to his liking. He tossed in two chips for the bring-in and waited as the other players matched him. Then Ryan asked for two cards to replace the two of spades and three of hearts he'd been dealt.

He placed the cards in his sweaty palm and wiped more sweat from his brow with the tail of his shirt.

"You make the bet," Herbert growled.

Ryan examined his cards again, then the pot. Ten thousand bolivars. Ryan calculated the exchange rate in his head. The pile of money wasn't even equivalent to two U.S. dollars.

He tossed a few chips on the pile, wiped sweat from his brow again, and licked his lips.

"He has a good hand," José taunted.

"Call it, *chamo*," Ryan said.

José leaned in and whispered in English, "I'm not your dude. I will slit your throat and screw your mother." He leaned back and smiled. "I call, gringo."

Ryan laid his first card, a two of clubs. The men giggled. Then he laid the queen of hearts. He glanced around the table as he placed the queen of diamonds beside the regal lady.

The laughter died. Ryan laid a queen of clubs and their faces grew hard. Finally, he slapped down the queen of spades.

Reverting to Spanish, he said, "Four royal ladies holding court today."

Herbert cursed and threw his cards. José flexed his jaw muscles and furrowed his brow. Manuel grinned and began collecting cards.

"Another hand, gentlemen?" Ryan asked.

Herbert stood and stormed away. Mateo, a gaunt Italian, sat in his place.

"You don't want to do that," José warned. "This guy has a hot hand."

Mateo rubbed his hands together as he sat. "He will be my first victim."

José gathered the cards and began to shuffle them. Ryan absentmindedly stacked his chips and gazed around at the other prisoners. While he'd come to terms with being in prison, he still couldn't get used to the view every time he glanced at the horizon. There were solid walls instead of beautiful sunsets and vast curving vistas of empty blue ocean. While some men wanted to stay behind the safety of the walls, Ryan wanted nothing more than to scale them and run free.

Ryan glanced up to see Isaac stop at the table. He was lean and short; Spanish blood mingled with Indian, giving him black hair and dark eyes in a square face. An angry scar curved around his neck where soldiers had tortured him using a method called *castigos*, in which they hung a prisoner until he passed out then revived him to do it all over again.

"My friend," Isaac said to Ryan in his raspy voice. "You have a visitor."

Thinking Navarro had sent the woman from the coffee shop to be his concubine, he replied, "I'm busy," and went back to counting chips. While he appreciated her beauty, he didn't want a prison wife.

"You do not want to be busy for this one. She is very beautiful." Isaac used his hands to imitate the curves of a luscious woman.

Ryan glanced up sharply.

The other men laughed.

"Is it Maria from the coffee stand?" Ryan asked.

"No, *señor*, I have never seen this one before," Isaac said.

"You dog," José said. "You've been holding out on us."

Ryan gathered his chips into his shirt and stood. To Isaac, he said, "I'll be there in a few minutes."

Isaac trotted toward the administration building while Ryan walked to his cell. He dumped the chips into a small box and placed it in the stand under the mirror. His reputation as a fighter and a killer along with his status as Navarro's lieutenant would keep the thieves away.

Ryan pulled on his shirt as he strolled to the visitor area.

He raised an arm and sniffed his pit. There wasn't much he could do about the funk emanating from his body. He longed to take a hot shower and put on clean clothes. Who was the visitor? He knew no woman who would risk her life to visit him in this wretched place.

At the office, a guard led him along a hallway to the same room he visited each time his lawyer brought him money.

When Ryan hesitated in the open door, the guard shoved him inside. The woman, who'd been sitting at the table stood as he stumbled into the room. She was five-foot-six with dusky brown skin, silky black hair, and doe-brown eyes. She wore khaki shorts and a blue shirt, which did little to hide her stunning curves. Ryan's breath caught in his chest, and his jaw dropped open as he recognized Kendra Diaz.

ABOUT THE AUTHOR

Evan Graver has worked in construction, as a security guard, a motorcycle and car technician, a property manager, and in the scuba industry. He served in the U.S. Navy, where he was an aviation electronics technician until they medically retired him following a motorcycle accident which left him paralyzed. He found other avenues of adventure: riding ATVs, downhill skiing, skydiving, and bungee jumping. His passions are scuba diving and writing. He lives in Hollywood, Florida, with his wife and son.

Visit www.evangraver.com to learn more about Evan and sign up for his newsletter to receive a free short story.

Made in the USA
Monee, IL
22 February 2021